Thinwalker

David Nabhan

Thinwalker

Other books by David Nabhan (fiction)

The Pilots of Borealis

Other books by David Nabhan (nonfiction)

Earthquake Prediction: Dawn of the New Seismology (with Paolo
Palmieri)
*Forecasting the Catastrophe: An Analysis of When and Where the Next
Great Earthquake on the West Coast Will Strike*
Predicting the Next Great Quake
Earthquake Prediction: Answers in Plain Sight

www.earthquakepredictors.com

Print ISBN 978-1-960405-15-9
ebook ISBN 978-1-960405-16-6

Cover design by Guy D. Corp www.grafixCORP.com
Triskelion design by Nick Prol https://linktr.ee/nickjoseprol

STAIRWAY⫪PRESS
STAIRWAY PRESS—APACHE JUNCTION

www.stairwaypress.com
1000 West Apache Trail, Suite 126
Apache Junction, AZ 85120 USA

Chapter One: Under the Lash

We have all sufficient strength to support the misfortunes of others.
—Francois de La Rochefoucauld, Maxim No. 19

WHEN THE BLINDFOLD was removed, the shock of sudden light was intensified by his surroundings. The chamber was completely, starkly sterile—with absolutely nothing to absorb or soften the brilliance reflecting from the enamel-white walls, ceiling and floor.

"If this involves your wife or sister," he said to the man who yanked the covering off, "I did my best to resist her, I swear it. But I'll stay away. You have my word; good enough?"

As his eyes focused, the first thought crossing his mind was a strange one: how immaculate and clean the cell was. And it had to be a cell since he was a prisoner.

The man who removed the blindfold spoke.

"Don't ask any questions."

His handler was a handsome man, impeccably dressed, but most strikingly, his auburn hair was coiffed in a singularly unique fashion. He sported thick straight bangs across the forehead with the sides and back framed with tight curls. The oddly puckish cut lengthened his face, accentuating broad shoulders and long, sinewy arms.

"No questions." He placed his index finger on his lips as if chiding a schoolboy. "Not a word, understand?"

Enguerrand Duprey was in no position to ignore the advice—handcuffed, bruised, disoriented, and admittedly and obviously, as anyone in his place would be, afraid.

"You won't ask questions because you'll be listening carefully to what I'm requiring you to do. Your task will be simple—and hard."

The handsome man, Enguerrand thought, revealed unattractive attributes as he continued with the threats. His lips sneered as the words spilled out. It wasn't appealing at all.

"Your job is to watch. You'll watch the show from the beginning to end no matter what. Understand?"

The man raised an eyebrow and stuck out his jaw.

"If you look away—even for a moment…"

The man didn't complete the thought. He shook his head and rubbed his deeply clefted chin, trying to find the right words to finish. He found them finally, then slowly sidled up to his prisoner, looking him dead in the eyes, so close Enguerrand could see the pores in his face and smell his breath. Enguerrand had changed his mind. This fellow wasn't that handsome after all. In fact, right now he looked like a demon.

"If you look away, even for a moment, I promise you'll knock on Hell's door, and it *will* be answered." He crossed his arms and stepped back. "Any insipid jokes now? Any funny-man comments?"

Enguerrand silently agreed that comedy was out of place and bit his lip.

"So tell me," his captor demanded. "What are you going to do?"

"Watch," Enguerrand answered, defeated.

"For how long?"

"For as long as it takes."

Satisfied, the handsome demon strode out of the chamber, only turning back to call over his shoulder, "Transparent."

The white wall in front of the prisoner transmogrified. It wasn't there anymore; something else was…something beyond horrible.

The victim was a middle-aged man. Enguerrand couldn't tell too much about him because the attendants had already cuffed his ankles and wrists and fitted a casquette over his head. But it didn't take any time at all to realize what was going to happen. Few people had ever witnessed such a scene, but everyone, in their worst dreams, imagined what it must look like.

The man was being strapped into a controller.

This creation of man's genius, the part poets ignored, sent pain simultaneously into all nerve endings. With over a thousand probes on every square inch of the skin, controllers accessed literally billions of portals by which pain could be sent to invade and break into every citadel of every region of the body.

There was no greater agony than what these evil apparatuses doled out, but the real horror was that while the machine drove the victim to the furthest limits of endurance and far, far beyond, it would inflict no physical or biological damage.

That meant the torture could go on constantly, indefinitely—endlessly.

No real data existed on what the longest period "under the lash" might be because, of course, most of these monstrous occurrences took place deep in the middle of nowhere, far out in the Big Black. So, the worst had been left unrecorded, a fact no decent person regretted.

Put under the lash and left there, one conceivably might suffer unspeakably for—well, too long. Demise would have to come in the way Nature herself could not grant but on the rarest of occasions: the victim would have to will himself to death.

The attendants pinned a mouth guard in place, but not from concern for the victim's dental health. They had another purpose, tightening the screw until it was bolted into place so swallowing his tongue would not be an option.

Immediately, Enguerrand knew what he was looking at. With the wing nut secured over the mouth and the eyes fixed far too open to indicate anything but super-human terror, there wasn't the slightest doubt. Enguerrand watched though; he had to. He watched for a time too long to reckon, and of course, would never be the same for having witnessed it.

"Welcome, Mr. Duprey," the serenely elegant host spoke with his hands gesturing with a flourish given by Renaissance grandees of a dozen centuries or so ago on Old Earth.

A bright, gleaming smile of perfectly even teeth accompanied the salutation, just as false and vacuous as the tone.

"I'm sorry," he admitted, pausing. "I get mixed up with free-rangers' names. Is that what I should call you?" He wasn't being solicitous though; it was a prelude to sarcasm. Enguerrand, this implied, didn't have a proper name and since the ill-named man didn't answer quickly enough, a more important one was intoned. He gave his own. It rolled off his tongue like a page would announce as he made an entrance.

"I'm Brabec Van Maanen Alexis, Alpha C-15307."

Anyone would have recognized him; he was an infamous and very powerful man. "And you? What's your name?"

"Enguerrand Duprey."

Brabec let out an immediate and dismissive guffaw, almost under his breath but quite audible.

"Just that? Nothing more?" He had an instant epiphany though, so didn't wait. "As long as it's so short, you won't mind me cutting it down even further? I'll call you 'Gary.' How's that?"

Enguerrand's absurdly simple name marked him immediately as a free-ranger, and they had nicknames though no one ever called him "Gary." Everyone else was called something suitable—everyone but free-rangers. Their names alone advertised the unpleasant fact that not all of them had been quarantined into some remote sector. Civilization was finally getting the upper hand on what was left of these Luddites from centuries long past. Simply being around them was offensive to the average person.

Dismissing them as contemptible, yet harmless rubes, was a costly mistake. Society had been at war, one way or the other, for an interminable duration with these stubborn and dangerous hayseeds who walked, talked and thought differently.

Brabec Van Maanen Alexis, Alpha C-15307's name told a different story. "Brabec" was the surname, the formal cognomen. "Van Maanen" indicated the star system in which he'd been born. "Alexis" was his third name, his familiar handle, what had been in the past one's first name. The rest of it was a determinant—a flow chart identifying which planet, which moon, which department, which hospital...which individual.

Anyone christened simply "Enguerrand Duprey" had to have been born in the wilderness, perhaps even outside solar system-sized wireless electric fields which suffused space for billions of miles around stars.

Brabec still shook his head, eager to squeeze a little more comedy—and impose more discomfort—out of Enguerrand's status. He turned to the handsome demon hulking ominously over his guest.

"Ever hear the term 'dumb as plugs'?" Brabec's henchman shrugged his shoulders; he wasn't following. "Yeah, some of the trash living on the edge," Brabec explained, "actually use wires and plugs to rig their gear, just like in comedy skits."

He clapped his hands remembering one of the punch lines.

"What's the matter; are you searching for an outlet?"

Brabac looked Enguerrand up and down, the ugly stare followed by an even uglier query.

"Is that where you found him? Was he diddling some outlet?"

The handsome demon lost interest, shrugging again.

"I don't know what he was doing. We just grabbed him."

It dawned on the demon that he might want to pat himself on the back.

"He didn't give off too many pings though; it wasn't that easy at first."

Enguerrand didn't ping; he was a free-ranger—someone who would be hard to find. Brabec Van Maanen Alexis, Alpha C-15307, and everyone else, and everything else, was logged and registered, with activity everywhere about them electronically memorialized from nanosecond to nanosecond, from birth to death, no matter who, no matter where.

This unremittingly unfailing chronicle of every event was Nexus, moving its data everywhere at once at the infinite speed of entangled particle pixels, as fast as thought. Dyson spheres, held in place by light pressure around dozens of stellar systems, sucked energy from their host stars to power it and everything else. Not Gary though. His name said he had little part in that, and that's why hearing it was repellant to an incalculable number of ears.

"Have a seat, Gary."

Brabec had already taken his behind a fine crystalline dining table fashioned from pure, high-grade cratonite, set in the center of an impressive dining hall. It was piled high with an eye-popping assortment of the most exotic and expensive fruits, condiments and *hors d'oeuvres*.

Brabec's jocular smile flashed off, evaporating as quickly as ice on the oven-moon of Io. He was suddenly and extremely displeased.

"Oh, come on! Can't anyone see that Mr. Duprey has wet his pants?!"

It was true. Two very large and apparent advertisements of the same were plainly seen on both of the upper interior leggings of Enguerrand's trousers. Little wonder they were there. Witnessing someone put under the lash, it wouldn't have been remarkable to sweat blood.

Brabec let out a resigned sigh and raised both hands in frustration as would any magnate when dissatisfied with the service. His minions quickly set to the task of finding clean trousers for the host's guest. It didn't take long. This left the two men to fill the unusual silence, born of waiting for one of them to change his sodden pants. It was an uncomfortable hush, yet one that Brabec smiled through nonetheless, his grin coming back to him; apparently he wasn't that distressed about it.

"No need to be embarrassed, Gary. Not a pleasant experience watching someone being put under the lash, is it? Still, it's the maid's day off and I like things tidy."

Brabec Van Maanen Alexis nodded around him, urging Enguerrand to assess the ambient décor. This was just a dining room, but because of the man who sat at the head of the table, it was a distinctive one.

The most obvious feature of the space was that floor, ceilings, and walls were done in the most stunning, intensely blue Massurian chalcedony. It gave the feeling of being transported to a chamber that had been carved in a seam of sapphires massive enough to accept it.

Brabec was a connoisseur who appreciated finery and beauty, himself an attractive man as well. He had widely set eyes and a very narrow aquiline nose set between them. It gave him an intellectual, authoritative look. His hair was light brown with the top layers tapered and cut conservatively, appropriate for a man long past middle age. It was combed to the side, framing a prominent forehead. His mustache was slight and inconspicuous it seemed almost an afterthought even though it was perfectly symmetrical and impeccably trimmed. It provided a foil for the strong, jutting chin.

Below the neck, there wasn't much to admire. His average height was the best thing to note about a baggy, soft, ill-trained, and physically unimpressive body. It was wrapped nonetheless in expensive, avant-garde attire that made Brabec as pleasing to look at as possible with what was at hand. The accoutrements he wore—gloves, cravat and the rest—might have been seen as preening, but, like Nero, Hitler and so many before him, he was an artist too.

Enguerrand wasn't interested in the interior decoration; his eyes were fixed instead on the fruit in front of him. Brabec took note.

"Of course, you're my dinner guest. It's on its way." Brabec emphasized the next phrase, saying the words too loudly to fit with what had come before. "Along with your pants."

The bodyguards laughed. Brabec chuckled too, but didn't forget his manners completely.

"Please, if you're hungry, have anything you like," he offered solicitously. "That caviar there, it's roe from Amphipolan lancers—imported all the way from Arietis."

Enguerrand slowly shook his head in the negative while squirming in his wet pants. He did stare at the fruit though. He had no real idea how long he'd been held captive, but it must be going on the sixth or seventh day now. He didn't have anything bad to say about what his captors had fed him during that time— but that was because it had been nothing.

He insisted on the pretense that they hadn't gotten the best of him.

"If dinner's coming, I'll just wait for that."

The initially good-looking but now decidedly unattractive demon who'd abducted Enguerrand finally delivered the pants.

Immediately the host was nonplussed.

"Oh, Jupiter's beard! What?! Where did you get those things? Orion's Belt? They're hideous!"

The ugly man held them up for a better look. They were ridiculous pants—comical pants. Ankle tight at the shin, they ballooned out to resemble two wind-flushed spinnaker sails only to finish the insipid garment at the waist—a waist tailored for a fifteen-year-old anorexic girl—clown pants that even a genie would judge silly and over the top.

Turning his back on Brabec, Enguerrand pulled them on.

"You know what?" Brabec shook his head the way people do when they remember something they shouldn't forget. He looked over to the trio of bodyguards huddled nonplussed around the bar to one side, asking them to chime in. "What's wrong here? Anybody?"

His associates shrugged their wide shoulders and collectively pled ignorance.

"Where's his third eye?" He pointed to Enguerrand's hands. Free-rangers wore their third eyes on the left hand, around the thumb. Brabec had a finger up, pointing to his own eye, to the power of intellect that dwelt behind them and which saw to such detail. "He's a free-ranger. Without it he's 'third eye blind.' Can you imagine what barbarians he must take us for?"

His men looked to each other for an answer.

"Where is it, Mec?"

Mec. The repulsive man's nickname. Mec looked down apologetically.

"It got misplaced, or lost, or...something. I don't know. It's not around."

Brabec rolled his eyes.

"Rigel or Regulus, if it isn't this it's that." He repeated Mec's words, not to anyone in particular, just muttering them. "It's not around, I can see that. It's not around or else he'd be wearing it."

He made a great show of rolling his eyes some more.

"Well, go find it!" He frowned and used his palms to tamp down something imaginary yet obviously problematic that only he could see. He turned to Enguerrand—starving, wearing buffoon pants, and third eye blind. "We'll have you back to ram-jet ready in no time at all."

He gave Enguerrand a very friendly wink. This was a congenial host, the gesture said. Yet it was the same host who had only hours before ordered an opening created in the barrier holding back the infernal regions and invited the essence of pure evil in to visit. Then he zipped it back into its lair until next time. That somehow, yet obviously, left him human, human enough to provide clean pants, delectable, exotic refreshments and to restore a third eye.

Brabec spied something else as well: a small, silver token dangling around Enguerrand's neck.

"Aren't you the very picture of backwardness, Gary?" he chided. Brabec didn't even bother to hide a disgusted expression. "A free-ranger…" he paused, searching for the right word, settling for a term that allowed him to avoid even uttering the name. "And one of *those* too?"

Enguerrand had long since realized he was less than the perfect picture of morality. He hadn't killed as many men as someone like Zandruss II, the scourge of the Beta Hydri star system, nor done it as cruelly. But having survived the maelstroms of his young life, he'd already committed sufficient unforgivable acts to gain an enthusiastic welcome into any ruthless war band.

The medallion was a triskelion, a motif of three interlocking spirals with rotational symmetry symbolizing mind, body and spirit, and had belonged to his dead mother, bequeathed to him by his dead father and had come to him with a simple sentence to which his father made him swear.

"Never remove this, never hide it. Keep it around your

neck even as you meet those who would kill you to take it off."

Enguerrand had kept his word to his father, but not to all his ideals. He didn't have much notion about what he now accepted as true, but felt little compunction to explain to his captor.

"It's a triskelion," he admitted.

"So you're a believer in good and bad, right and wrong, and up and down, Gary?"

It was made to sound absolutely ridiculous.

Enguerrand answered immediately.

"I'm a courier, and haven't the slightest idea what you think I can do for you."

Brabec liked that.

"Yes," he agreed, "a courier. The lowest forms of life ever to wind up stuck to the soles of my boots have all turned out to be couriers."

Brabec made a disagreeable face thinking about it, but then smiled realizing he had the right candidate for the task at hand.

"Yes," he repeated, now more confidently, "you might just do fine." He leaned closer, ostensibly to reach for an incomparable Circinisian merlot. "I know you've had a rough time here lately on my account, Gary. Let's put that to the side for now."

The magnifico of the choicest *area incognita,* the gatekeeper of the next great push, the maker of opinion, the policy shaper, the one in a billion who owed obedience to no one, now gave him a hallmark, close-range smile. It said that even though he'd reached the top of the hill and gone over the hump he was doing his best to drag the descent out for as long as he could. He radiated power, wealth, vigor, health, intelligence and could even mimic, at least, conviviality.

Still, Enguerrand was more starving than impressed. To get his mind off hunger he fidgeted with the tableware.

Brabac, the perfectionist, didn't like that much.

"Those are Laguiole folding knives, imported all the way from old Earth. And," he fussed, "the tines are supposed to be set face down. That's called French style."

"My ancestry is French," Enguerrand answered quickly. "And I've seen a table set before."

A voice inside Enguerrand, from his deepest, atavistic parts, that had been speaking to him in French since his childhood, scolded him. He wasn't French, per se; he was Quebecois. What difference that would make to his captors, he understood, wasn't worth the trouble. He accepted the shorthand, even though his inner martinet screamed its dissent. Canada had long ago ceased to exist, taking the fiercely independent province, Quebec, into the mists of things that weren't real anymore. And Enguerrand, if nothing else, had long since become the realist.

This perked up Brabec.

"Hey, Mec, did you hear that? He's French. We're in the company of a French free-ranger, Monsieur Enguerrand Duprey."

He leaned back in his chair and clapped his hands. Unimpressed, Mec scratched his head.

"French?" Mec said. "What's that?"

Brabec seemed astounded but smiled.

"It was a country, Mec. On Old Earth, for Pete's sake."

That explanation did little to help.

"A country? What?"

The conversation may just well have been about electorates and duchies in long gone empires. For Mec, the nation of France was as nebulous and far off as the landgraviate of Hesse or the khanate of the Crimea.

Brabec didn't want to let it go.

"Mec, have a look. See?"

He inserted his hand in an imaginary waistcoat pocket and thrust his head back more like Mussolini than Napoleon. But the gesture worked; Mec got it.

"Oh, yeah," he smiled now. "Those guys."

"A French free-ranger," Brabec summed everything up. "And mystical channeler of the divine," he mocked whatever it was that Enguerrand supposed he believed. "How do you like that?"

The entirety and grandeur of French culture reduced to this caricature didn't annoy Enguerrand so much as give him an opening. Error had to be a constant companion with the lack of genius on display in those in the employ of his captor.

He looked straight at Mec.

"I don't know who you think I am but I'm pretty sure somebody has made a colossal mistake."

Brabec opened his eyes wide, as if really interested in giving this unusual news a fair hearing. Enguerrand started, just a little, to come back to himself, enough that his host's sarcastic look irritated him.

"Seriously, I'm nobody. I'm just a simple courier."

All of that was true, so it was easy for Enguerrand to lean forward and say the rest with the most patently honest face.

He looked directly at Mec again.

"Somebody screwed up."

Brabec put his index finger straight up, like a magistrate ready to judge.

"You're Enguerrand Duprey, free-range courier, aren't you?"

"Yes, I am."

"Then nobody screwed up," Brabec pronounced. "You're just the fellow I want to see."

He plastered a cracker with a gluttonous dollop of Amphipolan caviar.

"And as far as your so-called profession is concerned, everyone always said couriers were nothing more than part-time vagabonds. You've got a full-time reputation though."

The words were filtered through the incalculably pricy *hors d'oeuvre* still in his mouth.

"A courier will take anything for anyone anywhere, that's your stock in trade? Well, hopefully that leaves you available to contract your services with me."

Enguerrand Duprey's business wasn't a flattering profession, but it was one that flourished. There were millions of messages that couldn't be sent, but were necessary.

In humankind's ever-expanding sector of the Spiral Arm, where some dozens of star systems interacted and jockeyed for everything under a hundred suns, couriers moved threats, recriminations, pleas, proposals, plans, apologies, congratulations, curses, and calculations from one end of Creation to the other, in an informal way, without even Nexus itself being the wiser.

Couriers moved other things as well, from place to place—things unseen and without bills of lading.

Brabec sat and stared at Enguerrand, not smiling in the least, just chewing.

"You're not busy right now, are you, Gary? You weren't just in the middle of something, were you?"

Enguerrand declined to say, but convinced that he'd successfully resisted displaying how famished he was, nonchalantly slathered Amphipolan fish roe on a cracker. His hands trembled just slightly though, whether from hunger or fear or both, hard to say. The rush of nutrients after so long had the immediate effect of reawakening what he'd been forced to witness and caused a dark and disagreeable expression to come out on his face.

He had no power to control it.

That didn't seem to upset the host though; Brabec made light of it instead.

"Look, Gary, there's no reason for that. We need not be chums, but certainly you prefer the easy way over the hard?"

Again, he filled his flute. His manner was genteel and cultured. He swirled the wine gently in the glass, held it up to the light briefly and took another careful sip, appreciating the vintage.

"You know who I am, obviously?"

Enguerrand nodded—almost anyone would.

"Then you must realize you're probably already dead, yes?"

Enguerrand didn't nod, but the thought *had* passed through his mind.

Brabec pointed all around expansively.

"You're probably a dead man just because you're here, and I'm here, and Mec's here. Every decent man respects honesty, Gary, so I'm not going to lie to you. You were probably a dead man from the minute I decided to bring you here." He finished the last of the wine in his glass and licked his lips while Mec placed a fresh carafe on the table.

Following Brabec's nod, Mec, without words, poured a glass of this top drawer vintage and set it in front of Enguerrand.

"But that's no reason for gloom, is it? I hope you're not going to hold that against me and spoil the dinner?" Brabec tried hard to cheer him up. "That wine comes from a place not even registered on star charts. You'll love it. Please, have as much as you like."

Enguerrand put the glass to his lips. His hands shook, not slightly, but quite visibly.

However, the wine was delicious.

"And like I said," Brabec repeated, "I hope you have nothing else going on right now." He raised his glass politely to his guest. "Because," he said, fixing Enguerrand with unfeeling Cephalopod eyes, "I have a job for you."

Chapter Two: Feasting with Demons

Whatever great advantages nature may give, it is not she alone, but fortune also that makes the hero.
—Francois de La Rochefoucauld, Maxim No. 53

WHILE BRABAC WAITED for the main course, he did what other cultured diners did—changed things up for his guest by adjusting the ambience. He did this simply by *thinking* about it.

As spectacular were his dining hall's chalcedony walls, floors and ceilings, no matter how exotic, they were finished with splendid paint—a thin, acrylic, pixilated tempura as fine as any wall in any domicile anywhere.

They transformed according to the thoughts of the host—morphing into the abysmal depths of the oceans of Amphipolis, a moon in the Alpha Arietis system or amethyst waters lit by the glow from the molten nickel being extruded from its pockmarked sea floor.

It was almost like being there.

Brabec's thoughts rambled through others of the most

marvelous locales in existence, only pausing long enough for his own unimpressed grumbles. Then he had an idea.

"Hey, Gary, guess who I'm thinking about?"

Thinking about it was all he had to do. It was the first step anyway. This was New Modern and nanites had changed the world, altered history, overturned the calendar and transformed the very galaxy; there was no watershed like this one. A Babylonian astrologer, a medieval squire, or an Old Modern miner on the Moon—there wasn't much difference among any of them. They couldn't think things into existence and that made them a different species, and a lower one.

Brabec thought about Enguerrand's renowned grandmother. His interest scrolled across his inner third eye and simultaneously the query flooded through uncountable primary synapses, received and converted to metadata by an army of microscopic nanites. They had been injected into Brabec Van Maanen Alexis, Alpha C-15307 at birth and had ceaselessly served their assigned biological resource since that time.

Brabec's query was active and required an immediate response. Untold numbers of these marvels of nanoscale technology fetched an answer by accessing Nexus, broadcast everywhere within any habitable distance from any Dyson shell around any star. If Nexus didn't have the data, then the answer obviously didn't exist.

Aside from ferreting data from one end of Creation to the other, the new symbiosis between biology and technology affected not just answers but the questions themselves.

By adulthood, more than a few thoughts passed within civilized humans' brains that were at least partially engendered or a subtle side effect of one's nanites. It took time for young children to learn how to fully manipulate them. As with any endeavor, some were quicker or better than others. Human beings, though—at their very core—were becoming hybrids.

Anyone with a lick of sense breathed a sigh of relief.

Everyone, except, of course—the free-rangers. They ranged, as they would have everyone believe, "free." They didn't host nanites, refused to have their children inoculated and this was the beginning, middle and end of their great bone of contention.

"Not a single nanite in a single drop of blood!"

That was one of their rallying cries.

These anchorites still existed because of the few systems on the extreme edge of existence where newborns amazingly, foolishly, stubbornly were *not* assigned a batch of nanites to be programmed, registered and injected, to accompany the new citizen for life—a life made exponentially easier, more convenient, more fulfilling.

It was a disgrace, almost everyone thought, that such life-long impairment was allowed to be inflicted on defenseless babies, resulting in creatures such as Enguerrand. They had no internal third eye! To interact with them was eerie for the average person for they didn't possess that far-off, slightly blurred look others wore a lot of the time, taking in things meant only for their central cerebral cortex, focused on data that floated invisibly in front of them, seen only by their eyes.

But for physical devices—the third eyes free-rangers wore as a ring—access to every interaction would be lost due to their interface disability. They used them to fall under the umbrella of the Nexus too, just that they had to actively establish the connections that came and went at their discretion. They'd forsaken an automatic, smooth, and constant life in the face of everyone else and opted instead for an existence in fits and starts, in bits and pieces, switching their contacts on and off.

Thus did this strange sub-set of humanity stumble through their day to day life leaning on the bands around their left thumbs like crutches, but yet clinging to their supposed privacy, individuality, and freedom. Anyone with a funny bone found them great laughing-stock. Of course, that's not how

Enguerrand saw himself; he saw things differently.

For free-rangers, the melding of mankind's collective persona with microscopic automata was the greatest evil ever conceived. That it was taking over vast sections of humanity's bailiwick seemed to them a heart-breaking portent of the future. They were the last holdouts with everyone else enjoying the blessings of a number of generations of nanites.

"Mec has been known to make a mess of things, so you're making me a little bit nervous, Gary. I've got the right guy, I hope? Here, this is your blood, your own grandmother, isn't it?"

Brabec thought about her and a perfect three-dimensional holographic Adrienne Duprey appeared.

Enguerrand Duprey's grandmother was the preeminent free-ranger to have ever lived in the Vela Eridani system. This hotbed was either the birthplace or aided and abetted almost every confrontation between the two competing visions of the future of humanity.

"*Tu es Québécois*, Enguerrand." Adrienne said it to him so often and so early in life that it was the first phrase he could remember hearing. "You are Quebecois, Enguerrand."

But then German, Arabic, Japanese, Argentine, Maori, Russian and other grandmothers of a hundred different ethnicities said the same thing to their grandchildren in Enguerrand's boyhood star system, just in a hundred different languages. The free-rangers of Vela Eridani, no matter what language they spoke, no matter their customs and traditions, stuck together like Cyanoacrylate glue, supported each other against any foe, refused to abandon any of their alliances even in the face of unmitigated disaster, fought together to the very death with unparalleled courageousness, and shocked the entire galaxy with their death-defying refusal to submit.

Their seeming unbreakable camaraderie and collective fate was seen in a simple maxim: they would either all have their freedom or none would. They turned out to be astoundingly ferocious opponents, terrifically difficult to defeat. After all the byzantine conflicts and armistices, after endless rounds of compromises and revocations had collapsed, the two sides came together to try one last attempt to discover any scrap of common ground outside of all-out war.

The pixilated tempura worked its holographic magic, transforming Brabac's cobalt blue walls into the Great Hall of Creation at Tau Cygni; the peace conference was the setting for the beginning of the end.

"You're Enguerrand Duprey, grandson of Adrienne Duprey, aren't you?"

Brabec had thought up this watershed, this turning point in the colonization of the Milky Way, the great moment when history went one way and not the other. The Home Sector's ambassador, Earth's voice, speaking for the oldest power in the Milky War, gave a scathing appraisal of the opposition, his holographic avatar thundering scorn at Enguerrand's grandmother.

"To be a free-ranger is to want your cake, to eat it too— and then to send the bill to the rest of us. You want the safety of an informed and efficient security service, yet you'll afford it no way to collect vital data. You want to be part of the explosion of riches and the amazing, endless bounty of a whole galaxy opened to our economic system but it must be calculated with abacuses because you long for Doric columns and Delphic mysteries. You avail yourselves of the infinite advantages of science—and call yourselves rationalists who must bow to science—and yet count yourselves immune from paying the least respect when it displeases. How are you not like the rest of us?"

Brabec had called up the snippet of history most people thought of whenever Adrienne entered their minds. She was answering the delegate. Everyone who heard her rebuttal knew then and there exactly what must come next. Her response had been memorized by free-rangers. Certainly, Enguerrand knew the words by heart as well. It was his own grandmother speaking.

"The security you offer us is a fantastical and worthless trust since it requires safeguarding everything we have and are to be held in your safes, at your pleasure. Our share of the riches of Creation should have produced the wealthiest slaves to have ever existed, whether we lifted a finger for our freedoms or not. You must wonder at our reluctance to accept that status. Here is the simple explanation then, the right that we demand: it is to say 'no.' You may not know what we think, feel, see, say, fear or love. You may not access our faults and errors and pains and victories and tears and joys. We will not join you in the herd. Those on the edges of the flock will see that false comfort vanish as sooner or later the lions appear. We are not like you, we are the caretakers of a timeless ember that we'll defend to the end: we are human, the very reflection of God. And I? *Je suis Québécoise.* We choose death before inoculation."

With her words, another round, perhaps the last round, of The Wars had been declared.

"What a woman, your grandmother."

Brabec seemed to offer the compliment honestly. Then he almost jumped out of his chair with the realization.

"Isn't that you there, Gary?"

Fourteen-year-old Enguerrand Duprey's image could be seen in the audience by anyone accessing the data, sitting in the row behind his fiery grandmother. His father was absent, having already upheld, without asking quarter, the *grande dame's* slogan, to the letter. The French boy didn't look anything like an incarnation of his lionhearted father though, no Alexander eager to eclipse the fallen Philip of Macedon. Instead it was a sad boy in the images, difficult to look at without feeling a pang of sympathy.

It was painful also for Enguerrand to look at those old

images for he too saw himself for whom he was. He was no champion—but no coward either. He did his duty, no better or worse than millions of other young free-rangers. But he wasn't his father and couldn't live up to his grandmother's expectations. He had been just a scared, traumatized, young French boy—orphaned by the horrific conflict—thrust ready or not into the crucible of total war to do or die. Enguerrand Enguerrand in the end did what was most natural of all for a free-ranger: he poured his heart and soul into the decision, and without any high-powered nanotechnological help, made it.

Because of who he was, many expected him to toast the emperor with sake, strap on the family katana, and end his existence in a blaze of glory as part of a futile but nonetheless *Divine Wind*. A part of him wanted to, but in the end, he surrendered, just like anyone else. In the end, he walked away, just like everyone else. When it became clear that force of arms would change nothing, that the cause was lost, that to continue would be to march forward to suicide, he chose the only sane option. He threw down his arms and lived to fight another day.

"That *is* you, Gary," Brabec snickered. "You don't look like much of a hero there though. I'll say that."

He was no hero, this grandson of Adrienne Duprey. But in lieu of that and lest anyone underestimate him, there was something both very extraordinary and almost superhuman about Enguerrand Duprey, something bequeathed to him from another great tragedy.

Brabec was looking him over.

"They say you're dangerous though. They say there's something special about you. Is that true, Gary?"

Enguerrand Duprey was blessed, or cursed with something quite beyond normal human ability: speed beyond imaginable, only appreciated if glimpsed by one's own eyes. The tragic fact was his mother had contracted Lacaillian fever while he was *in utero*, delivering him prematurely and a critical case;

she expired almost immediately after giving birth. Rare survivors like Enguerrand bore both subtle and extreme marks for life. He didn't have "whites" in his eyes, for example; they were pale, pale green. His irises also were stained the deepest jade, the effect was quite striking, in truth, almost feminine.

Most remarkably though and certainly impossible to believe without seeing, he could move in a very feminine way too, just as long as it were compared to a lioness bursting out of cover in ambush or to the lightning-quick killing thrust of a black widow. His muscles didn't work like the average man's and he had no white in his eyes. Those were the first two things anyone ever said about him, and no one, male or female, could fail to notice these distinctive characteristics about Enguerrand Duprey.

Brabac rose now and with an odd foreboding reached across the table for a Gliesean peach.

"You know, Mec," he repeated more to himself, "they say Gary is a dangerous man." He corrected himself, holding up a finger. "A very dangerous man." He then cocked back and suddenly and unexpectedly launched the peach at Enguerrand, trying to judge Enguerrand's unbelievable reaction time, throwing it at him as hard as he could. Enguerrand's hand reflexively shot out as if pushed by the armature of a dynamo, easily snagging the fruit in mid-air and pleasing Brabec mightily.

"Blessed Betelgeuse!" Brabec marveled. "I'd have never believed that unless I'd seen it for myself." He sat for a moment studying his dinner guest with great interest and quietly mumbling the oath under his breath, "Blessed Betelgeuse…"

Nature and fate had marked Enguerrand in another way as well, and almost as striking. He wasn't just handsome but was favored with looks far to the extreme edges of attractiveness. The hypnotic eyes were mesmerizing on their own, yet made more so underpinned by cheekbones that pushed up from under the face like oaken roots, so high, sharp and strong, pulling up cheeks as taut and angular as the trimmed topgallants on a sailing ship.

Enguerrand's skin tone was the result of exposure to every color star in existence, a shock of very thick, very dark brown hair giving an accentuated contrast. It seemed to need combing hardly ever, the locks long enough to flow and move but almost always falling back in place, obedient to the parts. His was a long, thin Gallic nose. It was but the slightest bit too big yet this fit his face just right in a very pleasing, unique way.

He had a courier's physique. These anchorless nomads traveled light, traveled fast, and never stopped. It wasn't a profession renowned for its cuisine; he was thin, lean, hard—and as mentioned—fast.

Enguerrand wasn't a youngster anymore, now twenty-five, and was quite tall and well built, what there was of him devoted to muscle and bone. So it was fair to describe him as an extraordinarily handsome man...in a slightly feminine way.

And just for clarity, even though he was no great hero, he was no coward either. Enguerrand was a very attractive man with a slightly effeminate bearing but he could be, as Brabac said, a very dangerous man, too. As proof of that he was seriously considering the option now: maybe he should kill Brabec. He reasoned sanely that even if he didn't live through it, he only cared now that he couldn't allow himself to wind up under the lash. Dinner arrived though to put his homicidal musings on hold, hungry enough to force murder itself to wait its turn. All he wanted to do now was eat.

"Ah, Gary, you've got timing. I have to give you that." Brabec said while rubbing his hands together. "Feast your eyes."

Smiling from ear to ear, he reached over and removed the lid of the tureen.

"You have no idea, do you? Admit it. Take a look, oh, what a smell!" He had to close his eyes in rapture for a moment. "These are genuine alogostines," he didn't need to say "from

Tycho in the Sirius system." They could be from nowhere else.

"You thought they were extinct, didn't you?" He answered his own question. "Well, why wouldn't you? Anyone would. They *are* extinct, or very well may be after our dinner." He declared the next fact with a grandiose formality. "These could be the last alogostines in existence, and we're having them for dinner. What do you think of that, Gary?"

Enguerrand was hungry enough to eat the rocks under which these crustaceans were found. The smell of these delicious morsels—shrimp-like creatures sizzling in butter, cheese and saffron—was sufficient for him to grant himself complete and immediate absolution for the crime of eating them.

Enguerrand Duprey stuffed himself with the alogostines, oblivious to the offense. Gorging himself once in a while didn't do much damage. His courier's build didn't have an ounce of weight in the wrong place, the right body type to be wrenching and angling itself into the hard-to-reach places on his quantum cruiser that might need attention light years from the nearest harbor, moving at just under a hundred times the speed of light.

While they ate, a long period of silence descended, neither man saying a word for some time. The comforting, clinking sound of tableware in use reverberated throughout the room with no other noise to compete. Enguerrand was deep in thought though, and it was just as well that his plans weren't being holographically displayed to his host. One rogue thought kept calling out from the background, dismissed initially because of the seeming implausibility. But it continued popping to the front of his mind.

What about killing Brabec Van Maanen Alexis?

It sounded ridiculous at first, but he gave it real consideration, turning over tentative scenarios of how it might be accomplished. Brabec's neck, for instance, he'd surveyed carefully. It was a weak spindle for such a big head. He could break it, he was sure, in seconds. The thought of breaking this pathetic neck didn't bother him at all; it almost comforted him.

He had a rough idea what kind of sound it would make as it snapped and the shocked and dumbfounded noises he'd squeeze out of it. Enguerrand thought hard enough for Brabec to recognize murder written across Enguerrand's face.

"I've known quite a number of free-rangers in my life, so I've seen that look before," Brabec warned him. "You couldn't mistake one like that from the Crab Nebula. Seriously, Gary, all that nasty emotion and negative thinking inside," he chided, "just isn't healthy."

Enguerrand silently took another bite. Simultaneously he began to breathe deeply and rhythmically, tensing and then relaxing his muscles from fingertips to toes. Lacaillian fever lay dormant in him and when the adrenaline was running would produce brief moments of blindingly quick-firing musculature. He was already silently asking absolution in advance from heaven for the sin he was about to commit, imagining what Brabec was going to look like with a head twisted around the wrong way.

He slowly swallowed another delicious morsel, moments away from transforming into a verdant-eyed, panther-like blur. The whites of his eyes—always light green—now changed perceptibly with the blood up, to the color of Vandalucia's oceans. This was a color that not a few had seen when they'd seen last. Enguerrand didn't know how many men he had killed. His whole being now though was focused on just this number: he was going to kill one more, and then go down swinging.

"I have your daughter, by the way," Brabec said off-handedly, between bites, not even looking up. "Not here, of course, but I have her. Your wife, too."

He stared straight at Enguerrand for a long time, obviously trying to judge what effect this information produced. The reaction was profound. Enguerrand's eyes immediately lightened and his body relaxed. The submissive thoughts flooded into the control centers of his brain, running the daring ones out of town and cursing them as they fled from the disaster they came so close to causing.

"I'll do whatever you want. There's no need to involve my family in anything."

Enguerrand said it like someone who actually had a say. He didn't, but Brabec was willing to play along.

"Good, then," he said and clasped his hands together as if a deal had been struck. "*Bien, tres bien*," he repeated just to show off.

Brabec swallowed another prawn and drank more wine, not a word forming for a very uncomfortable time. When he next spoke it was in a tone of pure business.

"I want you to find someone for me. Find her and bring her back here. You're a courier; that should be easy for you."

Brabec had skipped over what mattered.

"I want to know about my wife and daughter, not about your girlfriend problems," Enguerrand demanded.

The instant he said it he wanted to pull the words back. He told himself that derision was simply the most insane tack to take here and now. His eyes flushed a fleeting pulse of aqua marine at the self-reproach.

Brabec let out a disparaging puff of air.

"Well, I'll answer this way. I'm giving you carte blanche. Bring her back here or kill her. Alive or dead, it doesn't matter to me."

He finished off the last of his shrimp, licking his fingers. To make sure Enguerrand understood he ran his hand across his throat and made a decapitating sound.

"What about my family?" Enguerrand asked.

Brabec thought it was a stupid question. He shook his head and rolled his eyes. "They're both in fine shape. They haven't been touched and won't be. They go free the minute I have what

I want." Only one point was a bit unclear to Brabec. "Did I misspeak? She's your ex-wife if I have this right?"

"We're separated."

"Oh, separated," Brabec intonation didn't compliment the word. "That's never good, is it? It's your profession. It's ruined a lot of marriages." A distinctly threatening look came straight through his eyes. "You still care about her though I hope, Gary, yes?"

"How am I supposed to trust you?" Enguerrand asked instead.

Brabec's answer agitated him; he leaned forward and let Enguerrand know why.

"You, Enguerrand Duprey, are hardly anything to me; I'm sorry to put it that way. I'm Brabec Van Maanen Alexis, Alpha C-15307. I can barely concern myself with treating with the likes of you much less rearrange my future schedule with the fate of your insignificant spouse and progeny. I have no interest whether they live or die, but if we are to make a deal and their freedom is part of the contract than that's how it will be."

"I have your word?"

Mec and the other bodyguards had a good laugh at that. Brabec smirked at the notion too. It did sound plainly stupid for Enguerrand to ask.

"Yes, you have my word. Good?"

It wasn't good but it was all he'd be getting.

Now Brabec scanned data only he could see, calling up information on Enguerrand's daughter. He shook his head disapprovingly.

"About your daughter, Gary," he began. "You've more or less abandoned her, haven't you?"

Enguerrand didn't respond; he only swallowed hard in silence.

"Poor thing, it's hard growing up with no father. We wondered if there'd be better insurance to be had, but it seems you don't have too many people in your life worth holding hostage."

Now he gave a mild rebuke.

"You should have someone in your life, Gary. This is a big galaxy to go through alone, with no wife, no family, no friends."

Enguerrand repeated the plea.

"I don't want them hurt."

He wasn't speaking to Brabec; he was just saying the words. Brabec gave Mec and the others a brusque nod and they surrounded Enguerrand. Maybe he'd read Enguerrand's mind over dinner and thought it more wise to have his muscle at the ready before saying the rest.

"Here's what I will promise you, Gary. If you run off and don't come back with what I want, I'll make them pay for it and I'll sell tickets to every sadist in this sector to come and watch. They won't know it will be your doing, but you will. You come back with what I want and within three periods—and not a moment more—or you'll know what you'll have done."

Enguerrand couldn't think of killing him now; he wasn't thinking at all.

Mec gave his boss an affectionate poke on the shoulder and spoke up.

"Come on, you'd wind up telling. Who are you kidding?"

Everyone laughed, especially Brabec.

"Yeah, you're right." He shrugged his shoulders. "He's right, Gary. I'd wind up telling. It's the last thing they'd know."

Brabec mentally clicked off all the three dimensional holographic accoutrements. They were back where they started in the stunningly beautiful hall of polished Massurian chalcedony.

"Here are the ground rules then," Brabec summed up for him. "One of these things is going to happen. You can run off and I'll never see you again and three periods after that your family will pay for it. Or else you'll be a husband and a father for the first time in your miserable life and you'll report back to me within the time allotted. You'll either have who I'm after or you won't. If you're not the courier I trust you are and you've failed, well, I'm a fair man. At least you will have tried. They go free and you'll have earned yourself a quick and easy death."

Brabec cleaned up in the finger bowl and wiped his lips with pristinely laundered linen.

"If you *are* the man I hope you are, you'll come back with what I want and within the time frame. That would be best."

Enguerrand's look seemed to hold the question he now answered. It was offered very honestly.

"Gary, I can't promise that you'll get to walk away even then. It's fifty-fifty. I really won't even know myself until then." He shook his head and frowned, turning over too many things in his mind to give a straight answer. "It's complicated. You'll see what I mean. But there's a chance that if you come through with flying colors—well…"

He laughed as he motioned to each of his henchmen.

"I was going to kill every one of these jackanapes! That's how anyone comes on board *this* crew. So do your best, don't double-cross me, and things may turn out for you in the end after all. Questions?"

Enguerrand started to pose one but Brabec interrupted him.

"Get him out of here."

As he was being led out, Brabec called a query of his own.

"By the way, Gary, those really were Tychonean prawns. For God's sake, those might have been the last in the entire galaxy. You ate them up like a ravenous wolf. Aren't you shamed about that in the least?"

Chapter Three: Fleeting Eternity

It is far better to accustom our mind to bear the ills we have than to speculate on those which may befall us.
—Francois de La Rochefoucauld, Maxim No. 174

MEC AND TWO other beefy attendants escorted Enguerrand down a long corridor, the clicks of their heels the only sound reverberating off the metallic deck. Enguerrand judged by the remarkably gentle degree of curvature along the floor that the size of Brabec's station was, as could be expected for one of the richest men within a parsec, ostentatiously overwhelming.

Around a sloping arc, the passageway finally terminated at an access portal. A woman stood before it waiting. She gave Enguerrand a look halfway between curt and unfriendly and immediately launched into her tutorial.

"Listen very carefully, Mr. Duprey. We're dealing with time constraints so you'll be embarking momentarily and it's my job to prepare you as best I can. The less you say and the more intently you listen the further your chances for success will be improved. Do we understand each other?"

She was past middle age, the kind of woman who had obviously been beautiful decades ago and who even now exhibited the vestiges of what must have been quite a hey-day. The wrinkles in her face had been cosmetically erased—the barely perceptible, faint lines that remained were somehow attractive and appealing. The lack of sparkle in her eyes was the surest sign of her age but even that was alluring—big, dull, deep brown eyes that must have pulled more than a few men down into them in her time.

Her tone and demeanor said she'd been around too.

"And you don't need to know my name."

Enguerrand judged her to be a specialist, doctor, technician—one of those or all three. She looked as out of place here as the flying fish he'd seen in the amethyst clouds of Devonia in the Epsilon Eridani system. There must be a real story here too he almost allowed himself to wonder, but his mind was otherwise occupied.

"If you don't mind, lady, the idea of putting a few light years between me and here doesn't require any convincing at all. Is that the exit?"

She gave a shrug as if to say that this was as good a way as any to explain.

"It is, in a way," she said.

The party boarded the elevator and was whisked straight up, leaving the spinning gravity well, losing their weight as they rose and arriving at the only fixed section of Brabec's station, the domed hub. The transparent observation pod was open for 360° to the immensity of black space all around it.

Immediately things became clear—in a muddled, inexplicably complicated, miraculously impossible way. As a courier, Enguerrand had witnessed countless vistas all across much of Creation; but he'd never seen a sight like this. The stars and nebulae and black ink of the void—it was all there, but only as background. What he was meant to see however was right before him now. It was beyond spectacular—and astonishing enough to make the blood pound even in zero gravity due to sheer shock.

"That's where you're going, Mr. Duprey," she said flatly. "Do I have your attention?"

Enguerrand stared at her as if she were insane, so she qualified it. "It's not what it looks like."

Her expression and tone were that of someone who had their wits about them even if her words were completely mad.

"That's a pulsar," he finally said after some dumb-struck moments, with the most matter of fact inflection, stunned beyond any reckoning, the words simply spilling out on their own, banking on the sheer weight of the obvious to validate the observation. "That can't be there."

She stood her ground, nonetheless, cocking her head to indicate that the answer was only half-right.

"It might have been at one time a normal pulsar, that part is right." She paused, and then dropped the weight. "It's been modified."

Enguerrand was so staggered by the words that he looked around instinctively, at anyone, even the mob of demons in his company. Mec and his cohorts didn't offer any comment. They weren't even paying attention, arguing instead about a bet that had turned out badly.

"Modified?" he asked.

"Modified," she repeated.

It took some time for his eyes to communicate other impossibilities to the brain. One was more urgent than others since certain fatality came with it.

"Why aren't we dead?"

"You're right, we should be, by any stretch of physics, shredded by the fields generated by that monster at this close range," she agreed. "But the energy that ought to be emanating in all directions out has instead been pulled into and focused within the beam."

Enguerrand couldn't take his eyes off the ferocious shaft of crackling rays that swung around wildly as the pulsar rotated. She asked him to shift his eyes.

"Don't look at the pulsar, Mr. Duprey." She pointed to the intensely blinking light receiving the blistering fury of the focused beacon. "That planetoid is dead in the path. Except the thing is, it's not a planet either. That's where you'll be going."

Enguerrand almost whispered the next sentence. The series of stunning blows now started to finally accumulate, settling on his voice, almost paralyzing it.

"Let me guess. It's been modified too?"

She gave him her first polite look. It said she appreciated that he could somehow attempt wit even now. Enguerrand, she knew, had for days been pulled from pillar to post, couldn't be far from where any man's courage and aplomb would fail. Somehow, he kept his bearing. She had to admire that.

"It's not modified. It's been constructed from whole cloth."

That did it; he'd had more than enough.

"That's where you're thinking of sending me?" he demanded to know, now plainly unnerved and not bothering to hide it. "What *is* that thing?"

It was a fair question and deserved the fair answer she gave.

"Two and a half decades into the past. That's where you're going."

They came back down from the gravitational null zone where Enguerrand recovered enough weight to sink into a couch. She had some straight Tartarusian tonic brought and insisted he throw back two draughts. Taking a seat next to him, from her bracelet she opened a tiny reservoir and tapped out the lightest sprinkling of amber dust on her hand.

"Here," she leaned toward him and placed her lightly freckled finger onto his lips. "Just take this little bit."

It was ambrosia. Enguerrand didn't hesitate.

She didn't say any more, having the decency to wait for the effects. She sat close to him, almost showing concern.

"I'll explain everything in a moment. Just relax for right now."

He thought she might be the only one with a soul among them, but wasn't sure if the notion was his intuition or the drug. As the ambrosia came on he imagined she was admiring his eyes and he perked right up, giving her a smile. She managed a smile back even though she wasn't smitten by the eyes. She was giving instructions to a dead man and she felt a little sorry for this young, unfortunate French free-ranger.

"Feeling better?" she asked.

"Yes, much!" he answered, completely under the effects. "So what about the pulsar? What were you saying?"

"Well, as I told you, every erg of power is being sent only one place—the faux planet. What is even more astounding, you can't see it now of course, you'd have to watch for a while, but the orbit is so synchronous that as the planetoid circles the pulsar it keeps moving into the next precise bull's eye. The celestial mechanics are incredible."

"I see," he murmured. "Yes, they would have to be. That's absolutely amazing," he agreed.

"That's nothing. Where do you think all that energy is going? That orb isn't even heating up, Mr. Duprey. Can you imagine that?"

"Wow...where is it going then?"

"Well," now she leaned back, enjoying the fact that she'd be able to get it all out without anyone fainting or asking a thousand questions. "That satellite was itself constructed. It's made of a class of materials we can't even begin to identify, but here it is. Its piezoelectric effect is stupendous. It absorbs the pulsar's blasts and modulates the energy through the entire globe. Everything goes to keeping the throat open inside the sphere—a throat that runs from pole to pole."

"A throat? I don't understand that."

"Of course you don't. We're not sure if the wormhole was constructed of exotic matter or if it was initially a nanoscale pathway that was extracted and augmented, but there's a wormhole that runs between those two poles, Mr. Duprey. Think about that for a minute; I'll be right back."

She and Mec exchanged some words. Enguerrand couldn't make everything out but it seemed to be a disagreement about the ambrosia. She had a defiant look on her face when she returned.

"Here." She wiped her finger again on Enguerrand's lips. "Now, do you remember where we were?"

He nodded and she continued, wiping on a last smudge of ambrosia while explaining.

"Well, the thing about wormholes is that you go in one end and come out the other no matter where the two ends are. You understand that, don't you?"

Enguerrand nodded.

"How silly it would be though, Mr. Duprey, to go to all the trouble of constructing a wormhole just to have the ends in the same place when they could be galaxies apart, wouldn't you say?" She raised an eyebrow and cocked her head slightly to the side. This was the important part her expression said.

"Hey!" Enguerrand exclaimed, open-mouthed and scratching his ear. "That would be so silly! Who would do that?"

"No one would. But these people," she stopped and shook her head, "the people who built this, these people were very, very clever and very, very advanced. They weren't interested in shrinking the distance in space—they created a way to disturb the time component in each of the ends of the wormhole. It's a time portal, Enguerrand. One end runs 25.7251 years faster than the other."

She had finally called him by his given name and that made him smile. Then he frowned, thinking hard.

"Who *were* these people and how'd they manage *that*?"

"I have no answer for the first question—we have no idea who they were or what happened to them. But this relic of their civilization is in fine working order. As to the second, as best can be surmised, they spun one end at close to the speed of light while the other was left undisturbed. When enough time dilation had accrued for their liking they maneuvered both terminals back into proximity, back here as it turns out, where there is eternal power pulsing to keep the throat open. It might be millions of years old already. There's no way to tell."

"So I'm going to go in one end..."

"It's the one we call 'north,' the one on 'top.'"

"And I'll come out the other..."

"Yes, you'll exit from 'south.'"

"And I'll be here?"

"Yes, you'll be right here."

"But it will be twenty five years ago?"

"25.7251 years ago, yes."

At length, Brabec entered in a huff and stood in front of them with his hands on his hips. He was nettled.

"If I had wanted to send an ambrosiac I'd have sent Mec! What is this?"

She was steadfast.

"You wanted this done fast. This is the best way."

Receptivity, inability to feel fear, complete jubilation, self-assurance—this is what ambrosiacs experienced, but so much more. For mind-bending forays into places perhaps best left unexplored, ambrosia could produce an odd lucidity too. This she'd banked on.

"He understands most of it now?" Brabec turned his gaze

on Enguerrand. "So you know what's expected?" he asked.

Enguerrand answered him calmly.

"I was going to kill you a while back. I'd already asked forgiveness for the sin I was about to commit. I would have done it but then you told me about my wife and daughter."

Brabec rolled his eyes and let out an exasperated puff.

"You see, Mec? You guys should take your jobs more seriously. I told you he was dangerous." He focused back on Enguerrand. "That's right. I've got them. Now you get back there and bring me what I want."

Enguerrand nodded his head in agreement and spoke without emotion.

"That's what I'm going to do."

"Well, good," Brabec said, calmer now. "I don't care how you do it, just do it."

"I'm going to," Enguerrand repeated.

Brabec clapped his hands.

"Is everything ready to go? What are we waiting for?"

She turned to Enguerrand and told him slowly, softly, reassuringly, "When you get to the other side you'll be able to access all you need. Everything is on board. Okay? Any questions?"

Enguerrand smiled at her and asked a candid one.

"What are you doing with these awful people?"

She didn't counter that she had a daughter too. Instead, she wished him *bon voyage*.

"Good luck, Enguerrand Duprey."

Chapter Four: Stacking the Deck

When our hatred is too bitter it places us below those whom we hate.
—Francois de La Rochefoucauld, Maxim No. 338

THE PASSAGE THROUGH the pulsar portal was surprisingly easy navigating. It was enough to simply nudge the beat-up, decades old quantum cruiser into barely the roughest direction of the wormhole. Nature took care of the rest save but that in these bizarre environs nature was angry. With less power to escape than a leaf passing over the edge of one of the thundering waterfalls on Eta Cassiopeia-6, not only the craft but the very ether of space-time that surrounded it, the actual fabric of existence, was washed into the gaping maw of this unquenchable drain.

To the extent that dark energy pushed space to expand and however much more cosmic volume was added to the universe, here was an escape valve for the pressure. Enguerrand, the ship that bore him and the void anywhere near it in every direction, were flushed down the cosmic culvert with more impetus than scales have readings to measure, and in the end, faster than the speed of thought for a duration of the journey.

For this phenomenon, the idea itself of what actually transpired was too slippery, too elusive, and required too much mental mercury to properly fathom. Some part of it was literally over both before and after it began.

Enguerrand was ejected out of the south pole of the ferociously pulsing sphere and pushed away, still in a rapidly decreasing slipstream of pure space, arriving twenty five years in the past.

It wouldn't be accurate to say he woke up in Nev's arms, because though not totally sensible, he was conscious during the transit through the wormhole, even if he felt like that interval could have been a microsecond or a decades-long journey with ambrosia not helping his judgment. And Nev didn't actually have her arms around him, although she was definitely dialed onto a very friendly setting.

"You've been through quite a few shocks lately." She purred the words. "But you need your wits about you at this moment, Enguerrand. May I suggest this?"

She popped an ampoule under his nostrils and two or three breaths later, the ambrosia antidote began its work. Enguerrand slowly started coming back to himself. Only now did he realize he'd been almost outside of himself, his own internal autopilot having been engaged so as to keep him in one piece mentally throughout the duration. He'd never stopped praying aloud from one end of the wormhole to the other, throughout the entire twenty-five years, without even really knowing it, the words coming out from a place over which he had no control at all. He still mumbled the entreaties as the android and her smelling salts brought him back to a much-improved place, in a terrified and bewildered state, true, but certainly better.

This Nev-igator, he realized immediately, was set on "flirtatious." Sappy, solicitous doe eyes made that conspicuous, as did the light brushing touches that went with everything she said. Worse, this model's seductive lure—considered sexy two and a half decades ago—seemed oddly dated. It was like waking up with a bright light in one's face.

"Go to *professional*," Enguerrand commanded as soon as he could think straight.

Nev morphed at the voice command, her now dour face hardened, hair shortened, and her measurements going from curvy to frumpy. Nev's attitude had changed too.

"I can go all the way to Otto-matic if you like."

Since that would be a far swing to the other end of the gradations, right through female to the flip side of the gender spectrum, it was a snarky query.

"One notch friendlier," he instructed, ignoring the insinuation. "One more click."

"How's this?"

This new Nev blossomed, but still wound up on the margin between mousy and boyish. She was pretty, but just so. He noticed a thin centimeter-long scar running from the corner of her lips into her right cheek. It was intended to give her character and make her seem flawed and approachable. The rest of her, softened but still advertising hoyden, wasn't too intimidating either.

"Don't speak. I want silence. I'll require your assistance shortly but don't speak now."

It wasn't shortly. The next hours were spent like no others in his life. He'd been held hard for a week and forced to watch a lashing. The rest piled on top of this—both his and his family's life in the gravest peril—and now being jettisoned into a place that most certainly couldn't even exist, was enough to push to the limit any man who breathed.

The psychological torment was worsened since no time, no focus, no thoughts could be spared for any of that. There were other things that, abominably, took precedence.

So, the first few hours in the past were spent doing everything in his power to keep from breaking down mentally. It took all he had just to convince himself that he wasn't dead, in limbo, in a coma, or insane. What reached down and pulled him to the air in the end was a terrible yet powerful thought: Brabec Van Maanen Alexis, Alpha C-15307 was going to die for this. To do that he'd have to live and he'd have to get back. He put pulsars, and wormholes, and their super advanced creators out of his mind. He was going to kill him and as long as he was shamed into admitting everything else to himself, this time he wasn't even going to ask for absolution.

"Weapons," was the next word he said to Nev.

Since Nev-igators didn't respirate, she'd been waiting patiently without breathing a word.

"Weapons?" She used shorthand for more information.

"What kinds are on board and where are they?"

"Well, I'm afraid, Mr. Duprey," Nev looked down and paused. "I won't be able to answer that question at this time."

"Did you just refuse an order?" It was a stupid thing to say. Of course, she had. Nev tried to be as diplomatic as possible.

"Oh, no, Mr. Duprey. You are obviously in command. I can assure you that anything…"

He interrupted; he'd heard this kind of speech before.

"Anything I want, save a core protocol you're following?"

She seemed happy he'd put the awkward business so succinctly for her.

"Your orders are to be obeyed explicitly, yes, except for that."

"And weapons are part of that?"

She looked him straight in the eyes.

"There are no weapons, Mr. Duprey."

Because his patience was at an all-time low, he increased the cadence of his speech.

"What else is off the table?"

"You'll excuse me if I'd rather not go into every possible exigency right now but would rather address each of your orders as they come, that way..."

"Oh, strangle you with Orion's Belt!" He'd rather talk man to man about all this, considering the unfriendly dialogue that was very apt to be scripted. "Go to Otto-matic, immediately!"

Everything that moved in the void, and of course without exception crafts superluminal, navigated by autopilot. Otto-matics or Nev-igators, physical touchable things, and other corporeal automations had their advantages over the classical yet ethereal three-D, holographic shape-shifters, called amanuenses, which performed the same tasks on many ships.

The androids—even in their timid gamine form like Nev now—were quite well equipped to deal with any task or emergency. They were walking, talking welding torch, vise grip, drill, pneumatic punch, x-ray machine, ultraviolet and infrared scanner and anything else.

No airy, cyber-born ghost of an amanuensis could do any of that. And the mechanicals were just as smart, since they were amanuenses at the core, intimately connected to the Nexus to receive petabytes of data every second, capable of solving any problem every conceived, yet contained within an amazing electromechanical chassis.

Enguerrand wasn't pleased with the standard, unintimidating, helpful Otto—actually Enguerrand wasn't pleased with anything. He had his wits about himself fully now and he was in a seething, murderous mood. His next order was due to pure spite.

"Go to Capellan pirate."

Enguerrand hated Capellans. Not all of them were assassins and cut-throats—not enough to condemn a whole star system—but they were scum in Enguerrand's mind. It didn't help that two friends, fellow couriers, had been killed by Capellans. He simply despised them. Otto-matic transmuted into an evil visage, and did an excellent job of it. The skull was misshapen, purposefully twisted and deformed, the result of cruel bindings around the head from birth. To highlight the ugliness, an unattractive tonsure left the distended crown bald, the fringes long and slick with Taursurian bearcat grease.

"Uglier," Enguerrand ordered.

Otto complied. Wrinkles, age, boils and scars adorned the new incarnation.

"There, now you look as ugly as your protocol—just as loathsome as the man who superimposed it. This will help us keep track of who the human is on board and who's the monster."

The monster didn't answer, but did acknowledge with a foul, low grumbling. Enguerrand motioned around himself.

"What ship is this and when was this old thing built?"

No quantum cruisers were created equal, even though they looked exactly the same—spinning tubular rings. The basic design couldn't change in order to use centrifugal force to act as artificial gravity. The only calculus was the radii and circumferences of these superluminal hoops along—with better classes of gyroscopical ballasters to smooth out the force to make it feel linear and Earth-like.

"This is the vessel *Ultramariner*. She was built twenty-five years ago," Otto growled. "Did you want to be cruising around the galaxy in a model that hadn't come out yet?"

"Well, what's to prevent it from falling to pieces when we step on the accelerator?"

"That's the least of your worries. This ship has been re-vamped from deck to hub. It's as fast as anything that moves, even back in the time you just left. It's just the shell and the registry that's old. She'd been left orbiting one of the moons in the Sigma Draconis system, destined for scrap and a target for micro-meteors for the last decade." Otto slowed down and waited for the human to catch up. It wasn't a genial and patient pause. "For anyone who'd care to scan there's nothing out of the ordinary here, free-ranger, except that you're traveling the galaxy in style in the 'newest' model cruiser. Can you savvy that?"

"Alright, that's good." Enguerrand ignored Otto's insolence. "Traveling unnoticed is good since I'd certainly rather not answer any official questions. I guess anything I'd say wouldn't add up correctly even in the best of circumstances."

Otto shook his head aggressively, like a brigand.

"You're thinking. If you'd like to go on breathing, you might want to keep that up. Because if you blunder into getting this ship forcibly boarded it will be scuttled." The android gave him a sneer that displayed the uninspiring probabilities he'd calculated in that regard. "Should I repeat that?"

It was almost as if Otto wanted to rub it in.

Enguerrand didn't ignore that second piece of impertinence.

"How dare you ask me a question without a prompt? Don't do it again."

The Capellan corsair gave him a dismissive shrug.

"Aye, captain."

"And why are weapons being withheld from me?"

Now Otto's indifferent air changed to one of peevish inquisitiveness.

"What would you do with a weapon? Are you planning on killing someone, Frenchman?"

Enguerrand allowed himself to forget for a moment that he wasn't talking to anyone really, answering incredulously.

"As a matter of fact, and as I'm sure your clinking memories will corroborate, that's pretty much not far from what I've been sent to do."

That brought the unadulterated churlishness out of Otto.

"My memories, human? Of such things you delude to concern yourself? Very well, I'll answer in the same way the architect of the Pyramid of Trans-Pegasi could respond to an ant, since they're both builders and to your mind must share an equal bond. At the risk of informing you without prompt, your eminence, it's part of protocol to counsel that your interactions over the next three periods should be kept to the absolute minimum. You are stomping around on a playing field that occurred twenty five years ago. You are forewarned to have a care, Enguerrand Duprey. Putting a weapon in your hands, courier, is too dangerous."

Otto-matic had earned his attention, all of it. Enguerrand sat silently and pondered every single bad-natured word. The Capellan had called him a courier and it stung that the machine hadn't meant it as a compliment. But the truth is that men of Enguerrand's sort, even among billions of humans, were unique.

Couriers were stellar nomads, not unlike pony express riders of a millennium ago, with the same drover's gaze in their eyes. They did nothing but roam the Big Black. It gave them a distinctive and hard-to-pin-down air, and not admired by everyone. But then couriers knew what they thought of themselves and that's the only thing that counted despite everyone else's opinion. Enguerrand had schemed, fought, bluffed, jury-rigged and finagled his way out of plenty of deathly jams and for the sake of his wife and child wasn't going to fail now either. He didn't regard the term as the slightest derisive, yet insofar as the machine were concerned, here insisted on the correct one.

"You'll refer to me as 'captain'," is all he said.

This wasn't a captain to be taken lightly either, young but very experienced. His never-say-die stamp was genuine, and this particular pilot's verve was intensified by the rare emerald-eyed beauty his prenatal fever had bestowed, in a shade of green nature often used as a warning. It was proof positive that something deadly had tried to kill him before he'd even been born, and failed.

He decided to clear up the ground rules doubtlessly.

"We seem to have at least established the fact that I'm in charge of this vessel. Are you to follow my orders?"

"Of course," Otto abided.

Enguerrand tested the breadth of his powers.

"Put in a trajectory for Epsilon Majoris VII and cast off immediately."

"That's not going to be possible; you'll have to select another destination," Otto countered, using a very truculent pitch. "In the periods we have available, we couldn't even reach that Sector much less return to the portal in time. You have all latitude, unless your directives are to plainly circumvent protocol. Choose a port-of-call within those strictures."

While it was strange listening to Otto speak like that, Capellan pirates not known for their refined communication skills, Enguerrand shook his head in wonder.

"No weapons, a potentially scuttled ship, and a three-period leash. Is there anything else?"

Otto-matic, no matter in whatever mode, had been superimposed with a protocol to help Enguerrand in any and every way. Here, its amanuensis determined, was an excellent place for a pep talk.

"Well, you're sitting at the helm of the fastest ship in the universe, by far, in this time. It's twenty-five years ago, remember. And, on board is enough ambrosia to purchase a moonlet. That's going to be your currency since Nexus won't recognize credits you don't have."

It was hard to see the mechanism as anything other than a buccaneer from light years across the galaxy. The way Otto paused and seemed to choose its words now gave it the aspect of a cagey bandit chieftain.

"You came to Brabec Van Maanen Alexis, Alpha C-15307's attention as a particularly daring and experienced courier. Your chances of successfully completing your task aren't terrible." He hesitated long enough to cough up a glob of hardened mucous, a disgusting habit prevalent among the riff-raff of Capella who suffered from endemic bouts of biliousness. Otto chewed on it for a moment and swallowed.

"However, you're wasting time. You have three periods and we're drifting."

Enguerrand took a few seconds to make the decision of his life, too long though for the liking of his Capellan auto-pilot.

"What's the matter, free-ranger? Can't think fast enough?"

The autopilot's poisoned arrow dug into Enguerrand's Achilles Heel. He was indeed part of a dwindling class of human beings who could form pure, unadulterated, pristinely biological—human—thoughts. Free-rangers gladly accepted their imperfect and cluttered notions as part of their individuality—far less offensive than what they deemed the toxic evil they bitterly opposed: the censoring of mankind's collective character. But strangling moods and other mental demons doesn't come easily or without a struggle, and the free-rangers weren't going down without a fight.

"There's no gadgetry to me," Enguerrand belittled, shooting back. "I'll do the thinking, and without any help from an elaborate can opener."

The mechanism shrugged off the insult and parried with one of its own.

"Just my luck, a free-ranger for a captain. Oh, well, I always wondered what the inside of a star was like. Is that where you'll be steering us?"

The robot had reason to view Enguerrand as a dysfunctional freak of nature. He lacked the blessings of a number of generations of nanites, and not just to keep the mind in check. They were necessary for handling all the mundane interactions and transactions of life that required accessing the Nexus: shopping, selling goods, entering contracts, booking passage, taking a job, paying taxes, attending school, joining a guild, transferring property, marrying, divorcing—those, and every other aspect of life outside of breathing.

But it was the indirect, passive, involuntary default work they did though that made for the Golden Age just dawning. Everyone's nanites interacted with each others' by the trillions, automatically, unobtrusively, brilliantly, incessantly. All that data—GPS, credit accounting, health status, sexual receptivity, level of depression or cheerfulness, and everything else—was collated nanosecond by nanosecond in every quadrant of the settled Milky Way, making everything go. Free-rangers just didn't get that. Or if they did the misanthrope in them didn't like it.

"If I set a course for the core of a star," the human replied, "you can believe I'll have a reason for doing so."

"Ha!" The autopilot motioned to the talisman around Enguerrand's neck, advertising his beliefs. "Sure you will. Mumbo jumbo always finds a way."

Believing, though, was the precious cinder kept alive by free-rangers. Being nanite-free they managed to keep that to themselves, along with their identity, location and everything else, but making decent people wonder why the suspicious person passing next to them had such an unseemly interest in refraining from sharing information properly, by default, as every other normal individual did. The only answer was the obvious one: they had to be up to no good.

When everyone else went about displaying their marital status, veracity, level of sexual excitement, profession, resume, passport history, and everything else, these outlaws, flimflammers and shirkers wouldn't even disclose their names to passers-by.

The required gall astounded respectable people who kept free-rangers at arms' length. Then too their insufferable insolence was matched by the outlandish mummery they kept alive with their inviolable connections to the cults of Jesus Christ, Jehovah, Gaia and others, with their crucifixes, crescents, stars, and triskelions. There were many who found much to despise in free-rangers.

The noises that accompanied Otto's phlegmatic mishaps, along with its intolerable insults, were sufficient to change the channel in the end.

Enguerrand had had enough.

"Go to Otto-matic 'universal.'"

Otto metamorphosed into what he was always intended to be: his normal, typical, nondescript, uncharacteristic, ordinary everyman self.

"Why no weapons?" Enguerrand tried again insistently.

Otto-matic continued in the most balanced, modulated speech, unaccented by any regionalism from any quadrant anywhere in Creation.

"There can be no settling of scores, Mr. Duprey, either from the past or the future. The subject of weapons brings with it a point you should well understand. Brabec Van Maanen Alexis, Alpha C-15307 has done this a few times; we've managed to garner the slightest bit of information about how to proceed. You're in a very precarious environment."

Enguerrand wouldn't relent.

"Elucidate, please."

"Well, you're walking around in a cosmos where your mother is pregnant with you, Mr. Duprey. Give that some thought. That's just the beginning though—there's much more if we start down that path. In this state, humans tend not to adapt well quickly if at all. You're advised to avert your gaze and accept counsel."

Enguerrand did though want a look at least in that direction.

"Yes, that *is* a strange state of affairs, isn't it? And what does your cyborg's logic say about *that*? I'm in a universe where my *in utero* self also resides. There's much more than that? This must confuse you, doesn't it, Otto, just like it baffles me, a mere human?"

Otto's electromechanical soul could rise above anything and carry on however.

"Not at all. I'm aware of many conundrums; existence seems built upon a foundation of enigmas. You could ask me to answer why there can be no such thing as a perfect sphere, how long the afterlife lasts, or why we're made of matter and not anti-matter and we'd be on the same ground. Any educated person knows that the scaffolding of the universe rests ultimately upon error, purely illogical contradictions. You've triggered an irresolvable rift to embed itself in space-time but one that is at least causative since the basis of which is your having exited through a wormhole."

So that's what an amanuensis looked like when it lied, Enguerrand thought to himself.

The electronic palpitations shone through the flowery claptrap, its primal functions making any and all attempts at processing the pernicious data while somehow upholding the pretense that a sensible output resulted.

It was a rare thing to see and was usually only taken in by those unfortunates on the brink. It's assumed that a few fibs had come out of amanuenses to soothe human nerves just before unavoidable and inescapable fatal accidents and mishaps took place—mercifully. This was different however. Otto knew Enguerrand was fully aware he was telling double-talking stories and yet was proceeding nonetheless.

"Oh, yeah, perfect spheres. This is a lot like that," Enguerrand scoffed sarcastically. "You haven't the faintest idea either of how to make sense of this, do you? You're as gobstruck as I am, yet no one coded into you any flow on any chart to deal with this."

Enguerrand wasn't buying and said so, flat out.

"You're actually pretending to be giving advice about things that turn every scientific and mathematical law into mush, and expecting me to nod my head? Where we are is where nothing can be; you must comprehend that as well as I do."

Otto coiled his thin lips into a guilty simper.

"Well, you have a point, but I've been programmed to override those kind of..." Otto paused and gathered those things he very much wanted to display now to his human charge: his thoughts. "Deterministic chaos?"

Otto gave that a shot; it missed completely, so he chose another tack.

"But a man like you who has intortion-jumped a thousand times between stellar systems understands that there are many things achieved about which not everything is known down to the last fractal. That needn't interfere with logically following protocol."

Otto only wished to move forward, pushed onward by ratiocinative code inscribed so profusely and deeply that it worked even in this invalid milieu. It didn't serve any purpose to dwell in these inexplicable and enigmatic places; there was a simple mission and objective to pursue. So he changed the subject to a more positive note.

Otto-matic's uncertain palpitations were replaced with a friendly set of agreeing nods, these having been determined the kind of signals that put humans at their ease.

"There are tools at your disposal though. In a matter of speaking, that is. There is on board fourteen full hekats of ambrosia. You should be able to barter your way through any exigency in any port-of-call with that kind of cargo."

Such a quantity of ambrosia could fund the recruitment of a mercenary army.

"Then there's something else that should lift a great weight from your shoulders," Otto promised. "And you could probably use some good news," it added solicitously. "Brabec Van Maanen Alexis, Alpha C-15307 is going to give you the opportunity to load the dice in your favor. Complete one simple piece of child's play before initiating the hunt for your bounty and even if things go badly for you afterwards and you should end up returning empty-handed, you'll have the hope of receiving quarter. You'd be very foolish to overlook this small housekeeping request."

Enguerrand's mind quickly saw the best reasons for a prince's ransom in ambrosia to have been stowed away in the ship's hold.

"Future commodity contracts, bets on winning teams that haven't taken the field yet, or real estate options on boondocks parcels destined for gentrification, which? Is it one of those or something else?"

 Otto admitted it was something else.

"You'll be purchasing stock as a proxy for Brabec Van Maanen Alexis, Alpha C-15307."

"In mega-corporations that in this time are in their infancies, I assume?"

Enguerrand had just seen an unusual example of android deception. Now he was treated to an exhibition of extra-human appeasement.

"It isn't just monetary, Mr. Duprey. Brabec Van Maanen Alexis, Alpha C-15307's control of the portal goes far beyond mere money."

"But there's plenty of that, no?" Enguerrand mocked.

"Yes, of course. But, well…the details are of no importance, but you realize slight changes in the past can affect the proper monumental results—political, cultural, monetary, military—in the present."

Enguerrand did grasp that.

"And that makes Brabec the closest thing there is to a divinity or wizard."

He apprehended the rest too very quickly. It was small wonder that Brabec always turned up on the right side of the river whenever the cavalry arrived at the last minute. His incredible propensity for having his finger on the pulse of everything was no knack at all. He not only possessed a crystal ball, he held the genie hostage who was compelled to call forth the visions Brabec desired.

"It's a simple matter. You can choose from a list of brokers who almost certainly will accept payment in the medium of exchange you have to offer. They'll take care of the details, placing the instruments in escrow until, well, the present...twenty five years from now."

Enguerrand understood perfectly.

"So, a windfall will magically pop into existence accruing to Brabec's accounts after I've done my job."

Otto smiled.

"Brabec Van Maanen Alexis, Alpha C-15307 will know immediately that his factotum will be acting in good faith." The smile vanished quickly. "You can be sure that good faith will purchase the best treatment for your family."

The next words struggled from between Enguerrand Duprey's clenching teeth.

"You're not to mention my family again."

"Yes, captain. Please accept my sincere apologies. That was untoward."

Enguerrand didn't give a thought to absurd contrition from a non-human offender. Instead, he turned to other weighty matters. Otto judged the time right to disclose the last details to his human charge, especially now that the subject of his family had been broached.

"Listen very carefully to this, Mr. Duprey, for more than you may realize depends on you not only fully comprehending but determining here and now to act ruthlessly to prevent causing yourself and others great and irremediable harm."

That preface didn't sound good to Enguerrand, and he let Otto know it.

"If you're attempting to scare me, I'd rather instead that you focus on informing me. I've already seen enough over the last few days to turn a hundred men's hair gray. Is there something *more?*"

"Oh, yes, there is quite a bit more, a whole universe more."

Otto actually paused to catch the breath he nonetheless couldn't hold. He must have done it for effect.

"Brabec Van Maanen Alexis, Alpha C-15307 has learned more about quantum mechanics in these last periods than all the greatest physicists of the last millennium combined. You see, he's had this age-old relic of a race of demi-gods with which to experiment and we've managed to ascertain quite a few important facts."

"Hurrah," Enguerrand responded, along with a slow hand clap. "Such as?"

"Quantum systems exist in a state of genuine indeterminacy; this has been known for centuries, of course, with all possible outcomes coexisting, each as eager to 'happen' as the next. However, the idea of separate universes coming into being as distinct versions of what we do or don't do, where we go or don't go, whether we turn right or left, requires a multiverse of infinite universes with infinite copies of all of us— rather a daunting and highly unappealing possibility for what reality looks like with the mask off. Many physicists don't like that view of existence. You probably aren't too fond of it either, I'm assuming."

Otto made a disagreeable face.

"It's so terrifyingly complicated," the machine allowed itself to put the finer points on this human emotion, "that the very meaning of life seems to cease. If everything is happening everywhere with untold trillions of copies of everyone doing anything in an infinite series of universes, well, that means that really nothing is occurring at all since there would be no specificity, no preferred reality, in essence, just illusion."

Otto paused for those words to sink in.

"You're following all this, Mr. Duprey?"

"Of course, I follow. Who hasn't heard this lecture before? What's the point you're making?"

He didn't say it with bravado; the tone betrayed more than a little concern.

"A simple one. It turns out that this view is the correct one, as difficult as that may be to accommodate. As you may have surmised from the very bounty you're currently pursuing, you're not the first to have been sent through the pulsar portal." Then Otto added gravely, "Not hardly."

"Are you telling me to be careful, Otto? Is that the shortcut version?"

"No, not exactly. Unfortunately, what I'm telling you is that whether you're careful or not, in this dangerously surreal, impossible, hyper-sensitive landscape of kaleidoscope reality in which you find yourself, just breathing, taking a step, allowing your heart to beat—indeed, the very act of thinking is going to be enough to push that indeterminacy one way or the other, and in this place—a past that can't exist with you in it but yet does— some very nasty results can occur from just the mildest brushes with what for a lack of a better term we'll call fate."

Enguerrand gave that some long, hard thought. He believed Otto. Just taking stock of where he was, simply reminding himself that he wasn't dreaming and his current circumstances were real, was enough to pump more veracity into Otto's words than if an archangel had been sent to deliver the warning.

"So you're cautioning me not to look back at Sodom or I'll be turned into salt. Something like that?"

Otto smiled at him.

"You're a brave man, Mr. Duprey. Others before you have reacted quite differently at this point. I have to tell you I admire that about you already. And your reference to the Bible is apropos. If there is some deity or sacred text which can provide you with guidance, now is an excellent time to solicit that aid."

Enguerrand, brave or not, didn't feel valiant. He answered with a trembling voice.

"And those others...what happened to them?"

Otto-matic shook his head sadly.

"They didn't fare so well, not at all."

He left it at that.

Enguerrand, of course, wasn't satisfied.

"Care to be a bit more specific? Did they burst into flame, implode, explode, come down with a cold, lose their hair? Just exactly what misstep did they take and what price did they pay for it?"

The deadly serious look on the mechanical's face was matched by the perfectly accentuated tone of extreme caution that carried the words.

"Try not to interact with anyone, Mr. Duprey. Do the least you can to effect the most. On no account should you give anyone an indication of who and what you are; that might be the worst thing you could do. It would most certainly cause a chain of unforeseen repercussions that would pile up to await you over the next twenty-five years, sufficient to create some great and insoluble problems if and when you return. You're making a new reality for yourself at this very moment, both here and in the future and any other place and time as well. And you're constructing it blindfolded. You shouldn't be too surprised if not all the pieces come to fit well in the end or whether some of the pieces turn out to be missing, or worse, from some other completely different puzzle. *Me comprenez-vous?*"

"I comprehend," Enguerrand answered, "that I've been converted into a 'what' *and* a 'who' at the same time. And my coming out of this is being described as 'if' and 'when.' *Mais oui, je comprends.*

Enguerrand tried to buck up; strangely, he was concerned that the mechanical should see him both scared and depressed. So instead of soliciting pity he opted for one more bit of useful information.

"With no interaction, no introductions, no breathing, no stepping, no pumping of blood," Enguerrand checked off the list of forbidden options, "that could make it a bit difficult to find one particular person hiding anywhere in the Spiral Arm— much less contract Brabec's business for him as well. That should be a neat trick, won't it?"

Otto spoke sincerely.

"I have faith in you, Mr. Duprey. You're different from the others."

"Oh, really?" Enguerrand asked. "How so?"

"I already said you were a brave man," the ship's amanuensis complimented a second time, "and a good one too. Anyone can tell that."

"Ah, well, I'd just as soon you'd have included 'smart.'"

Enguerrand reconsidered his initial prospectus on Brabec's scheme before speaking.

"I have an idea how well the prior Frankenstein investments attempted by others before me worked out. Not too well? Brabec Van Maanen Alexis, Alpha C-15307, you tell me, is currently the leading candidate for galaxy-class physicist laureate thanks to information gleaned by his ham-handed misuse of the greatest artifact ever discovered being put to use as a million-year-old, extraterrestrial fraud machine. I doubt such a miscreant and villain has turned a single credit profit after deducting for all the inherent pitfalls you've just warned me about. Be honest with me, has he turned his first credit yet?"

Otto shrugged sheepishly.

"We do keep trying, Mr. Duprey. We keep trying."

Otto then placed his hands together the way humans do when a conversation is coming to an end.

"Just to be clear then, Mr. Duprey, where all this comes together insofar as what you've been tasked to do, I'm to have constant access to your third eye during every nanosecond of our time here. You're an interloper walking around a minefield. If I see you starting to stumble, if I judge that you have lost the mental edge required to successfully continue, this enterprise will be brought to an immediate end."

Otto pursed his lips.

"If I need to make that clearer, please, now is the time to ask for clarification."

Enguerrand needed none.

"I understand very clearly."

They sat silently for a moment while Enguerrand collected his final thoughts. As daunting and terrible as the tasks in front of him were, he made up his mind very quickly.

"Lay in a course for Tau Corvus. I'll contract with the broker there. Cast off immediately."

"At once, Captain. Casting off, in three…two…one."

Within seconds, the craft, *Ultramariner*, was surrounded by a superluminal multidimensional vortex, but revamping the space between the ship and the Tau Corvus star system, equivalent to ten times, now twenty, now dozens of times the speed of light. As the vessel settled at maximum velocity Otto turned and offered a last piece of advice.

"Indiscriminate killing isn't the only pitfall to avoid. Creation of life—but born out of place, as it were—isn't something to be counseled either. If abstinence becomes overwhelming, I can be anything you like, man or woman, or anything else, in any way you desire."

The offer was more disgusting to Enguerrand Duprey than listening to a Capellan pirate chew his cud.

Chapter Five: Cosmic Onion

Some disguised lies so resemble truth that we should judge badly were we not deceived.
—Francois de La Rochefoucauld, Maxim No. 282

THERE WAS A sizeable intorsion lag between the pulsar portal and Tau Corvus even at *Ultramariner's* mind-boggling pace. In point of fact, quantum cruisers didn't move in any conventional way at all.

To be more precise, it was the black of space that was twisted, poked and broken into, treading areas where there is neither proper time nor distance, nor then subsequently the speed that should describe ratios between the two. Humanity had gotten used to the notion that velocity itself was an untrustworthy concept used to describe its movements around the mind-numbingly gigantic celestial empire it had created.

The space between mankind's far, far-ranging outposts was the slippery customer that refused to obey the old-fashioned calculations between here and there. And it was this space that quantum comprimers violated, forcing entry down to its incalculable Plank length—a billionth of a trillionth of a trillionth of an inch—and then pushed some more past that frenetic boundary.

Poking around this incredible region, the void showed itself as just what anyone should expect of something built of nothing. Beyond the Plank length, what was there couldn't suitably be called "nothing." It was the place where distance, time, dimension had no limit—no start, duration or terminus—so it was no real place at all. It was called "quantum foam," but it was brash that science even gave it a name.

Couriers' opinions on all this counted for at least something since no one traveled more than they did. Their nickname for the indescribable ether through which they piloted their crafts was "marrow," as if they wormed their way through the innards of the bones of a pantheistic godhead. It was as good an explanation as any for it was realized that anyone who said they understood all the nuts and bolts was quite simply lying. No one did.

Otto quipped as they hurtled through the marrow.

"She's quite a ship, isn't she, Mr. Duprey?"

How such speed could be realized was the result of playing amazing games with the laws of nature at the heart of everything—and cheating. Manipulating space in eleven dimensional vectors temporarily thwarted even the bosons of the Higgs field that gave the vessel mass, allowing *Ultramariner* to move through a thin conduit of space rendered fleetingly devoid of the normal rules for inertia, mass—and speed.

Newton's and Einstein's bylaws weren't broken but only bruised such that the craft, seemingly without mass insofar as a Nature were concerned, could cruise through sections of space in which time and distance had no real calculus, and hence speed left at end a word that could wind up registering at almost any value.

Enguerrand nodded appreciatively.

"It's a first-rate vessel," he agreed. He put the autopilot to use though; he had other things to do. "Take the tiller, Otto. The bridge is yours."

Enguerrand used the transit time, settling into his cabin for one of the few exercises now left to humans with so much of everything else dominated by their contrivances: thinking. His task now was to get to know the quarry he'd been sent to hunt, one Vanessa Braverman, to scrutinize everything about her, to find a way to catch up to her.

She actually *had* a story, as opposed to any particular single human unit in the Home Sector or many robotic souls from one of the hundred star systems in Creation. She was a free-ranger, born and raised in the third and outer layer of the four million cubic light year celestial spheroid that was humanity's great and stupendously far-flung domain.

He hoped this would make his search easier. He banked on the fact that free-rangers felt very ill at ease at any locale within Creation, especially ones on the run from twenty five years in the future.

The two inner concentric spheres weren't very appealing for a free-ranger. And as for entering the dense core, the Home Sector—Earth and the nasty, crowded, chaotic inner light year out to the Oort Cloud of comets—a free-ranger would rather visit purgatory than go anywhere near Earth. The cradle of the human race was as alluring as the rotting skin shed from animals that had moved on to some other form. Hundreds of billions of resumes from Earth were exactly the same: void, save vital statistics and subsidy allotment data. Individuals within the Home Sector simply were born, ate and breathed for a while at state expense, reproduced, and then expired.

What those on Earth did was precisely nothing. Everything had long since been unconditionally surrendered to automation. Machines seeded and harvested the great oceans, processed, transported and distributed the food, smelted the ores, built the constructs, and did everything else in between. The age-old automata was a self-supporting, colossal reticulation of apparatuses that now did nothing more than sustain and repair itself—and preserve mankind on the home planet.

So, humanity in this ancient zone had come full circle back to its origins, reduced to the status of benign fungus that coated the cogs of the machinery it had built in a past stage. Like all parasites, hundreds of billions of people on Earth periodically perished in great die-offs—caused either by raging epidemics or intermittent and unavoidable famines—to be replenished in time by the next wave of booming newborn hordes.

The Home Sector was a great, ongoing, Malthusian trap and the cycle had gone unbroken for centuries now. No one imagined it would ever change. This was one image of the face of humanity—thankfully festering in but one star system, Sol—destined to leave a very unflattering fossil of its pointless yet prolific imprint on one small segment of the Milky Way.

Investigating someone from Earth then would be a bizarre task as their amoeba-like dossiers wouldn't be far different. Vanessa Braverman wasn't from the Old Planet though; and there were other faces.

Around the Home Sector for a hundred light years in all directions was the vast sphere of Creation, the true mainstream habitat of mankind. The great mistakes that had condemned squalid Earth and robbed it of its decency, of its heart and mind, were scrupulously avoided here. Automation was even more advanced and widespread everywhere throughout Creation but was kept at bay by design, by custom, by law.

What had destroyed society in the Home Sector wouldn't be allowed to spread beyond the Oort Cloud. It was a plain and simple expedient that held machines in check and protected the soul of humankind throughout Creation: guilds and unions. No single screw could be turned from Alpha Centauri to Xi Scorpii without a human being present and in charge. No hole was dug on any moonlet anywhere unless under the eyes of a living, breathing man or woman supervising. Fleets and armies of drones could certainly and exponentially out-produce the relatively slow-paced economy of Creation were they simply turned loose. For once, mankind spoke in one voice for its collective heart rather than its purse—the horror of dead-eyed Earth serving its great purpose. It was a terrifying and constant reminder of what awaited any race that put efficiency and economy above humanity.

If Vanessa Braverman had been born within the vast bubble of Creation she would have been rich, an entrepreneur, a supervisor. This population, no more than a few billion of them, had done an awe-inspiring job. There had never been supervisors such as these. Inside a sphere with a diameter of two hundred light years, even the stars shone differently in the wake of these human managers and their machines. Dyson shells had been erected around them, putting an end to the wasteful flood of squandered energy that had poured out unimpeded since the birth of the Milky Way.

The shells powered staggeringly far-flung electromagnetic Tesla Fields, even past the furthest reaches, the heliopauses, of each star, the crests of the waves of all the fields meeting finally with each other and filling this entire vast region of the universe with crackling electricity. Information, communication and profligate power through the Nexus knit together hundred-star systems, creating an ordered, vibrant, bountiful, green knot of life halfway out from the galactic core in one of the Milky Way's spiral arms.

Mankind's domain didn't end here though. Some thought that it only just began at the thirty-parsec radius from Earth at the extreme far periphery of the orb of civilization. Hovering like a wispy halo around Creation was the Free Range.

Free-rangers pointed at the Home Sector and then asked what sort of dystopian horror was in store for those in Creation. The way they saw it, a terrible misstep had already sown the seed for their end: the insane marriage with nanites.

It may not have cast the citizens of Creation into the species of paramecium with their pathetic brethren on Earth, only that their category was in the eyes of free-rangers a few steps higher, more like the insect phylum. While it was an insulting exaggeration to say that the citizens of Creation were little removed from ants or hornets, those however inoculated with the newest and tenth generation of nanites, Gen-teners, *were* creepily wasp-like.

What mankind would look like by Gen-twenty no one could say. Free-rangers, however, were already making their opinion clear. They wouldn't take that ride with the rest of humanity to find out.

If the Free Range could hold the line, its culture, its vision would be the face of mankind a thousand years hence as Homo sapiens expanded into the rest of the galaxy. The two prior failed versions—the Home Sector and Creation—would be insignificant museums to show how humans profited and learned from their past errors. Beyond the Free Range began the bone-chilling boundlessness of the Big Black—terra incognita, untouched, unexplored, unclaimed. This, the future, was the prize.

The pulsar portal was some distance out into the Big Black, obviously still undiscovered. That made sense to Enguerrand now, thinking back to how the orb eclipsed and occluded the pulsar's beam, swallowing all the energy, endowing the portal with invisibility at long range. One would have to almost physically brush space with it to come to know of its existence.

Brabec was fortunate indeed to have stumbled upon it.

There was no Nexus or Tesla field out in these lonely and remote environs and everything was run on auxiliary. Enguerrand knew when he'd pierced the periphery of the nearest star system as his third eye switched to "engaged." He was back in civilization again. Anything he wanted to know he now only need think about. There was one thought crowding out all others. He wanted to know everything there was about Vanessa Braverman.

He started with the child Vanessa, scrutinizing every clue. Family, home, schooling, awards, demerits, interests; year by year, layer by layer, he built up an image of who she was. Everything, at first, made perfect sense—for the adolescent and teenage Vanessa. She was a child of an impeccably respectable extended family, among the richest in all of the Free Range, with quite detailed records going all the way back to the Home Sector. Hers was a clan of expert glacio-prospectors, their original hunting ground for floating icebergs of precious volatiles was the Oort Cloud itself.

That was three centuries ago, though. The Bravermans had moved on, wrangling mountain-sized chunks of frozen carbon dioxide, methane, ammonia and other sought after icy commodities. They had prowled the comet belts around a dozen star systems for generations, slowly moving further out from Earth and thereby avoiding the great catastrophes as they unfolded. It didn't strike Enguerrand as strange that they now should have opted to quit Creation and establish their home in the Free Range.

Above their profession, their livelihood, their reason for being, ahead of their very lives they placed something else. The Bravermans were Jewish to their very marrow, devout, implacable, orthodox adherents to their creed and mores. They wished nothing more at end than to be left in peace to practice their traditions and religion.

The Free Range welcomed them, and all others wishing to keep the embers of their own culture and religion alive, with open arms. However, something bothered Enguerrand. It was more than incongruous that Vanessa Braverman, the scion of one of the finest families in the entire Free Range, should be found in the company of the likes of Brabec Van Maanen Alexis, Alpha C-15307.

"Take it back to her Bat Mitzvah," Enguerrand thought and the Nexus responded, scrolling data, projecting the holographic representation of just what was asked, no matter the request.

The smiling, fresh-faced innocent was frocked in her *tallit* prayer shawl, bright-eyed, scrubbed clean, the image of the daughter that any man would love to father. She finished giving the reading in perfect Hebrew and began to explain her *tzedakah*. This particular charitable project was charming enough to bring a faint smile to Enguerrand's face as he watched and listened. By hand, she'd constructed a dozen enclosures for the species of aschimopoulites that inhabited her home planet.

"They're God's creatures and with as much right to their place as any other living thing," the twelve-year old angelic version of Vanessa Braverman explained. Her grandfather, the stoic, iron-faced paterfamilias of the clan, stood beside her and was none too pleased by the childish focus of his granddaughter's compassion. His gaze softened somewhat when she skillfully quoted the passage from the Torah that justified her empathy.

"Just as the Holy One, blessed be He, has mercy on human beings, so does He have mercy on animals."

Enguerrand moved on, pushing the years forward. By the time she turned eighteen, Vanessa had bloomed into a stunning, sultry, dark-eyed beauty, her outside matching and then surpassing the inner charm. Also, she'd done remarkably well with an impressive course of advanced honors studies, earning exceptional scores, very much on track to take the reins of her family's concerns one day.

"Medical," Enguerrand inquired.

There was absolutely nothing. She'd never been sick at any time in her young life.

"Mental," he didn't want to leave that stone unturned.

There was no hint of any infirmity here either.

"Criminal history?" He felt silly even pondering this question, viewing the ravishing, highly intelligent heiress of one of the Free Range's patrician families. Her record was absolutely pristine.

None of this made any sense, which set Enguerrand's internal pistons firing. This motor could be quite a dynamo. Enguerrand's pre-natal bout with Lacaillian fever was the great watershed of his life—bizarrely also an event having taken place prior to his birth. Whoever he had been meant to be, Enguerrand bore the marks, good and bad, of the distemper. His metabolism raced, all the time, like an engine idling on high and poised to be slipped into gear and let loose in a flash. That energy bled out in a unique way when he concentrated deeply. All the fiddling, toe-tapping, hair twirling, finger play and other nervous outlets were then shut down, the effervescence sucked up by the paramount biological agent in any human: his brain.

Now he sat motionless, his green, green eyes staring intently, absolutely frozen, save but for the languid and methodical movement of his balled-up fist slowly rubbing against the groove in his upper lip under the nose. The philtrum develops in the womb and often displays signs of developmental problems. Enguerrand's was extraordinary—deep, chiseled, overtly masculine. No matter the shocking disbelief that registered in the few people's eyes who'd witnessed Enguerrand Duprey moving at his highest gears in an emergency, far fewer ever saw this even more stunning exhibition.

Alone with his thoughts he pushed an internal lever and unleashed the greediest and most powerful organ in his body. The synapses firing within his cerebrum were super-charged, the electric tracery no mere trickle as with normal brains but instead a raging voltaic flood. He of course couldn't hold his own against even the most primitive quantum computer, but whatever original spark mortal men possessed in the beginning, whatever had pushed forward the clever and gutsy clan of anthropoids from the interior of caves on prehistoric Earth to the far limits of Creation, he had—in spades. The power was sufficient to change the features of his face, sucking in the cheeks, raising the brow, narrowing the eyes.

"List of friends and associates," he demanded, now speaking aloud.

"Travel itinerary," he called out even though Nexus didn't need to hear him to respond.

"Teachers' evaluations," he required.

There was just simply—nothing.

When he was certain he'd done his due diligence for anything hidden in Vanessa's youth, he moved on to assess the train wreck of her current life. However, this was as far as he could go with the Nexus, whose information on Vanessa Braverman was up to date—but only for a time twenty five years ago. As far as the Nexus was concerned—and according to the simple reality invested within the unalterable ticks of spacetime that moved inexorably forward from past to future— that was everything there was to know about the 19.2014 year old Vanessa Braverman. If Enguerrand wanted a picture of the forty-four year old version, he'd have to rely on what the ship's amanuensis' archives brought along from two and a half decades into the future.

"Otto, display Vanessa Braverman, current," he prompted.

Ultramariner's amanuensis didn't dwell solely within the man-drone stationed at the ship's bridge. It was everywhere, permeating the diodes and capacitors, imbued in the transistors and semiconductors, infused in every circuit of all the automata on board. It was never out of ear shot. A very unfavorable avatar appeared, actually quite shocking as compared to the cherubic visions of Vanessa that it replaced. True, she hadn't lost her looks, the stark beauty was still there, only it had been overwhelmed by an overt and flagrantly deviant sexuality that had spun wildly out of control, playing havoc with everything she touched or that brushed up against her.

Otto droned on dispassionately as the data scrolled beneath Vanessa's avatar.

"The subject is banned from entering five star systems, *persona non grata* from Ophiuchus to Piscium109, having been accused of indecency, fraud, sexual misconduct, perjury, contraband trafficking, and contributing to minors' delinquency." Her medical record was just as scandalous. "At one time or presently, this individual contracted and or is a carrier of seven venereal infirmities." Otto paused to go over old ground. "The authorities on Aquila M-1 are currently assessing whether to bring charges for the intentional and reckless infection of the public with a sexually transmitted disease, in this case, genital septomoniasis."

This was the newest of a series of virulent viruses that had mutated and run rampant across vast sections of Creation. Enguerrand had never heard of it, but he got the gist nonetheless.

"Distinguishing marks?"

Otto rattled them off.

"Eight piercings, fourteen tattoos, five brandings and three acid washes. Would you care to scan the visuals?"

Enguerrand didn't answer and instead let out an incredulous yet sympathetic sigh. He wasn't speaking to Otto; he was just saying the words.

"I wonder what happened to you, Vanessa Braverman," he said softly to himself.

Otto heard it and cued a coded response prompt. The smutty avatar disappeared, replaced now by one far uglier. It was the image of Brabec Van Maanen Alexis, Alpha C-15307.

"She's quite a piece of work, isn't she, Gary? Take Salome, mix with Jezebel, add a helping of trollop, a pinch of lying vamp, and *voila*, what you have is perhaps one of the most sluttish harlots ever produced this side of the Home Sector."

It grated on Enguerrand to hear Brabec throw out his French *bons mots*. Brabec's avatar was determined to display its deftness in Gallic history and culture and had more to say about Enguerrand's ancient ancestry on Earth.

He gave Enguerrand a thoroughly repellant smirk, just curling one side of the lips, an unmistakable sign of the contrived cognoscente.

"You Frenchmen, though, you're the ones who helped make Vanessa what she is."

Enguerrand almost answered by inquiring why the holographic Brabec had more hair, less flab and smelled better. But, he was going to kill Brabec when he got back and preferred that he should be aware of it too late, only just before it happened.

Enguerrand couldn't restrain his tongue entirely.

"Your avatar must be exercising regularly; the results are impressive."

Holographic Brabec let the insult wash over his cyber-electric back. His point about Enguerrand's forebears took precedence.

"The thing is she's Ashkenazi. You'd better have a care with her. She's Ashkenazi and smart, smart, smart. Her IQ is off the charts."

Enguerrand, of course, didn't understand the connection.

"It's your people, Gary, who bred her line for intelligence, some two thousand years ago. That transformative advantage was stamped into them. Your pot-walloping ancestors gave her that gift. Naturally, your brainless progenitors in the Dark Ages couldn't imagine what they were doing since all they were really good at was killing. The Jews in their midst they assumed were to burn for eternity anyway in the afterlife, so medieval France determined to get some use out of them before consigning them to the hell fires. Usury, money lending, Gary, and the laws against it in that backward age planted the seeds for Ashkenazi mental powers. Banking, finance, credit and all the mathematics and critical thinking needed to go with it, though sins, your dim-witted ancestors needed to fund their endless wars. Countless generations of European Jews were forced to exercise their brains while your forefathers lopped off heads in alcoholic stupors."

Enguerrand wasn't going for any of it.

"That's the history of the world according to Brabec, otherwise categorized under nonsense. And, by the way, what is your obsession with Old Earth and France? Isn't that the accusation leveled at free-rangers?"

The wraithlike Brabec shook his head and wagged a finger.

"Here's the kicker, Gary. If that weren't enough, the slow-witted Askkenazi who weren't clever enough to talk their way out of pogroms or who weren't worthwhile enough to be shielded by noble protectors were culled from the herd, ensuring that the survivors became even more intelligent. It's the classic evolutionary strategy for producing the desired effect."

Brabec shrugged his shoulders and winced.

"Not that those things that shambled around on two legs in the *ancien regime* had any idea at all about a desire much less an effect. That's just the way things turned out. And, now the sins of the father are visited on the son. She's smart, smart, smart, Gary."

Enguerrand was pretty smart too though.

"She's obviously sharp enough to have run off with your ambrosia, ignoring whatever plan you gave her for whatever investment, turning your sure-fire windfall in the future into a bust and using you as her taxi ride into the past since she apparently has no interest in coming back. Is that how smart she is?"

Brabec smiled.

"That's why I chose you, Gary. You're a pretty quick learner yourself. You think you have the whole picture now?"

Enguerrand paused and collected his thoughts. A faint pulse of green slightly pixilated his eyes. It was hardly discernible. Brabec's avatar noted it though and logged it.

"There are only one or two nagging loose ends," Enguerrand began.

Brabec clapped his thermionic hands together.

"Well, fire away. It wouldn't do for you to proceed with your eyes half open. I, of course, want you to succeed, Gary. Ask away, anything."

"Well," Enguerrand began slowly, "it's not that the insurance you chose to hold was insufficient to bring her back. That reflects on the fact that you're none too smart, smart, smart. I assume that poor man I watched you kill was someone you judged she couldn't live without—and you judged incorrectly."

The condescending look was wiped clean. It was listening quite intently.

"Her boyfriend," Brabec said flatly.

"So that's not it," Enguerrand continued. "Here's my problem: none of this makes any sense at all."

Enguerrand left it at that, not saying another word, simply staring at the photovoltaic apparition. Finally it responded.

"Do you intend to be more specific?"

Enguerrand did.

"Why doesn't Brabec take care of his own business?" Enguerrand fired back quickly. "There's no reason to involve anyone else. The simple and sure way for Brabec to steer the future so that he makes fortunes from the past, or puts political power in his hands, is to just go back and do it himself. The absurdly complicated and failure-prone method is to rely on criminals and couriers to pull it off for him—or maybe not."

"Your point is well taken, Gary." It gave the critique in

such a way as to assure that it wasn't. "Anything else?" it asked in a slightly defeated tone.

"Actually, there is one other point—equally absurd. What does Brabec care whether he's lost some ambrosia to a pathetic nobody in the past? I'm going to make that financial loss up for him and then some. I assume there will be others after me to fix anything and everything for him. Why is there the great and overriding necessity to bring back Vanessa Braverman?"

"I'm afraid I can't answer those questions for you, Gary," Brabec said flatly.

Enguerrand treated the avatar to the same sort of repudiating smile that had previously graced its ghostly visage.

"Of course you can't. I was quite sure you couldn't."

Amanuenses didn't usually pause this long; its internal wheels were definitely turning. When it inquired next of Enguerrand Duprey it wasn't as an overbearing, infinitely superior, omniscient, infallible overlord. It sounded very human, very concerned, very unsure.

"You think you have the answers to those questions, Gary?"

Enguerrand turned one side of his lips up, mimicking Brabec's unseemly simper, and sent the same comment back.

"I'm afraid I can't answer that question for you," Enguerrand said flatly.

Brabec's avatar had no recourse other than to accept that.

"Alright, Gary, I guess I can live with that." It wasn't alive but knew just what to say to make it seem so, and act so. "One way or the other, you have three periods to figure it all out," it smirked. "Just like that ancient prophet of yours who got swallowed up by a whale, or the other one that rose from the dead and all in three Earth days. Any sort of tricks you can learn from them, or does your particular voodoo advertised by that thing hanging around your neck come from some other magic book?"

"It was a great fish, and a lot can happen in three periods,"

Enguerrand corrected. "And, Jonah learned what hope is, that's all."

Brabec bowed to the answer.

The avatar spoke with an evil wink in its photo-coherent eye.

"If you've got hope, that's enough for me. Does that about cover it then, Gary?"

There was one other thing.

"Just this, stop calling me French; I'm Quebecois."

Enguerrand Duprey finally set him straight.

Chapter Six: Unscannable

We should only be astonished at being able to be astonished.
—Francois de La Rochefoucauld, Maxim No. 384

PRESTON BETA-HYDRI VINCENT, Gamma D-25417 had a foot in both worlds. His name indicated he was a properly inscribed, duly recognized citizen of Creation. His residence, place of employment, and professional licenses were all in Tau Corvus however, one of the leading star systems at the very edge of Creation, right at the boundary of the Free Range.

His entrepreneurial intermediation had served him well, providing him with wealth, position, reputation and respect. Working with both realms though, he never lost a certain edge. He had contacts everywhere and was the man to see for any sticky financial problem that needed fixing with a deft hand.

Though Preston was no free-ranger, he perhaps understood them as well as any. He too could trace his lineage all the way back to the *gbeto* of his maternal parentage, the military and hunting units of the so-called Amazons of West Africa. These female palace guards of the kings of Dahomey were selected for their physique, courage, and family pedigree.

Preston's bearing seemed to suit his heritage well. When not raking in credits, the dapifer's great avocation in uncovering the millennia old traces of his ancestry was perhaps the result of his not joining the rest of his extended family in the Free Range— that was a line too far to cross for this highly cultured, extremely wealthy, and patently fastidious man.

He was also something of a *bon vivant* and his offices were proof of the fact. Waiting for the majordomo himself to conduct the business, Enguerrand's comfort was seen to quite elegantly. He sat in plush luxury, sipping piping hot Charan khat, helping himself to Aquilian fudge. And Pavonian gingerberries were quite rare to see anywhere, especially out here so close to the Free Range.

He tried to restrain himself for decorum's sake but by the time Preston made his entrance, the compote was embarrassingly devoid of the delicious nuggets. Enguerrand's host didn't give that the slightest note, focusing on his client with welcoming, outstretched hands and a beaming, toothy smile.

"I'm Preston Beta-Hydri Vincent, Gamma D-25417, at your service, sir. Welcome to Tau Corvus."

Preston waited for Enguerrand to introduce himself. There was no way for him to do that, so Enguerrand simply smiled back and pumped his hand. An uncomfortable interval passed while the realization took hold that this particular walk-in wasn't going to offer a name. It was odd in the extreme, but Preston had customers that hailed from some quite bizarre quarters of the galaxy.

He let it pass and moved on to business.

"So, I understand you have quite a large consignment of product you wish to liquidate. Fourteen hekats is some quantity. What grade?"

Enguerrand could speak from his recent experiences.

"It's triple A."

Preston whistled softly.

"Fourteen hekats of triple A ambrosia should fetch a decent price. You've come to the right place. We'll treat you right."

Preston punctuated his promise with a forcefully executed nod of his perfectly coiffed head. He was salesman from tip to toe, from gleaming, ten thousand credit and immaculately shined footwear to the gold filigree meticulously applied to the braids on his epaulettes. Not a hair or a thread was out of place.

"Seven hekats," Enguerrand corrected. "That's the amount to be traded."

The diminution in bulk didn't affect Preston's good mood.

"As you wish, seven hekats it is then. Will you be taking the proceeds in currency credits, merchandise vouchers, or other instruments?"

"Futures contracts," Enguerrand replied.

"All of it?"

"All of it. Here's the list of concerns, the sums to be converted to stocks in each, the date of maturity and the name of the bearer."

Enguerrand's third eye relayed the data to the pixilated tempura coating the office walls. Preston took his time reviewing the contracts. The genial bearing quickly evaporated. This was an unusual transaction and he was concerned enough to jettison courtesy for candor.

"Those instruments will mature twenty-five years from now." Deadpan seriousness had replaced jocularity. "And you're not Brabec Van Maanen Alexis, Alpha C-15307. If this is some kind of joke, I don't appreciate it. I'm a very busy man."

Preston Beta-Hydri Vincent, Gamma D-25417 cleared his throat giving the implication that he wished his impending request to be understood in no uncertain terms.

"If you don't mind, I'd like to start this all over. You'll please identify yourself."

"I can't," Enguerrand admitted.

Preston didn't comprehend; the confusion was apparent. Also obvious was the fact that he wasn't at all pleased by it.

"Excuse me?"

"I can't," Enguerrand repeated.

Preston furrowed his brow.

"Of course you can," he said as if scolding a child. "If you'll be kind enough to remove the block from your third eye we can proceed with this transaction with some semblance of normalcy. I insist upon it."

"As you wish." He shrugged and "unzipped," pulling down the shield. Now Nexus was able to access his third eye, scanning and broadcasting everything there was to know about him. Nexus recognized absolutely nothing about Enguerrand Duprey. There was no match with anyone. DNA, blood type, fingerprints, iris recognition, voice patterns, facial modalities, and every other biometric identifier came up blank for any human in existence. That, of course, made sense, since Nexus was scanning someone who didn't—exist.

Preston was visibly knocked back.

"You're unscannable," he said in a faint, low voice, speaking more to himself than to Enguerrand, in complete disbelief. The well-traveled impressario had been to every settled quadrant within the Milky Way's spiral arm and had thought he'd seen everything. "I've heard about this sort of thing. I always assumed it was utter nonsense." He paused, catching his breath. "You're actually…unscannable?"

Preston put on an expression that said he himself couldn't believe these very words were coming out of his own mouth. "Who…or what…are you? He didn't wait for a response. "Some sort of…'Thinwalker'?"

Instantly he seemed to regret using the term.

"I don't mean to be brusque; it's just that I've never seen anything like this before. Never."

Enguerrand realized, in a way, that he was exactly what

he'd been called—and even more so. There were quite a few unexplained things that happened across the immense domain of mankind, under the light of every kind of colored star, but as far as Enguerrand knew there was nothing to match the impossible set of footsteps he was laying down.

He was a specter to rival any spine-tingling tale he'd ever heard. And far from disappearing, the ghost stories of old had been replaced with other more frightening—and much more believable—tales. In those "thin places" between heaven and earth, between the infinitesimally small and the immeasurably large, the human imagination still spied inexplicable things out of the corner of the eye.

Entities said to flit back and forth between our dimension and theirs, accounted for quite a few enigmas and mysteries that abounded from one end of the galaxy to the other—Thinwalkers. Whether or not these phantoms and apparitions existed, coming from places where branes might go bump in the night in the multi-dimensional bulk, squeezing through cracks where one reality met another, the other humankind most certainly did.

The name was also applied to those rarest of individuals, who by hook or by crook, through extreme alchemy, physics and biology, had managed to acquire the ability to cast no shadow at all: the unscannable. Enguerrand wasn't sure if allowing Preston to think he'd come from another dimension would help but he also determined that it sure couldn't hurt.

"I can't identify myself," Enguerrand repeated nonchalantly. "You see now?"

Preston wanted to know.

"How is that possible?"

To allay Preston's concerns, Enguerrand pushed up his sleeves, offering his dearth of tattoos.

"I'm not yakuza, *hassassin*, Capellan pirate or connected to any other criminal organization. I'm not wanted for anything in any star system in Creation or the Free Range. I'm just unscannable and let's leave it at that."

Preston's broker's mind recovered quickly from the shock, acquiescing to what was factual if he were to believe his own eyes, the potential for an incredible margin on the impending negotiation helping to bring him around.

"So how do you intend to effect the contract?"

Enguerrand nodded toward an artifact on display, set in an alcove to their side.

"Is that what I think it is?"

It obviously pleased Preston greatly that his potential client had taken note of the item, appreciated its provenance, and now remarked upon it. Enguerrand could see that immediately by the way his eyes came more alive and how he now sat even more ramrod erect.

Preston put him to the test.

"And what do you imagine it is?"

Enguerrand was a courier, however, and had done his fair share of trading. He'd actually seen one of these before—once. "Is it genuine," Enguerrand answered with his own question, "or simply a replica?"

Preston couldn't restrain the smile.

"It's an authentic trade stick, dating back to circa 1750 AD. It's pre-Old Modern." Preston paused. "It's quite a piece. I commend you for recognizing its value." Preston rewarded Enguerrand with a slight, but distinguishable bow. "That's real ebony," the host determined his guest would appreciate knowing.

Trade sticks were used to represent the firms or great houses of Ewe-speaking peoples on the coast of West Africa—a totem to stand for the good graces, fair-dealings and excellence of the merchandise they proffered.

Enguerrand understood all that.

"What it comes down to is the fact that it says I can trust

you?"

Preston was both very slightly piqued and yet just as eager to make certain of where the answer lay.

"You most certainly can!" Preston's eyes then alit on Enguerrand's triskelion. "Does that indicate that I can do the same with you?"

"Then put the transaction down under your mark," Enguerrand said, spoken like a courier well-versed in legal twilight zones. "In-house."

Preston Beta-Hydri Vincent, Gamma D-25417 tapped his fingers together, thinking.

"That's highly irregular, almost under the table."

The two men sat quietly while the buyer turned numbers, liabilities, arbitrage, risks and rewards over in his mind.

Preston's verdict was finally pronounced.

"The product will have to be discounted."

"Of course," Enguerrand agreed.

"Deeply discounted," Preston clarified.

Enguerrand was no stranger to negotiation. His occupation had taken him everywhere men could go in quantum cruisers. He knew how to dicker his way out of close calls and tight corners.

"Invest the market value of seven hekats, minus your commission, and take the eighth hekat gratis."

Preston was already shaking his head.

"No, I'll need at least ten."

"You have a deal at nine," Enguerrand countered, stretching out his hand to close the contract.

Preston ruminated on the offer for a moment, cocked his head to the side, and let out a sigh of surrender.

"Nine it is." The two men shook on it.

Now that the business was very near to settled, Preston Beta-Hydri Vincent, Gamma D-25417 wanted to put something else right.

"I didn't mean anything by the 'Thinwalker' remark," he half-apologized. "I don't really believe in such things, not all the way, at least."

Those in Enguerrand Duprey's line of work though had heard—or seen, if they could be believed—inexplicable and incredible arcana that was thought to exist in those veiled places in the cosmos now being disturbed. Mariners plying the seas of Old Earth declared that rogue waves existed, with everyone doubting their word for centuries. And couriers spoke in hushed tones of similar petrifying and inconceivable things and swore they were as real as the stupendous liquid nitrogen geysers on Mu Cassiopeiae-A8 that in fact could actually be seen with the naked eye from as far away as six million kilometers.

Horrors, yarns, fables and legends go back to spellbound listeners huddled around primordial campfires. Little had changed from the foreboding and danger-filled nights of Neolithic Earth to the present, even at the furthest edge of humanity's colossal habitat, now pushing out a hundred light years in every direction from those ancient cave dwellings tens of thousands of years later. In fact, the night terrors now could be worse. There was no Serengeti like the Milky Way, and truly, no human alive who could say for sure what was lurking in that dark—or wasn't.

"My brother-in-law was in the Beta Hydris system, only three AUs from Cardanis-5 when the 'Ripple Event' took place," Preston volunteered. He kept his voice down, along with his eyes, almost embarrassed to bring up the topic. "I can vouch for that. I'm absolutely certain he was there. No more than three AUs away, if that."

"I see," Enguerrand offered in reply, and nothing more.

Preston was irritated by the seeming lack of interest.

"There isn't the slightest doubt in his mind that those ships were there one moment, and then gone—just gone—the next."

Enguerrand had heard the story, a hundred times. A

cosmic string would be a trillion times more deadly and powerful than a rogue wave. If such a thing existed and washed over a ship's bow, it wouldn't matter what sort of ballast steadied the craft's yaw; anything in its vicinity would be doomed.

These hypothetical monsters were just the sort of phenomenon to cause the worst sort of space terrors among voyagers throughout Creation. According to many thousands of witnesses near to the Cardanis-5 sector, a cosmic string did, in fact, ripple through the Beta Hydris system, wiping the quite sizeable traffic en route there clean off every scanner out to Beta Hydris' heliopause. Nexus itself went down in the system for almost an entire quarter-period.

"The ones that will talk about it say it was a passing cosmic string. They also say they're one-dimensional and are as old as the cosmos itself—formed during the symmetry breaking phase of the universe." Preston looked mystified. "Can you imagine? A one-dimensional...thing? How is that even remotely possible? And weighing as much as a bevy of black holes and as aged as time itself, a full fourteen billion years old."

He whistled and said the next as if he were mostly speaking to himself. "We sure haven't any idea what's out there, not really anyway."

He thought Enguerrand might have an idea what was really out there.

"You strike me as someone who has seen his fair share of Creation." Preston politely left off referencing once again the fact that his client was also, quite astoundingly, unscannable, and the factotum of someone who could be as bad for business as a cosmic string, at least close up and personal. "I'd venture to guess you've had an experience or two that left you at a loss for an explanation?"

Enguerrand answered immediately.

"A streaking blue light, more blue than the deepest violet,

a blue that can't belong on the spectrum, intensely focused, laser sharp and stretched across what seemed to be an entire parsec of space."

Preston's mouth fell open at once. "A Karnifex? You actually saw a Karnifex?"

"I don't know what it was," Enguerrand admitted, "but it came crackling from what appeared to be one end of the galaxy to the other, and then just as quickly it was gone."

Enguerrand honestly wasn't sure what he'd seen, and never chalked it up to the streaking Bifrost-esque inter-dimensional bridges that "Karnifexes" were imputed to utilize as they made their forays between nowhere and somewhere. Of all the sundry genres of Thinwalkers, these were the ones most likely to chill the blood of children—and adults too. Karnifexes were willed into existence when something had gone wrong, when an energy debt had somehow gone unpaid, when something or someone broke a law that couldn't go unrequited. They came to take things away that didn't belong anymore.

"But, I *did* see that impossible ray of blue light." Enguerrand paused, collecting his thoughts, as if more convincing himself than Preston. "It shot across the entire celestial horizon in an instant."

"And then?" Preston asked on the edge of his seat.

"That's all," Enguerrand answered, neither satisfying himself nor his listener.

Because there was more, quite a bit more. For one the light wasn't blue, not really. Blue would be the closest word in any language to describe the shade, but it wasn't really even a color. It was something else from some other segment of the light spectrum yet somehow seen by eyes—his eyes.

Preston didn't want to let it go.

"It moved across the whole sky, just like that?"

That too was the only way Enguerrand had to explain it, but that's not precisely how the beam behaved. It didn't travel as any other ray of light from source to target in the straightest line possible in this universe because, Enguerrand thought in his bones, it wasn't from this universe.

"It was taking quantum paths," Enguerrand blurted out.

Preston, of course, didn't fully understand such an incongruous description, his slight frown prompting Enguerrand to explain.

"It seemed to taking all possible paths, the way quantum waves do, neither here nor there, in two places or in all places at once, moving in an infinite directions, and somehow making it look like a straight line. Just like quantum paths."

Now Preston's frown morphed slowly to a smile.

"Quantum paths are unseen, my friend. We can't perceive them."

Enguerrand shrugged.

"It looked to me that I could perceive them."

Preston's frown returned.

"If you truly witnessed a Karnifex breaking into this reality from..." he paused. "From wherever they hail. Well..." he paused again, leaning close to Enguerrand and speaking softly, with big, black, languid eyes wide. "You must know as well as I that if you've seen them once you'll see them again whether one is unscannable or not." After a much longer and uncomfortable silence he finished the thought. "They stalk you, and like no bloodhound from any Hell could. They'll track you from one end of the Milky Way to the other, to the Andromeda next door. There's no escape. If you see their trail once, you'll see them again."

Suddenly Preston was all smiles again.

"At least that's what they say anyway."

Enguerrand smiled back.

"Yes, I've heard that."

"They take you away," Preston said quite off-handedly. "They take those away that are here...but yet...shouldn't be."

Enguerrand was still smiling back.

"Yes, I've heard that too."

Whether he'd seen a Karnifex or not, it served his purpose right now to allow Preston Beta-Hydri Vincent, Gamma D-25417 to wonder if he had. There were, indeed, monsters in the cosmos and it couldn't hurt of apprise the broker of one with whom he had just concluded business.

"Brabec Van Maanen Alexis, Alpha C-15307 asks that you see that this matter is correctly submitted personally," Enguerrand concluded, "and considers it a favor."

It was a reminder, and a polite warning.

Brabec, even twenty five years in the past and in his early thirties in this time period, had already begun tearing a path across more than a few systems. Preston was very much aware of who he was and that it would be in anyone's interest to stay away from his bad side.

"I'm happy to oblige." Preston gave his word to Enguerrand that he'd comply with the request. "Just in case, in the unlikely event some detail needs your attention and I have to post a notice to that effect, may I at least ask where you'll be heading?"

Enguerrand apprised him of his next port-of-call.

"Arcadia."

Nothing more was required to designate the second planet in the neighboring Vela Eridani star system. Everyone knew where Arcadia was.

"Ah, Arcadia," Preston sighed as anyone did when mentioning the bewitchingly beautiful planet. "A most lovely world; an excellent choice. Have you been there before?"

"I was born there," Enguerrand divulged.

Preston, very much a family man himself, approved.

"You'll be visiting your relations there?"

Enguerrand nodded affirmatively. His eyes went dark, dark green at the thought. He would indeed.

Their business now completed, as Enguerrand prepared to take his leave, Preston Beta-Hydri Vincent, Gamma D-25417, broached a last favor of his own, giving it one last try.

Preston made a sweeping gesture with his hand as if wiping clean from his client all the trillions of bytes of identifying data that accompanied every other human being he'd ever met and quoted Scripture to explain the miracle.

"I don't suppose you'd consider explaining but I'd sure be interested to know how it's done."

"We fix our eyes not on what is seen, but on what is unseen, since what is seen is temporary, but what is unseen is eternal." The line was delivered with aplomb, in the hope it might loosen Enguerrand's lips. "That is from one of Earth's sacred texts."

It did, in fact, make an impression on Enguerrand; he'd heard the words before, just not cited by a futures broker from Tau Corvus angling for the inside scoop on unscannability.

"Civilization spent all of history devising ways for things not really there to be seen," Enguerrand reminded him, accented with a wink of one of his hypnotically green eyes. "Just this once it's the other way around."

Chapter Seven: Paterfamilias

We are never so happy or unhappy as we suppose.
—Francois de La Rochefoucauld, Maxim No. 49

THOUGH THAT LOCALE was a little over a hundred light years away, Enguerrand Duprey's father could have been called the salt of the Earth. He was a farmer and the elected foreman and *gildenleiter* of one of the largest collections of agricultural consortiums on Arcadia.

They produced prodigious quantities of the two oldest staples of the old mother planet: bread and wine, enough of it to fill the pantries and cellars of every living soul in the Vela Eridani system, and then some. It was a good life out here and that could be seen in Louis Duprey and his beautiful wife, Sophie.

They were quintessential Arcadians—vigorous, strong, fit—reflecting the healthful, life-giving bounty of the planet their great, great, great grandparents had chosen for them as home. Things simply sprang to life on Arcadia, the word for "paradise" in Greek.

It was complained, and with cause, that the only reason it

wasn't christened Eden was due to the fact that the name was already taken—by the moon orbiting the first planet around Barnard's Star. The truth was, though, that this second planet from Vela Eridani, with its amethyst sky, orange sun, and pale pink colored clouds was more paradisiacal than that moon in the Barnardian system, or any other known planet.

Arcadia's benevolence surpassed even that of Earth's in its heyday—possessing all the life-nurturing qualities of the mother planet with none of her flaws. There were no deserts, tundra, or badlands on Arcadia, only a lush carpet of fruit-giving vegetation from equator to poles. Science marveled at the amazing jackpot that Arcadia was, imagining that Earth had been about as far as one could hope to push the odds in favor of a habitable abode for life transformed out of the chaos of the cosmos. Earth wasn't though, nor Eden; Arcadia was the reigning champion of freakishly lucky planets.

Though sizably smaller than Earth, Arcadia was so much denser that the gravity was only slightly weaker. A thick atmosphere, rich in oxygen, carbon dioxide and nitrogen securely enveloped the smaller, condensed sphere.

This world also was nearer to Vela Eridani than Earth was to Sol but that too was in perfect harmony. The planet huddled just near enough to the lesser, cooler orange star for its red-shifted light to bathe Arcadia's vegetation in the optimal color. All the countervailing forces were ideally balanced on Arcadia as if perfectly tuned by some cosmic deity amusing himself with a transcendent chemistry set.

Temperature, pressure, atmospheric composition, the intensity and wavelength of the sunlight, the perfectly synchronized cycles of water, nitrogen and carbon—all those parameters and a hundred others had been adroitly calibrated in such a way as to put out the most famous welcome sign for life in the known Milky Way. But the greatest long shot that had come in for Arcadia was her absolutely unique celestial mechanics. No other planet yet discovered spun in just the way Arcadia did.

Revolving around Vela Eridani and spinning on her axis, there were years and days, like on any planet. Here, though, there was only one season, stuck just where spring turns into summer. Most cosmologists believed a collision in Arcadia's past struck the planet an extremely unlikely, but lucky blow. The missile, either a comet or meteor, would have clipped the planet with the most extreme pool-table English, glancing one of her poles at just barely above zero degrees, causing Arcadia to flip end over end, pole over pole, while she rotated in front of and revolved around Vela Eridani.

Some rare dynamic, in any event, was the cause of the current slow, lethargic, blessed cartwheel Arcadia turned while gliding in orbit around her star. The gentle, favored roll that gave each latitudinal swath of Arcadia its equal moments at the equator, at both poles, and at every parallel between, was unknown anywhere else in existence. It was as if colonists had come upon Arcadia on the very night of her prom and captivated by the most beautiful belle around any star seen anywhere, immediately promised themselves to this virginal territory.

Arcadia—pristine, untouched, fertile, gorgeous—might be compared to a virgin, but a unique virgin, one constantly pregnant. It was said things sprouted on Arcadia just by *thinking* about growing them and that was only a slight exaggeration. Rain came every night, falling gently in a baby-light mist, everywhere—but storms were unknown. Since it was springtime everywhere every day on Arcadia, and with the rich, plentiful carbon dioxide for plants and the super abundance of oxygen for its creatures, this planet of eternal summer was the scene of an explosion of life of all kinds.

As the farmstead of his father came into view, it was just as he'd recalled it, but from recollections of an age when he was barely old enough to remember. It was a fine holding in a splendidly rustic setting. Naturally, an incredibly strong nostalgia swept over and almost overpowered him since he was reliving moments that were just before his own birth. He realized what sort of mental power would be required to cope with it and imagined he'd prepared himself. He, of course, hadn't.

The Duprey plantation was proof of a familial bond between Vela Eridani and many other star systems. It was strong, with no distance capable of stamping out the age-old, atavistic need to trade. Some of Arcadia's products were among the most sought-after merchandise bartered back and forth over the mind-numbing distances of interstellar space. Wine from Arcadia was shipped to its stellar neighbors, and more prosaically, but in such staggering profusion, its wheat too.

Goods baked with plump, maltose-rich Arcadian wheat were the most delicious of any that had been tasted since the first loaf came out of the brick ovens of pharaonic Egypt. As for Arcadian wines, words were useless. It was the opinion of many connoisseurs that it was best, for those who couldn't import it, to never let it pass one's lips lest either a lifetime of appreciation for other quite pedigreed vintages be irrevocably lost or one's finances strained in crippling imports.

However, Arcadia exported a much more important commodity. There were many new things to get used to living out in the stars dozens of parsecs from Earth. At the far edges, in the Free Range, there was a barely tangible malaise born from lying adjacent to the Big Black, a subtle melancholy conceived of distance and solitude. It was just this sort of soil though, this domain of autarchy of the individual that rubbed at people's souls, in which the seeds for the last great struggle for freedom and grace were planted.

This was Arcadia's real claim to fame, not her wine nor her pastries. On a thousand different planets and moons, where there were equal numbers of shades of politics and culture in all the extra-solar worlds, on Arcadia it was liberty, the greatness of the human spirit, the belief in an inner eternal soul that grew to a rigorous philosophy and then merged with religion.

The Vatican, Mecca, Tibet were all on a fetid Earth that itself was hanging on by its fingernails. The ancient fonts which soothed the collective consciousness of humanity were too far away, too remote, too sapped of their former power—but there was Arcadia. Her greatest export, like classical Athens more than three millennia before, swept through a hard-won area of the spiral arm of the galaxy where mankind had laid down roots: words and ideas.

Where vast areas of Creation were being turned into honeycombed sections of a cosmic hive, beautiful, bountiful Arcadia held the shining beacon pointing to a different vision, steadfastly lighting the way for those who lost sight of the true image of humankind. The heart and soul of the Free Range was indisputably on Arcadia—free, God-fearing, moral, pious, spiritual, inviolable Arcadia.

Even by Arcadian standards the Duprey estate was unique and remarkably handsome.

Enguerrand's family had maintained it for one hundred and twelve years—counting from this time, a quarter of a century ago. It had the distinct and genuine feel of a stately ancestral home.

Indeed, that's what it was.

Enguerrand made his way to the front door seated behind the buckboard of a curricle pulled by a tandem of heavily muscled gray and black Percherons. The carriage was escorted by two distinctly silent and surly riders who were armed to the teeth. Louis Duprey wasn't the only homesteader to use horses on Arcadia. Even with dozens of droids tending the vineyards, wheat fields, vegetable gardens, and animal pens, the incongruity of men on horseback made perfect sense for quick movement over the patchwork of terraced grounds.

Enguerrand wasn't greeted by his waiting father on the entry veranda as he'd remembered fondly from so many times in the past. Instead, he was marched inside and through the long hall leading to Louis' study. It was just as it was when he'd played here as a toddler, triggering the most intense *déjà vu* possible.

His father's office was a hexagonal space cut in half, the shape of a cell in an apiary parted in two. In the center, having burst straight up through the floor from the foundations, was the stump of a wisely selected Billoghany wood. There was nothing but the stump now and in just the right proportions. A facet of this beautiful timber was that its trunks grew in just the right proportions, perfectly attuned as with many other florae on Arcadia, to the golden ratio.

The original tree had been sawed over a century ago at table level and converted to a desk one and two thirds as long as it was wide, the surface the same ratio as a Renaissance painting laid flat. The sylvan desktop had been shellacked with pixilated tempura, as had the walls behind him and to either side and was itself a portal to anywhere.

Louis Duprey sat behind it as if on a throne. In lieu of a crown, he had thick, luxurious, chestnut brown hair which he attempted to comb straight back, but being so dense and ample it overflowed in gently curving locks, the symmetric cascades falling to his shoulders and rebounding there. This russet mane was a striking contour for the chiseled almond face it framed, with his slender yet strong nose and piercing emerald green eyes exuding intelligence. The much lighter colored, sharply pointed goatee and mustache, an attractive foil for thick sensual lips, gave him a profoundly cavalier appearance.

He was dressed in rough yet perfectly fitted leathers and buckskins, the hard-worked and steel-corded muscles beneath filling the chamois in an impressive way. He wore elaborately stippled cuissardes, buckled above his knees with the breeches tucked in. Across his breast were half a dozen ribbons, badges and marks of the honors he had earned among his peers on Arcadia. He was thirty years old, in the peak of his powers, and as dashing as any landgrave who ever held court anywhere, especially here, augustly seated behind the same sort of furnishings as the legendary king of Ithaca, Odysseus, had crafted for his palace.

"Qui êtes-vous, et que voulez-vous?"

It wasn't a friendly greeting. "Who are you, and what do you want?"

Immediately, however, Louis' combative demeanor softened, and greatly. He could see the young man with the odd, bewitching, olive eyes had tears coming out of them. Indeed, Enguerrand was right in front of his dead father, it wasn't a dream; it was the mythical, atavistic chance to go back and say all the things never spoken to one's deceased father in life. He struggled to keep his composure in this ferocious emotional storm and a few tears did break through. Louis' men flanking Enguerrand shrugged their shoulders.

"Est-il fou?" He demanded to know of them. "Is he crazy? Has he been doing that all along?"

Unashamedly, Enguerrand wiped the tears and collected his wits.

"My apologies, I'm alright now. Pardon, Monsieur Duprey."

Louis, still wearing an incredulous frown, repeated his initial question.

"Who are you and what do you want?"

"Will you accept half-payment? Enguerrand proposed.

"Meaning what?"

"Meaning I don't have a name, but I have important business with you."

Louis breathed out a little more strongly; the riddle was unappreciated.

"I'm not a man to trifle with," he cautioned. "And you'd better have some tough husk on you to walk in here like this and start out with ridiculous answers."

Louis was taken aback when Enguerrand removed his shirt completely making plain there was only skin, and not the slightest indication of criminal tattoos and markings.

"Not tough husk, and no other marks either."

Louis didn't appreciate the informality either.

"Put it back on." He did though welcome this step in the right direction. "Alright, that might say who you aren't. I asked though who you were. Identify yourself."

Enguerrand breathed out now more strongly likewise. Repeating himself wasn't going to change anything.

"Choose a name if you like. Anything will do. I'm unscannable, as you certainly must already have been briefed. My identity is no concern of yours. I do, however, have an extremely profitable proposition for you."

That was enough for Louis.

"You're lucky to be leaving here without bruises," he threatened. "Get him out of here."

That was enough for Enguerrand as well. Lately he'd been shanghaied, beaten, starved, and pushed through a wormhole, his family threatened. He'd been on the receiving end without lifting a finger to defend himself.

The reaction was automatic when the nearer of the two men attempted to place a hand on Enguerrand's shoulder. Kinetic energy is not so much mass, but very more a function of speed, which is why Enguerrand's slaps, punches, and pushes landed so strongly.

Nature weighs matter but multiplies it times velocity *squared,* so his shoves registered exponentially, just like earthquakes on the Richter scale. His arm shot out to ward off yet another invasion of personal space, as lightning quick as a droid's extremity set on punch press. Louis' attendants were shocked by it, giving Enguerrand a final moment to plead his case.

Enguerrand, armed with the history of events past, present, and future, possessing a son's intimate knowledge of his own father's personality now took command.

"I can't tell you my name, Monsieur Duprey. A man like you should comprehend that. *Comment prétendons-nous qu'un autre puisse garder notre secret, si nous ne pouvons le garder nous-mêmes?* How can we expect others to keep our secrets if we cannot keep them ourselves?"

Louis was surprised enough at the words to put his hand up, signaling to his adjutants to belay the last order.

"François de La Rochefoucauld wrote that eleven hundred years ago. He was a duke, one of the Sun King's courtiers at Versailles." Enguerrand now asked his father, "Have you ever heard of him?"

That was like asking Courier if he'd ever heard of Ives. Louis had. He was enthralled by Rochefoucauld's maxims and had memorized hundreds of them. Monsieur Duprey was disconcerted by Enguerrand's tack but rebounded quickly.

"I'll give you credit. At least you bothered to investigate me before traipsing in here." He decided to be gracious. "You may walk out on your own. Please escort him."

Enguerrand knew his own father, of course. He realized it needed a few strong cannonades at the door before it crashed open. He fired another dose of Rochefoucauld.

"People who hate to be wrong are those most apt to err. Are you sure you won't hear me out?"

Louis smiled and decided he'd sit back and enjoy the caprice.

"I'll admit these tricks of yours aren't too boring. But if you're going to repeat yourself, can you do the one with your arm again instead?"

"They aren't tricks. I know quite a bit about you, Monsieur

Duprey," Enguerrand contended. "For example, from the way you're sitting I can tell your shoulder is bothering you, the one you injured when you were thrown by that Akal-Teke stallion."

Louis smiled even wider and addressed his entourage.

"Would you like to bring your children in to watch this?"

His men seemed agreeable judging from their smiling faces, so Enguerrand addressed them too.

"Yes, call in the children. I'll explain the story of how *Tornade* threw your boss and why it is that he determined from that moment that Akal-Tekes are a breed banned from this homestead."

Louis clapped his hands together at that.

"Bravo, now that is approaching first class! Please, go on."

Of a sudden, Louis' chuckles melted away, replaced with a truly sullen air. He was transfixed by the triskelion around Enguerrand's neck, taking it in with great interest. Enguerrand grasped instantly his blundering mistake. He'd neglected to remove it, oddly compliant to the oath made to his father when he was eleven, and now it was being recognized—as the pendant Louis Duprey's wife wore!

They were in fact one and the same.

Louis said not a single word, but his eyes told Enguerrand that he'd seen it, noted the bizarre and unmistakable similarity, and wasn't sure what to make of it.

Enguerrand raised an eyebrow and leaned a bit closer.

"The same *Tornade* whom you compare to Sophie, since you say neither ever were tamed."

Louis Duprey's face went stone cold. Enguerrand could see that his father had finally come to realize that no investigation on Nexus could provide these personal nuggets.

"That's my wife of whom you're speaking," he warned.

"*Oui*," Enguerrand as a boy was terrified of the look his father was giving him now. Taking it in as a full-grown man, he could easily see why it had kept him in line. "*Oui*, I'm speaking of Madame Duprey, the woman you compared to a Paradaysan carnation when you first met."

He called for his wife to come with such animus she'd have heard the summons anywhere within a distance of a lightsecond.

Louis sprang to his feet.

"Viens ici, Sophie!"

She was much closer in the cavernous scullery overseeing the exacting garnishment of simmering cauldrons of paella, sufficient to feed the cohort employed on the demesne. Enduring the silence of his father's glowering stare and waiting for his mother to appear was difficult in the extreme. Enguerrand kept repeating to himself that the lives of the mother of his child and his only daughter depended on him somehow keeping his head. He gamely fought off the quiet, whether Louis Duprey would deign to entertain his feelers or not.

"I'd request little of you," he tempted his father, "and pay handsomely for it," Enguerrand offered. "I need to find someone—quickly—and I know you're one of the few who can reliably provide that."

Louis Duprey blanched ever so slightly and feigned ignorance.

"I'm aware," Enguerrand said slowly, deliberately, refusing to flinch from his father's gaze, "I'm aware of le système. I know it's real and I'll pay generously for two simple words sent out upon it, Monsieur."

Louis tried to veil his utter discomfiture at hearing this brazen accusation from this complete stranger—flummoxed that the allegation was nonetheless completely true and accurate. His pretense at nonchalant indifference was absurdly awkward. Enguerrand had never seen his indefatigable father so perplexed.

"You can't actually believe that folderol?" Louis chided, faking bemusement. "You converted some nonsense you've heard into fact and have gone so far as to even assume there is a price posted for the imaginary service. I'm a farmer, not some fantasy telegrapher. *Quelle absurdité.*"

Enguerrand did think that.

"I'll pay a hekat of ambrosia per word: Vanessa Braverman. I need her location, in real time. She's a free-ranger in hiding, blocking her third eye and invisible to Nexus, giving off no pings, but she's no doubt moving around. Just a location with a name, that's all I require."

"And what makes you take for granted," Louis chastised the presumptuous, nameless, unscannable stranger, "that anything like that exists at all, much less that I can access it even if it did?"

Enguerrand couldn't justify that—it would have meant explaining that Louis was going to tell his yet unborn son all about it when the boy came of age in ten years.

Le système was ingenious, built up over decades, involving a stupendous network of biological and mechanical working parts, spies, face-catching satellites orbiting around hubs, DNA and biometric "sniffers," and other methods about which the child Enguerrand hadn't understood or wasn't aware so many years ago. But he knew it existed. *Le système* was the closest thing to old-fashioned shoe leather detective work that existed in the hyper-technological world of the twenty-eighth century. It was reserved for the highest, most important matters having to do with freedom or tyranny, life or death, riches or ruin.

"I'll double it," Enguerrand upped the ante. "Two per word, making four hekats."

Two other words were still nagging at the front of Louis Enguerrand's mind.

"How did you know I compared my wife to a Paradaysan carnation when I first met her? Explain that first."

Enguerrand declined to elucidate.

"In just the same way I know that I'm talking to the only man who can help me."

"Help you do *what?*" Louis emphasis was plain, as if he already had a fair idea of the villainy that must be in play. "Who is she to you, this Vanessa Braverman? Do you plan to murder her, kidnap her, rob her, to do her harm?"

Enguerrand knew that lying to his father had never succeeded; the son decided to give it one more try nonetheless. He concocted a whopper.

"You can consider me a bounty hunter. A gigantic quantity of ambrosia has been stolen. Vanessa Braverman can definitely lead me to the next step in recovering it. I have no intention of harming her, just moving on, following the tracks."

This interested Louis. He seemed truly engaged for the first time.

"A gigantic amount? How much would that be?"

Enguerrand gave the first huge figure that came to mind.

"A hundred hekats."

Louis whistled.

"*Ca alors*, that's quite a pile." He ruminated on the number. "She has it? That's why you need to find her; it's in her possession?"

Enguerrand was making it up as he went along.

"No, but she can put me in the right direction. I'm pretty sure of that."

Louis surprised him now.

"Alright, double it again and you have a deal."

"Eight hekats? I don't have that much," Enguerrand admitted.

"How much do you have then?"

"Counting to the last gram, on my word, there's five on board. Would you take five?"

Louis Duprey calmly took his seat again, sat back and confided something to his guest.

"Distrust justifies deception Rochefoucauld warned, but he lived a long, long time ago and he wasn't right about everything.

For example, according to *le duc*, I should be ashamed to entertain misgivings rather than to have been taken in by you. I'm not embarrassed however; it's you who ought to be. You're lying."

Just then Sophie Duprey entered, still wearing silicon oven gloves.

"*Mon Dieu!,*" she'd arrived just in time to hear her spouse's accusation. However, she addressed Enguerrand. "My husband is well known for speaking very plainly. I hope you can forgive the offense."

Enguerrand had, of course, seen images of his mother, but here she was in the very flesh, although it was the hair that commanded one's immediate attention when Sophie Duprey made an entrance. It was her glory and required much devoted attention. A thick, lustrous chignon was pinned at the nape of a delicate alabaster neck, accented by an equally copious crown plait that twisted from side to side across the top of her head. Delicate finger waves curled from either side, framing voluminous fringe bangs, perfectly straight, hanging to just above the eyebrows. Somehow there were strands enough still for two symmetric braids that caressed the sunken, feminine collar bones, coming to rest on breasts enlarged by lactogenesis.

She was with child.

The surging hormones and increased blood flow didn't just account for swollen bosom and lustrous tresses. She took very well to pregnancy and her skin was radiant, giving rise to melasmas that were unabashedly female and charming. These bruised areas are usually light brown, but the ones on Sophie's cheeks were lovely, subtle pink splotches, rouge genially applied by nature. The soft curves, wider hips and rounded abdomen revealed she had passed into her third trimester. She was pregnant...with *him*.

Sophie was immediately riveted by the newcomer, sufficiently for her husband to see.

"Do you know this man?" her husband asked her. "Have you ever laid eyes on him before?"

Those inquiries, put to her quite strongly and demanding attention, were just as quickly sidetracked. Enguerrand was manfully doing his best, standing erect, as motionless as granite, and couldn't be faulted that only the involuntary muscles and ducts disobeyed his will: torrents of salty tears streamed down both cheeks. It was a very strange weeping, silent yet obviously emanating from the very marrow of his bones.

Louis slapped his palms down on the face of his Homeric desk.

"*Oh, la vache,* there he goes again."

The weeping affected Sophie much more deeply.

"Why are you crying?" She asked him compassionately, a part of her somehow immediately, yet not unreasoned, drawn to her yet to be born son without consciously knowing why.

"Do you know him, Sophie?"

Louis was more curious about this than the reasons for the unbridled tears.

She ignored Louis.

"What is your name?" she asked her son softly.

He couldn't have the first thing ever said to his mother be a lie.

"Enguerrand," he wiped the tears away and stood straighter. "My name is Enguerrand, madame."

Louis let out an irritated harrumph; *now* all of a sudden he had a name.

"That may or may not be his name, Sophie. He's unscannable and more tears come out of him than straight answers. Do you know who this man is? Have you ever seen him before?"

She didn't know him, but yet experienced the strangest epiphany. Sophie's pregnancy was one which produced a high level of oxytocin, the bonding hormone that cemented mother with child. Hers was now put to an impossible task—yet responding nonetheless by innately recognizing the fruit of her own body—but from over decades hence.

"*Non, je ne le connais pas.*" She didn't know him, but turned to her husband and made the bizarre admission. "Louis, a chill just came over me." She intoned Enguerrand's name, pronouncing it with a thick Gallic accent. "It is a beautiful, noble and unique name. Do you not agree, *mon mari?*"

Louis rolled his eyes.

"I'm not sure what his name is or whether it's beautiful or ugly." Brandished, waving hands were helping now, emphasizing the next hard words. "But he's lying, of that I'm convinced. He just offered to pay all he has, willing to squander everything with no reserve to find a certain woman, but she's supposedly only the next step in his search and not the quarry herself. He's contradicted himself already."

Louis Duprey, the up-and-coming leader of the Free Range's most obdurate hardliners, had a great many followers as well as an equal number of enemies. Most inexplicable enigmas that found their way to his doorstep were in one way or the other connected to that dangerous business. Louis was leaning toward ruling this perjury of a different sort for other reasons.

"I don't think he's with the opposition. He's not a good enough liar for that. This is obviously some sort of revenge plot, to what end and to benefit whom I have no idea, nor do I care."

Sophie turned to her son and asked him so simply.

"Did you lie to my husband?" She paused and then said the name again, obviously delighting in the sound for reasons she couldn't fathom. "*Enguerrand, avez-vous menti à mon mari?*

Enguerrand had to think. He'd already blundered—twice. Here he was interacting with his formidable father, and not as a child but in an arena he'd never entered before, facing the intimidating man as an opponent rather than as a child's *le paternal.*

What unnerved him more was what he'd just inadvertently done with his mother, in spite of the warnings about walking lightly through the past and to cause no leaf to be overturned. He'd just named himself! He'd just planted the seed in the mind of his own mother, for his own name, within arms' reach of his fetal self, before his birth.

It scared the truth right out of him.

"*Oui, madame.* I had to lie."

Before he could say more Sophie's eyes fell upon his triskelion; that was her adornment around the stranger's neck.

"But I have a triskelion exactly like yours, *monsieur*, exactly. Where did you get that?" She pulled the pendant away from her breast, foisting it toward him, giving Enguerrand a better look.

Enguerrand continued with the truth.

"My father gave it to me. It's a family heirloom."

He tried to brush it off as something with no great meaning, as if he had his mind elsewhere, since he did. How could there be two versions of the same thing in the same place at the same time in the same universe? That awful thought made him focus all the more intently on the swollen belly of his mother before him. There were two of *him*, here and now, just as inexplicably.

His father wordlessly measured the stranger and his icon. Taking in his departed *père* before him in person again, resurrected from the dead, Enguerrand's mind couldn't be prevented from wandering from pillar to post, now for a fleeting moment back to his father's stories about King Louis IX, later Saint Louis, and his exploits in bringing back to France from the Crusades a sliver of the True Cross to be venerated in the church he built at Sainte-Chapelle.

He now though, and not a French king who'd been canonized, possessed the religious emblem with a provenance to merit mention with any that ever existed. It was here and there, making ripples in worldlines in the past and the future. There was nothing worn around anyone's neck anywhere to equal it, excluding of course whatever might be adorning Vanessa Braverman's.

"Why then," Sophie asked, "did you lie to my husband?"

"It *is* a personal matter, as he correctly surmised, madame, but something far above revenge or honor or profit. A terrible wickedness is being perpetrated upon two innocent people who will suffer horribly for it unless I can stop it."

His mother followed all of that.

"Which two people?"

"My wife and my daughter. Their lives are lost unless I can find Vanessa Braverman."

Sophie had another epiphany. It came to her over several silent moments of peering deeply into the hypnotic eyes of the extraordinary outlander. This one was even stronger.

"I believe him, Louis."

Louis Duprey, slowly stroking his beard, bored a hole in his son with a decidedly penetrating vision.

"I believe him too, Sophie." He paused, looked down for a moment in thought and then delivered the verdict with finality. "Unfortunately, whatever you've gotten yourself into won't be rectified here. I don't busy myself with chasing people down, be they villains or saints, whether they deserve it or not. I can only wish you luck and good day."

Louis put both palms flat on his desk as if sounding a gavel; this interview was at a close.

Enguerrand struck now with everything he had.

"You're going to want to summon 'Fumeux' before saying no to me."

Here was yet another confidential facet of Louis Duprey's life dangled in front of him. "Smokey" was the premiere mastermind, tinkerer *par excellence*, techie jerry-builder and the only man on Arcadia to approach with an impossible engineering problem to solve. If "Smokey" couldn't make it work, he'd burn it up trying, hence the moniker.

"*On y va encore une fois,*" Louis exclaimed dejectedly. "Here we go again."

"Yes, one more time, but now with a twist. You turned down double the ambrosia; let's see if you can reject this. I'll double the speed of your ships." Enguerrand waited for the offer to sink in. He repeated it. "You heard me correctly. I'm offering something worth millions of hekats of ambrosia. I can provide you with the technology to turn your cruisers into the fastest things moving in the universe. All it will cost you is two words sent out on your channels: Vanessa Braverman." It was time to make it inescapable as an epitaph chiseled in stone. "I'm not leaving until I have her location."

Sophie started to demur, the unequivocally absurd ravings of the poor man pleading his case before them she judged too crazy and beneath the dignity of a fellow French free-ranger to allow continue.

"*S'il vous plaît, monsieur…*"

Louis had just the opposite reaction and put his hand up. He wasn't so quick to dismiss the bid.

"Not so fast, Sophie. He knows the names of my horses, the nickname of my chief engineer, the authors I've read, that my shoulder is bothering me, what I said to you when we first met. And, he's unscannable. I can't decline the offer so quickly. This fellow may actually turn out to be quite sane after all."

Sophie heard mostly one part of it.

"What you said to me when we first met? *Qu'est-ce que c'est?*"

Louis gave the first real consideration to coming to terms with the unsearchable stranger and ignored his wife.

"How would you manage to do a thing like that…Enguerrand?"

Louis put a little distance between the question and the

name to leave no doubt that he viewed the moniker as almost certainly a pseudonym.

Enguerrand snapped his fingers.

"Like that, that's how. Get 'Fumeux' here; he'll understand."

It was an assurance he could certainly back up, having arrived in a ship from twenty-five years in the future, *Ultramariner* was the fastest craft in existence.

There was nothing for Louis Duprey to do but agree.

"*Nous pouvons faire un accord.*" He did. "We can make a deal." Louis added then, "And the five hekats of ambrosia," almost as an afterthought.

"Hardly," Enguerrand's face bristled. "I'm doubling the speed of your vessels, not doubling the ambrosia, not both," the son countered.

"Four, then," Louis bent.

Enguerrand pushed back.

"Two."

Louis Duprey spit on his hand and stretched it out to his son.

"Three and we have a deal."

"*Oui, trois,*" Enguerrand spit on his too, the way his father had taught him, the old-fashioned way, the way men did it in the days when Le Duc de la Rouchefoucauld was putting his skillful observations onto paper and clasped hands with his father like a true free-ranger. His father's word when given freely was a bond still more durable than anything even in the titanium-alloyed, carbon fiber strong world, as obdurate as the titans that had shook like that before him. He'd never pumped hands with anyone with a more tenacious grip in his life.

"*D'accord,*" each man said to the other.

Chapter Eight: Question of Honor

It is more disgraceful to distrust than to be deceived by our friends.
—Francois de La Rochefoucauld, Maxim No. 84

THE NEXT FEW days were the best by far of any in his life, spent with his young father and the mother he had never known in a place that he realized now, as he hungrily took in every sight, smell and nuance, was even truly more beautiful than his memories. Crushingly, this was the life that had been snatched from him, never to be shared with his young child and the wife whom he loved deeply. He couldn't look out across his ancestral demesne without also weighing the tremendous loss.

He was given the finer of the two guesthouses, the one further away from the stables. But, the faint and musky aroma of the horses not only didn't bother him, he found it deeply pleasing.

It reminded him of home.

Dusk fell and ushered in another perfect evening on fruitful Arcadia when Enguerrand made his way across the pasture to the arena doors of the stables.

It was a high point; from here the vista was rolling vineyards and ochre and henna grain fields to the horizon. Arcadia's degree of curvature was slightly less than terrestrial and its sun orange so the fall of darkness had its own unique and particular charisma, the fading light refracting in sublime hues of amaranth, marigold and vermilion.

These were the grandparents of the horses Enguerrand knew from his childhood. He chose an attractive speckled mare and groomed her with a curry comb, brushing aggressively enough to camouflage the sound of his father's footsteps in the litter on the floor. Enguerrand felt him over his shoulder rather than hearing him. It surprised him that his father appeared alone; for some reason, this said Louis trusted him to a degree.

"I never got to ask you. Why so many horses?" the son asked the father.

The question seemed all the more strange to Louis since they'd never exchanged a word about horses and wouldn't for another four or five years at least, when Enguerrand as a toddler would repeat the query to his father so often. He knew of course what his father's response would be since it was chiseled in his memory. He only wanted to hear his father tell it to him again.

"One can't have enough horses; *ils sont des créatures nobles*." he told him simply. "They are such noble creatures."

Louis cleared his throat the way Enguerrand remembered him doing before making serious points. He had something important to say.

"I had a very long talk with Fumeux." He cleared his throat again. "He's beside himself. I can't get him away from that gizmo of yours. He's satisfied he can create an adapter for my cruiser. If you've convinced him, as far as I'm concerned you've completed your side of the bargain." He bowed his head to Enguerrand, just slightly. "I'm indebted to you, *merci*."

Enguerrand returned the nod.

"*De rien*, and as far as your end of the deal? You have my information?"

Louis furrowed his brow at his son's undisguised eagerness.

"You shouldn't be so enthusiastic, *chargeur dur*, about spilling blood. There seems always time enough for that."

Enguerrand heard the disdain in his father's voice and it displeased.

"I didn't say I was going to kill anyone."

Louis shook his head in faked agreement.

"*Oui, mai oui*, I don't know what made me say that." He thought deeply for a moment, scratching the end of his patrician nose. "Perhaps it's just the idea of killing women or children that causes one to err on the side of caution."

Enguerrand repeated himself grimly.

"I didn't say I was going to kill her."

Louis made a sweep of his hand, a grand gesture of compromise.

"Of course, you didn't. You left it unsaid," he specified. Louis Duprey hadn't fully decoded the glowers, the jerky tone of denial, and everything else that spoke plainer, but nonetheless moved on. "And we'll just leave it there." He was more interested anyway in Enguerrand's access to miraculous technology. "I don't suppose there's any rationale for me to ask how you got your hands on that thing?"

The stark truth was that the rotodynamic magneto he'd cannibalized from *Ultramariner* was the simplest part he could dismantle and bypass without crippling his ship. It was no big deal so that's exactly how he put it.

"*Il n'était pas grand-chose.*"

Louis kicked up a divot of turf and laughed.

"It's hard not to like you some, Enguerrand."

It was bitter-sweet bliss hearing his dead father calling him again by his given name, something impossible, yet happening.

111

Enguerrand asked again.

"So you've found her then? You intend to keep your end of the bargain, *n'est-ce pas?*"

For a second time Louis seemed to dissemble. "We've found her," is all he said.

His son couldn't restrain the great burden that fell immediately from his shoulders.

This was the victory he needed. Without his father's help his mission would have been as hopeless as making entropy decrease. He at least now had a chance, and a real one.

"*Grâce à Dieu,*" he said softly under his breath, the most fervent prayer he'd ever intoned in this life.

His father noted and let his eyes castigate his son for the blasphemy of thanking God for abetting whatever crime was being hatched.

"Come with me," he beckoned curtly, turning and exiting the stables, "it's time for you to collect the debt."

The Dupreys' baronial oak great hall was the jewel of their home. It was crowned with a magnificent open-timbered hammerbeam roof, a dodecagonal truss consisting of an arc of six gorgeously grained wooden corbels. It spanned venerable plank and panel walls framed into place decades ago, and unlike almost any walls anywhere, were devoid of pixilated tempura. They'd been hand carved, hewn with stunning pastoral bas-relief by masterfully talented artists, and were left untouched.

It was a mark of the Dupreys' much vaunted and old-fashioned stubbornness. There was nothing to think up that could improve *this* room and *this* company is what that particular omission in interior decorating implied. The fireplace was another. It was not only unnecessary on clement Arcadia, but it bordered on illogicality. This *faux pas* was intended then again. Such a meeting place required a hearth however the climate may contend otherwise.

A string-turned leg of lamb, *gigot a la Ficelle*, filled the room with aromas that permeated the mortar, wood and even stone of the chamber. It smelled just like home because it was home, right down to the *poutine*, the fried potatoes served much like it was made in ancient Quebec almost a millennium ago save that the Arcadian version called for grated favilla root, grown only here, sprinkled as a flourish.

This was indeed a special place, where something untranslatable, something only said in French—*mesnie*—drew Arcadians to the household in avouchment of the quality and leadership of the Dupreys.

It was crowded, a bit noisy, even raucous.

Everyone enjoyed a new sampling of one of the estate's just decanted vintages. This Malbec was blended with an excellent Barbera and tasted faintly of plums and Arcadian spices. Louis filled a large glass for himself and one for his son and escorted him to the grand dame standing next to the fireplace. There was neither smile nor anything even hinting at a frown to come from Adrienne Duprey as they approached. Her countenance never changed. It was pure business, no matter concerning her opinion on how to swirl the wine in the glass or whether to hand over the coordinates of the stalked to its hunter.

"*Bienvenue*," she greeted him properly. "Welcome to our *soiree*."

A hush immediately descended as she began speaking, snuffing every other conversation within earshot among family, trusted grounds foremen, guards and advisors. The famed leader of the Arcadian phalange needed no introduction, but she made it nonetheless and bid him to be at his ease and to accept the hospitality at her disposal. The presentation was unnecessary; Enguerrand knew his own grandmother and this time he was ready.

He'd been doing quite a bit of self-appraisal over the last hours and was well aware of nail-biting blunders he'd already made.

Not only had he named himself with his mother but, much, much worse, it dawned on him that he'd might have played the inconsistent, self-contradictory pivot in building the bridge his father would take to his own death. There had always been a great mystery about how Louis Duprey had somehow managed inexplicably to take part in the insurrection on Gilese a decade from now, when it was thought he was too far away when the firestorm exploded.

He now thought of trading the rotodynamic magneto for a noose with which to hang himself and tried to convince himself it would have happened anyway, that it already *had* happened. Whether right or wrong there wasn't any turning it around now. There would *not* be a third gaffe.

He was as laconic as the most tight-lipped Spartan ephor who ever reigned and had to be with painful truths playing out so indisputably in front of his eyes. Neither would tears be wrenched from him so easily tonight, melancholy proof that he obviously hadn't loved his grandmother as much as he'd told himself all these years. It was very odd and quite embarrassing to catch oneself lying to oneself. All that mentally dovetailed together, the entirety of it incongruously adding up to just the single word he spoke back to her.

"*Merci*," he thanked her.

Adrienne Duprey was still a most attractive woman. There was nothing though to prevent the shrinking of her jaw or the widening of her eye sockets over time. Age and gravity had done its work there; descending cheekbones were now unable to support the eyes as before and allowed them to sink.

But her face was a full one in her youth and had taken the unkind treatment without appearing much gaunt now. The apples of her cheeks were still plump and almost youthful. The cartilage and connective tissues around a much-admired regal nose had weathered every storm, the scaffolding refusing to buckle and allow it to droop a millimeter.

She shared the Duprey luck for beautiful tresses, so the face was framed with the thickest shock of abundantly healthy, lustrous argent hair, enough that her coiffure was the only thing too youngish for such an awe-inspiring gentlewoman. Above all, though, with the long practiced airs of someone born to be the lady of the manor, she was an imposing and formidable personage.

"My son assures me that asking you the same questions over and again will get us nowhere. So, I'll dispense with quizzing you about the first few sensational phenomena." She gave Enguerrand a practiced, coy moue. "We'll take for granted that you haven't the single faintest footprint anywhere in Creation or the Free Range, that you're unscannable, that you don't exist as far as anyone anywhere can say. Since that's quite a trick, why shouldn't a man like that arrive likewise with a device sufficient to push quantum cruisers to unheard of speeds?" She had both of her palms outstretched and upturned to heaven, a gesture of perfect acceptance. "That's all your business you contend though, n'est-ce pas?"

Adrienne was clearly troubled about by the complete lack of anything at all resembling knowledge about Enguerrand, his sympathies, his access to bewilderingly superior technology, and not least, whom or what he was desperately chasing and why. Adrienne settled on what she considered the most important point.

"You are a true free-ranger?"

"To the death, madam," he answered honestly.

Such a simple reply, just those few words, but it seemed to get by as an answer for everyone listening. Some time passed before anyone spoke again, all silently enjoying the fruits of their labors in the vineyards.

"And you are an upright and decent man? You're a believer in eternal things greater than and beyond yourself as well, too?"

Her eyes were on the advertisement of his faith hanging

about his neck.

Enguerrand hadn't known the answer to this question for years, but he now was forced to find the words, and say them out loud, in front of quite a coterie of witnesses. After being pushed through a tortuous purgatory, witnessing the destruction of everything dear to him, having either lost or seemingly been abandoned by everyone and everything including parents, wife, child, destiny, and most of humanity, had he remained faithful? He truly didn't know, and said as much.

"I can't say I'm any perfect example of integrity, madame."

"That is certainly the most believable part of this whole matter," she scoffed. "Your candor is a step in the right direction at least. There are limits, however, young man and I'm quite sure we've reached them and far surpassed that ground."

She wagged her finger at him as a matriarch would to enforce her will on a grandson and fixed him with a look he remembered all too well from his childhood. This would not be pleasant; he buckled in for a very rough ride.

"We'll make a fresh start beginning with your name, my unscannable young friend. You'll please be kind enough to identify yourself."

Duprey gave her a slight bow.

"Enguerrand, madame. *Enchanté.*"

Adrienne didn't like that answer, not at all.

"*Quel est ton surnom?*" "What is your surname?" she demanded, using the familiar address, even though the query was hardly friendly in the least.

"*Je suis désolé,*" he apologized. "I'm sorry. I'm not able to provide that to you at this time."

"At this time?" she mocked him instantly. "What an idiotic qualifier. Is the hour somehow inappropriate? Will you be at your ease to disclose your unmentionable and taboo name if we wait for the clock to strike midnight? Or will the morning see you better disposed, at your leisure, to accomplish this most basic of civil tasks? *Mon Dieu*, I can't imagine why my son hasn't placed you under arrest and left you confined until some plain answers starting coming out of your mouth."

Louis Duprey sat silently, looking into the fire and frowning, swishing the wine in his glass. He looked as uncomfortable and small as Enguerrand remembered ever seeing him in his life.

"I have an agreement with your son, madame," Enguerrand protested, plainly alarmed at her tone and the flagrant allusion to his arrest.

She ignored her grandson completely.

"I'll ask once more. Your name, young man. Your full name. We'll start there."

Enguerrand swallowed hard, shuffling his feet, as would a chastised youngster being rebuked by his grandmother. He didn't even bother to reply but only shook his head in the negative.

"Monsieur Broussard!" Adrienne thundered.

That was Smokey's true name Enguerrand knew, though he hardly ever heard anyone call him that. Fumeux came forward instantly though, as disheveled as ever, just as Enguerrand remembered him, immediately ill at ease under Adrienne's gaze. His unruly shock of dishwater-colored hair was uncombed and looked like it could use a shampoo. He clutched his cap, pressing it to his chest in an unconscious but silly attempt at reverence in Adrienne's presence. He obviously had forgotten to remove it while indoors and had just pulled it off at the last moment. Even from where he stood, Enguerrand could see that Smokey's fingernails were dirty and one oozed a little blood, having dug into something metal that bit back. His face didn't have quite as many scars and burn marks, but this was twenty-five years ago, Enguerrand reminded himself, and Fumeux had plenty of time to still acquire them.

"*Oui, madame, a votre service*," he said respectfully.

"That device you've been examining. What was the word you used to describe it?" She looked straight into the eyes of Enguerrand as he put the query, only sending the words in Smokey's direction, not her steely gaze.

"*Extraterrestre?* Is that the word I used?" When she didn't answer he realized he had guessed right. "Yes, ma'am, that is exactly the word I used."

"And why did you choose that term?"

"Well," he blinked his eyes at the obviousness. "There's no way any human constructed that. There is no device in existence like that thing—not here, not anywhere. I've never seen anything even remotely like it."

Now Adrienne Duprey put on a look of mock shock and came to a flabbergasted realization.

"Maybe we should dispense with the name, after all, and concentrate on your origins, Enguerrand?" She turned to Louis and reproached him directly. "You seemed willing enough to just accept willy-nilly that this complete and utter stranger among us is unscannable and in possession of impossibly advanced technology, so I wonder if anyone thought to see if this individual has a beating heart and to determine whether his blood is red or green?"

Louis Duprey cleared his throat, in an aggressively irritated manner—yet said not a single word, still staring at the fire.

Enguerrand spoke up and for the first time with verve.

"Oh, my goodness, Fumeux, *quelle absurdité*, what nonsense." He gave but the slightest thought to attempting to insinuate the same that he had implied with Preston Beta-Hydri Vincent, Gamma D-25417—that Thinwalkers, extraterrestrials or the like might be involved here. That might have worked on Fumeux; it would only have infuriated his grandmother.

"Extraterrestrials, indeed. How could you embarrass yourself by saying such a thing? Many of those parts—the aggregation coil and the continuum chipsets, for example—those are stock items made on Leonis Minoris A-7 by the millions. Don't you recognize them?"

"Well, yes, of course I recognize them," he admitted.

"Then how did such a silly idea rattle around in your head and find its way out of your mouth?"

Fumeux bristled.

"Those parts—some of them anyway—were certainly fabricated on Leonis Minoris A-7. There are quite a few others though, I must say, whose provenance I can't speak for in the least. And as to who or what managed to assemble the whole apparatus, I can swear there's no engineer in the galaxy who could have accomplished that."

Fumeux was so flummoxed he slid his cap back on his head as if to punctuate his critique.

"No sir, no engineer alive put that device together."

Enguerrand had an excellent rejoinder.

"Some engineer obviously did just that. You are in error and the proof is that the device is in your workshop."

Adrienne wished to know.

"And does this device have a name or does it bounce around Creation incognito as you do?"

Enguerrand could answer that.

"It's a rotodynamic magneto." Then he added, "Hexagonal gradient class," he paused, "for specificity," he clarified cheekily.

Nothing caught her off guard.

"*Merci*," she shot back immediately, "I am a great proponent of specificity. I insist upon it whenever possible."

Adrienne was nodding appreciatively for that snippet of solid information and thought she'd push her luck.

"Any chance you'd be gracious enough to inform us where this magneto was constructed?"

He gave her a bit of a cheeky reply.

"It's not from Leonis Minoris A-7, but also not from any

warehouse run by any species of little green men anywhere."

Enguerrand folded his arms and stepped closer to his grandmother. He had an issue of his own.

"I made an agreement with your son, madame. We shook on the deal and gave each other our bonds. I trusted in the word of Louis Duprey, given freely, witnessed by his own wife. I have acted in complete good faith and kept my word to the letter."

His voice trembled as he was forced to reproach his own father on the thing he held the most sacred: his honor.

"I am stunned, madame, and quite far beyond the bounds of disbelief that someone so respected as Louis Duprey should sell his oath so cheaply."

His father, of course, heard every stinging word and visibly cringed while listening, but still remaining dead silent, unmoved, seemingly transfixed by the fire.

"You accuse my son, unscannable stranger?"

"*Oui, j'accuse,*" he stood his ground.

At that moment, Sophie Duprey entered the hall. At first she seemed pleased to see him, but then Enguerrand saw that she realized he was in yet another quite serious imbroglio with both her husband and mother-in-law. Still, she didn't abandon him; she came straight away to the scene of the discussion, immediately saw the discomfiture of Louis and whispered something in his ear, finishing by kissing her husband on the cheek.

She took a seat right next to Adrienne and reached over and affectionately took the woman's hand. she wasn't angry but she wasn't pleased either

"I must say, Enguerrand, I can hardly enter a room without you being accused or accusing. That's an unusual flair."

In her voice, there was a mixture of shock, pique, annoyance and reprimand.

"How did you come by that?"

Enguerrand leaned on his mother as any son would.

"Madame Duprey is a witness. She heard every word your son and I exchanged. She saw us spit and shake. She will not lie; ask her."

Now Louis Duprey spoke, rumbling like a bear over his shoulder.

"Leave my wife out of this. This has nothing at all to do with her."

Enguerrand turned and had the temerity to place his hand on Louis' shoulder.

"You gave me your word, *monsieur*," he recriminated, "you gave me your bond."

Louis shrugged it off, both the words and his son's hand.

"As you gave me yours, Enguerrand." He couldn't bring himself to make eye contact with his son, but gave his tepid defense with his gaze still focused on the dancing flames. "It isn't I who muddied this *affaire honnête,* but you."

That knocked the wind out of Enguerrand.

"I beg your pardon?"

The wind that left Enguerrand's sails filled Adrienne's with a startling vengeance. She was an expert negotiator, a lioness who sat growling behind mediators' roundtables just waiting for the perfect moment to pounce. It had arrived, she judged. She didn't pounce but sprang to her feet, pointing her perfectly manicured index finger at her grandson.

"Any pardon begged of the free-rangers of Arcadia, you insolent young man, shall be asked of...*moi.*"

She paced slowly back and forth in front of him, reading him the riot act.

"Let's go over this bargain you made with my son, shall we?"

Enguerrand was all for it.

"*Oui*, indeed, let's."

"But," she held up her impeccably polished finger again, "let us examine it piece by piece, word by word. *D'accord?*"

Enguerrand stood silently, fuming, yet nodding his head in agreement.

"You were to provide my son with three hekats of that infernal ambrosia and that..."

She was at a loss for words.

Enguerrand helped her out.

"Rotodynamic magneto."

She held up four fingers on her right hand.

"Yes, three hekats of ambrosia and one rotodynamic magneto. And we? What were we to repay you in kind? Can you please refresh all of our memories? What is it that we owe you?"

Enguerrand said it loudly, clearly, rudely.

"Vanessa Braverman. You owe me the whereabouts of Vanessa Braverman. It's really quite simple, madame. I can't understand what all this fuss is about."

Adrienne smirked. It was the same smug grin that caused countless ambassadors to finally lose their patience. It was a truly ugly grin, one that said that she was certain a snare had been tripped. She slowly, and with great pomp, held up one...one finger. She wanted to be certain so she asked again. Holding her one finger in front of his face she inquired.

"This is all we owe you, just this, just the location of one Vanessa Braverman? If this were delivered, you would hold us harmless and happily depart? You would consider my son's honor and word intact and leave our homestead and never come back? Will this send you on your way, along with your very disagreeable truculence?"

He raised his voice.

"*Oui, madame!*"

"Very well, then, just this, monsieur, just this one question I'd like answered, so we can make you whole, settle this affair, and put this matter behind us. This Vanessa Braverman whom you seek: why are there two of her—and none of you?"

She held two fingers up.

"*Deux*," she emphasized, "There are *two* of her. And there isn't even *one* of you. Can you explain that?"

The blood rushed to his face, his eyes flushed a deeper green, his pulse raced. He had been caught. He was in trouble and there didn't seem to be a way out. He lowered his voice.

"No, madam, I cannot."

"No?" She opened her eyes wide. "Well, which one is it that you seek? Which one is it that you paid for? Should we settle it by tossing a coin, *pile ou face*? Heads or tails, shall we call it that way then?"

"I'll be satisfied to have the whereabouts of both, Madame Duprey, if you please."

"*Deux pour le prix d'un*," she understood that plainly enough. "Two for the price of one. But of course, who wouldn't want that? I shop the same way myself whenever I can. But that *isn't* what you paid for, and that isn't what you'll be getting."

She sat down, took a sip of her wine and threw Enguerrand a more conciliatory lifeline.

"Now, we aren't ogres. There seems to have been nothing more than a slight misunderstanding. If you'll be so kind as to clear up a few things for us, well, by all means, we have the whereabouts of..." She stopped and shook her head incredulously as if she was constrained to speak gibberish. "We have the whereabouts of...both...of them, and we're very eager to renegotiate."

She rose, adroitly pressed back a lock of her hair that had fallen across her forehead, picked up her wine glass and made for the exit to the veranda.

"I'm going out for a bit of evening air. Think about it, Enguerrand."

Her grandson did think about it, and thought quite hard.

Chapter Nine: Across the Great Divide into Lacaillia

The simplest man who has passion persuades better than the most eloquent man who lacks it.
—Francois de La Rochefoucauld, Maxim No. 8

HIS GRANDMOTHER'S WORDS stuck in his ears and stung, and they wore him out. Enguerrand felt very tired and took a seat; this was a real problem.

Adrienne's words echoed in his ears.

"Can you explain why there are *two* of her…and yet none of you?"

He could explain, of course, but yet dare not. Aside from immediately being considered a raving madman, he was caught between the horns of other more mind-bogglingly twisted dilemmas, *entre le marteau et l'enclume*, between the hammer and the anvil.

Turning it over in circles in his mind wasn't going to open any doors for him, unfortunately. His grandmother, he saw now, was as hard as spent tetraprismane. Crossing swords with

Adrienne, not as her darling *petit chou,* but as an adult adversary, as a potential enemy in her mind, made him realize what a formidable woman she truly was.

He wouldn't be able to dance his way around her. The liveliest *gallop* would be required for him to try to manage that. Yet just then the choreography for those sorts of steps arrived, within the rucksack delivered by one of Sophie's household staff.

Sophie spoke.

"I had this prepared for you, Enguerrand," She blushed slightly catching the impenetrable gaze of her husband looking on silently. "I assumed you would be departing shortly," she clarified for both her son and husband, "and wanted you to have this before I'm on my way as well."

Her gift came at an uncomfortable moment, she realized.

"Whoever you are, Enguerrand," Sophie felt constrained to add, "you must have a mother and I'm sure she worries about your lack of home-cooked meals." She placed the bundle of wonderful aromas before her son. "There are croissants, baguettes, beignets and a few carafes of our private pressings." Her smile was both humble and proud, as honest and good as any face he'd ever seen in his life. "It's nothing really. *Bon voyage,* Enguerrand."

The irony struck him.

"Bread and wine, that's like a communion of sorts. *Merci,* Madam Duprey."

He thought back to what she had just said.

"You are going somewhere?" Enguerrand asked.

She nodded affably.

"To my sister's wedding in Lacaillia, on the far side of the Continental Ridge."

She described the geography of her planet for someone who really needed no tutorial. Enguerrand was born and raised on Arcadia and knew quite well where Lacaillia was. He was the only one in the cosmos though who knew what was waiting for his mother there.

His heart jumped straight into his throat.

Sophie, as well as Louis, saw it.

"My goodness, Enguerrand," she laughed, "I've seen men wince at the thought of marriage, but I don't believe I've ever seen a man nearly faint at the mere mention of the word. *Sacre bleu!*"

Now the mental axe fell within Enguerrand's quick-firing brain. It cut swiftly and deeply. This was the legacy of his dead mother, taken from him by the same fever that was bequeathed to him as both the curse and blessing of the dangerous fires that burned within him.

The logic was inescapable.

Finding Vanessa Braverman—either of her!—without his father's and grandmother's help would be impossible. And, they had already come through with the very information he desperately needed. All they had to do was say the single word giving her—their—location.

He would never be closer than this.

Unless he could manage to pry Vanessa Braverman's coordinates from the iron grip of his grandmother, he might just as well return now through the pulsar portal in defeat to throw himself and his family on the mercy of someone who had no inkling of the meaning of the word.

This unattractive option condemned himself to death—and his wife and child to who knew what fate. Just as heart-wrenching, if he didn't do something and allowed this opportunity to slip away he would be standing by idly and watching his own mother heading off to her certain death.

On the other hand, if he surrendered and accepted the terms of his grandmother and divulged who he was, he may very well change the fate of his mother and give her back the life she lost so young. He'd have the whereabouts of his quarry to boot, and would be one final step away from success, preserving the real chance of rescuing his wife and daughter.

On the face of things, he really had little choice. Only one peripheral caution kept making its strident disagreement heard above the hum of perfectly tuned logic drumming out the supposed obvious path to take. He went over each word of Otto's warning, striving hard to remember every syllable when he'd first punched through the portal into the past, still fighting off the effects of ambrosia. He turned Otto's ominous caveat inside out and back again looking for the meaning behind it all.

"Try not to interact with anyone in this dangerously impossible landscape of kaleidoscope reality in which you find yourself, Mr. Duprey. Do the least you can to effect the most. On no account should you give anyone an indication of who and what you are; that might possibly be the worst thing you could do. You're making a new reality for yourself both here and in the future and any other place and time as well and doing it blindfolded. You shouldn't be too surprised if not all the pieces come to fit well in the end. Some very nasty results can occur from just the mildest brushes with what for a lack of a better term we'll call fate. *Me comprenez-vous?*"

Those thoughts scared Enguerrand down to the marrow in the hollows of his bones—yet he was a man with no real choice. So he wasn't sure if his heroic or cowardly side was in charge but a decision was made.

He said the words aloud, speaking to himself, or not, feeling obliged to pronounce something to someone at least, realizing he was entering into the most dangerous territory this side of forever.

"*Quand le vin est tiré, il faut le boire.* When the wine is opened it must be drunk."

Sophie couldn't understand how this—in any way—had the slightest to do with men's matrimonial terrors but she smiled anyway out of politeness. It evaporated when she heard his next bizarrely inexplicable command.

"You cannot go to Lacaillia."

Sophie didn't understand him, but Louis did.

"What did you just say to my wife?"

Adrienne, returning from the veranda, hadn't made out the precise nature of Enguerrand's order but saw the look in Louis' eyes and had an idea.

"Have I missed yet another fiat delivered imperiously from this unknown, unscannable, impudent stranger?"

Faster than any other man, Enguerrand leapt to his feet. The fever against which he was foolishly attempting to inoculate his mother was beginning to rise. It alarmed everyone. So did his tone.

"You wish to know who I am, Adrienne? Is that your demand in order to step aside and refrain from causing your son to injure his honor by defrauding me? Is that what you require?"

That brought a response from the taciturn Louis Duprey.

"How dare you say that to my face in my own home?" he thundered.

The score of free-rangers throughout every corner of the hall heard it reverberate in their chests. Every conversation ceased; every pair of eyes fixed on the contest of wills taking place. Louis' face flushed beet red.

Enguerrand would not back down.

"You have dishonored yourself, sir. It has nothing to do with my saying so or not. You defrauded me, blatantly, to the discredit of your word, putting my wife and daughter in grave danger. If you have no care for keeping your trust revered it's not my concern to worry about offending you by making it known."

Louis bolted from his chair and would have made for Enguerrand had Sophie not thrown herself on him.

"You will apologize," he menaced. You will retract that," Louis said in a much lower tone, a much more threatening one.

Enguerrand would not.

"Whatever disgrace we may have deserved," he quoted *le duc* at his father, "it is almost always in our power to re-establish our character." He displayed his right hand, stretching it out as evidence of the injury, and continued in a more conciliatory tone. "We shook hands, Monsieur Duprey. We gave each other our bond. It *is* in your power to make that right."

Now the verbal assault came from another quarter.

"What did you say to my daughter-in-law?" Adrienne was fuming. "Answer my son!"

Enguerrand fumed as well.

"She can't go to Lacaillia. She must not go to her sister's wedding."

Adrienne had had far more than enough. She visibly trembled.

"This man," she said to Louis, "should be placed under arrest immediately. He is a raving lunatic, or in league with scum who use such pathetic creatures. This can go no further. You see he is intimating that Sophie will be ambushed or kidnapped or…"

She turned to Enguerrand, and as if in afterthought, spoke.

"You wouldn't care to elucidate why Sophie can't go to Lacaillia?"

She enunciated the query as absurdly as she could.

He was already wading up to his neck in the Rubicon he was crossing, too late to go back and with no recourse other than to make it to the other side. He snatched a carafe from a passing member of the staff who let it go without the slightest demur, happy to fetch another and in so doing gladly absenting himself from this discussion of possible murder of the lady of the house.

Enguerrand impertinently splashed the malbec up to the rim of the glass Adrienne was holding.

"You'll need this." He pointed down the stairwell to their

right. "And in the infirmary, down one flight and two doors to the left you'll find smelling salts. They're kept in the closet—not the large repository at the back of the room but the small one at the side of the desk."

He waited for the arrow to find the target and draw blood. He was close enough to watch her pupils dilate ever so slightly.

"Smelling salts. You'll need them."

That hushed everyone. A languid, palpable silence descended on the furious exchange and extinguished the threats and insults. Sophie felt confident enough to release Louis and approach Enguerrand, standing so close mother and son could smell each other's breath.

"Why shouldn't I go to Lacaillia? Am I in danger?"

He answered in a low tone. "Yes, Madame Duprey, grave danger."

"You will explain all this to me, and to my husband and mother-in-law, *oui*, Enguerrand?"

Enguerrand nodded. "*Mais oui*, of course." Enguerrand now gave his stunned relations to realize he knew much, much more about their homestead than just where to find the smelling salts. "But not here. We must speak in complete confidence—in the second cellar, the one below the wine."

Sophie was stunned beyond belief, and now was equally frightened. Before she could ask how he could know of such a hidden basement existed, he gave his reasoning.

"It's completely enclosed and protected with a tessellated Janssen cage. Nothing can get through, not Nexus, nor anything else, not in or out."

He took in the reactions on the faces of Louis and Adrienne—pure flummoxed bewilderment.

"You've been after me to explain things." He gave a quick glance in the direction of the stairwell leading down. "After you?"

Chapter Ten: Prodigal Son

Passion sometimes renders the most clever man a fool, and even sometimes renders the most foolish man clever.
—Francois de La Rochefoucauld, Maxim No. 6

SUPREMELY IMPORTANT HISTORIC conferences and plans had been hatched in this very locale, *The Cave*. No conversation had ever taken place like the one currently though, as one of the four participants had yet to be born.

By now, Enguerrand had come to grips with this. In a way, it was a great relief for him to spill out his predicament to another human being—anyone—since up to this point only a clinking amanuensis of an Otto-matic had been a confidant.

The doyenne of the hundreds of millions of free-rangers from Creation to the Big Black didn't hold court this time, nor did her heir apparent, her hard-charging and fearless son, Louis Duprey.

This *tête-à-tête* was under the undisputed thumb of a twenty-five-year-old courier who had accomplished exactly nothing in his entire life—a life which had yet to come into being to be precise.

Enguerrand, the "impudent young man," had taken the center chair of the semi-circular conference station that dominated the hidden chamber two levels below the homestead. This seat was the exclusive reserve of Louis but on this occasion of the strangest conversation to take place underground, above ground on Arcadia or anywhere else, Enguerrand would need to hold the court and make dead-certain eye contact with his three listeners.

Enguerrand paid his last heed to caution, said farewell to the remnant of every care and turned to Sophie and began saying everything to his dead mother that he had dreamed of his entire life.

"I was born and raised on Arcadia, the great, great, great grandson of Arcadians. My family is held in the highest esteem of any other on the planet."

Adrienne gave an audible harrumph. It didn't need explaining. The Dupreys were the family Enguerrand described and she herself was intimately acquainted with every family ranking anywhere close to theirs. This unscannable rogue was no scion of any revered family.

"I was raised to adhere to the best traditions of Arcadia, my father constantly explaining what it meant to be a free-ranger and how that decency and dignity set us apart from others." He paused and looked directly at Adrienne. "My grandmother as well."

That elicited another harrumph from Adrienne.

"Does this esteemed family have a surname?" Sophie asked plainly.

Enguerrand held up his finger to indicate that it did, that all the details would be forthcoming in due time.

"When I was ten years old, my father caught me doing something which he strongly disapproved. It didn't matter to him that so many other boys used slingshots to pursue sludgeskimmers."

Sophie, Adrienne and Louis knew how much fun Arcadian boys got out of targeting sludgeskimmers. These bizarre creatures—part insect, part bird and part firefly, but mostly alien hummingbird—actually exploded if they were hit properly, puncturing bladders that fizzled like fireworks in the oxygen-rich air.

Enguerrand thought back to the incident.

"I told my father that they were just sludgeskimmers and he gave me the lecture of my young life. He told me that all sins, every piece of ugliness that ever existed or ever would, all the dark, evil, debilitating defeats and failures of mankind, in every age, all stemmed from the same primal, spiteful poison: unreasoned violence. This was not only a great offense to the good, but brute force hid the true shortcomings of laziness and stagnation, since it was easier for the dull and sluggish to steal and threaten than to create it. Envy, theft, murder and finally warfare and annihilation—these and other weaknesses, vices, and crimes were nothing but the exposed gangrene of violence, let loose on the body of humankind."

After all these years Enguerrand remembered his father's words to the letter.

"If others needed nanites to restrain this terrible flaw in humanity's character, that marked we free-rangers as all the more noble. Violence and death would hold no terror for the man he would see me become, that I should fight to the death when it was required of me but that no son of his would ever treat the killing of any creature as sport."

"Your father was a wise man," Sophie complimented.

"Indeed, he was," Enguerrand agreed. "He confiscated my slingshot and put me on restriction for a period."

Adrienne wasn't interested in the story.

"You brought us here for this?" She tapped her finger impatiently on the conference table veneer. "Is this is leading somewhere?"

It was.

"I swore to my father that I understood the reason for my punishment and that I had learned my lesson."

"Bravo," Adrienne mocked.

"But I hadn't," Enguerrand ignored the slight. "I lied to my father."

Enguerrand explained that another slingshot, his favorite, had been safely ensconced in the makeshift fort in which he and his companions played. The boy legionnaires had toiled diligently on their secret citadel, constructed of twisted and woven briars, vines and branches, and camouflaged perfectly within the thicket of which it was made.

He didn't like disobeying his father, but the thrill he experienced tramping about in the wilds with his comrades appealed to him too strongly to ignore easily.

And, popping sludgeskimmers was the most fun a boy could have on Arcadia. He wasn't about to give that up—no matter how many boring lectures his father made him sit and swallow. He would just be more careful not to get caught. Because nothing could change the fact that he was happiest when testing his strength and agility in the bush, pitting his skills against the creatures that flew in and out of his slingshot's sight, and doing it all in competition with his friends who loved it too.

"I never got the chance to confess that to my father."

Enguerrand sat back and said nothing.

However, no one had truly understood. His three listeners stared at him blank-faced. He would have to make the confession more overt.

"My father warned me that the black sheep of our family— a cruel man who delighted in causing pain—he had also killed sludgeskimmers for sport as a child." Enguerrand looked at his mother whose face was flushed with a mixture of toxic emotions. It was her brother and his own uncle to whom Enguerrand referred, her tormentor as a child.

It didn't please him to open this old wound in his mother's past, but if he was to pry open Louis' steely reluctance he'd need a crowbar made of visions he never could have glimpsed, but could prove he did.

"Do you know anyone like that, Madame Duprey?"

Sophie's shocked eyes said she most certainly did.

He took a deep breath, girded himself and let loose the naked truth, knowing full well it would be as difficult to either explain or understand as a naked singularity.

"So, I never got the chance to confess that to my father— until just now."

He locked eyes with Louis Duprey.

"I'm sorry I disobeyed you, father," he apologized. "Because I looked up to you like no other man. I tried to listen to everything you ever told me and live up to the titan you were. I knew I could never be you, but I loved you even more for that. No boy ever had a father equal to you."

Even such blatantly explicit language was insufficient.

"Why are you calling my husband... *father*?" Sophie spoke as if she were sleepwalking, but as an angry somnambulist. "And your allusion to my brother with that tale of yours, it's the height of cheek and rudeness. Regardless of how you came to know about it, it's disgraceful and insulting to hear you retelling that story. What do you hope to gain by that?"

Enguerrand ignored all her queries save the first.

"Why am I calling your husband 'father'? Because, I am Enguerrand Duprey, son of Louis and Sophie Duprey, grandson of none other than Adrienne of Arcadia."

There, he said it, it was out.

Louis was ashen and frozen. Sophie gave a very pained, low cry from a place inside that seemed tender to the very touch, much less manhandled like this. Only Adrienne had her wits about her. She stood ramrod erect and emitted a string of curses in French that would have taken aback a platoon of hardened

Alshanian mercenaries. And then she raised back and slapped Enguerrand hard across the face. Even though they were within the impenetrable confines of a tensilated Janssen cage, it struck with such force that the reverberations must have pressed mightily against the field surrounding the cellar trying to escape.

She turned to her son and reproached him as well.

"How can you sit and listen to this?"

Louis was indeed sitting still, petrified, as stiff as the Monoliths of frozen oxygen covering the bitterly cold surface of the glacial moon Niflheim in the Geminorum system.

"Go on." That was all he could manage. "Go on," he said to Enguerrand.

His son should have pitied Louis in this state, but instead, Enguerrand was more concerned for his own wife and daughter. He sprang to the attack.

"Yes, gladly, Monsieur Duprey, I'd very much like to finish the tale. My father was such a man who would surrender his right hand rather than give it falsely to a fellow free-ranger. He was someone who held his own honor far above life itself. The idea of breaking his oath always seemed to me as impossible as rain falling upward. Have you ever met a man like that?"

Adrienne chimed in.

"This man needs to be put under arrest. Immediately."

Before Louis could comment on the possibility of a warrant Sophie brought up something far more important.

"You just now said that I was your mother, Enguerrand?"

Enguerrand looked at her swollen midsection.

"You're pregnant...with me." He said it as a matter of fact.

"Have you lost your mind?" Sophie asked just as matter-of-factly.

Enguerrand nodded.

"*Oui*, madame. If you had been through what I have been enduring I can promise that you would be a bit worse for wear as well."

"You're from my future?" Then she corrected herself. "You're from *our* future?"

Enguerrand breathed out hard.

"I truly don't know if I am alive or dead, competent or insane, your son or someone else's. I do know that my wife and daughter are in the hands of a monster. I can only change that by finding Vanessa Braverman. I contracted in good faith with your husband and kept my end of the bargain. I implore you to compel your husband to honor his word."

Sophie turned to her husband and managed just a single word.

"Louis?"

Louis hadn't taken his eyes off Enguerrand, boring a hole through him with a gaze as sharp and focused as a supracoherent laser.

"Why should she cancel her trip to Lacaillia?" Louis demanded to know.

Otto's stern warning came flooding back to him. The amanuensis hadn't gone into detail as to what dreadful consequences might be engendered should Enguerrand carelessly "interact."

The problem was, however, that it was far too late to worry about any of that now. He had put his name into his mother's mind and put into Louis' hands the apparatus that might have caused his father's death. What else he had or hadn't done especially now with his complete and open shedding of subterfuge he couldn't begin to fathom.

He put the best face on it though. If the glowering, shocked, and alarmed expressions before him were any indication, Sophie and Louis Duprey might well end up choosing another name for their son after all. There was no telling how this future-past-present enigma worked anyway. One thing was certain, his own mother was about to embark on a journey that would end in her death.

He intended to stop it.

"If she goes there, she'll come back with Lacaillian fever and she'll die from it."

Adrienne was beside herself and her words dripped with venom.

"Oh, there is no end to what this desperate man will say!" She slapped her hands on the table. "What a fiend, to say such a thing to a pregnant woman. How despicable to attempt to terrify Sophie in her state."

Louis shook his head.

"You must realize…"

Enguerrand cut him off.

"Yes, I do realize how implausible and unlikely it is to still contract Lacaillian fever in this day and age. I'm well aware it's as close to extinct as Denebolan pox. It happens though. That's how my mother died."

Enguerrand turned to Sophie.

"If you go Lacaillia you *will* contract the fever."

Sophie had been trying to collect her thoughts.

"I should miss my sister's wedding because an unscannable outlander appears at my door to tell me he is the grown version of the fetus I'm carrying, having come back through the mists of time to warn me that I'll be infected with the rarest disease in this sector and will die if I attend. Have I summarized that properly?"

Enguerrand flushed hearing his mother's critique; it was almost enough to convince him too that he was as batty as a rabid Circinian vole. Still, he put in all his chips; he wasn't going to fold.

"I can prove it."

Adrienne liked that.

"Oh, another trick? You ferreted out where we keep our smelling salts and the name of a stallion that threw my son. What else do you have up your sleeve?"

138

"My DNA. That will prove who I am."

That caused Adrienne to laugh.

"Your DNA? You foolish amateur. You've deluded yourself that you've spent time as our guest—eating, drinking, sleeping and grooming yourself at our estate—and that your DNA hasn't been collected? That and quite a few other biometric markers of yours have been run in every manner conceivable." She admitted a contradictory compliment. "Whoever put you up to this, I'll grant, did a better job than just wrapping a matching replica of Sophie's triskelion around your neck. They've obviously invested an exceptional amount of time, effort, credits and expertise because there isn't a trace of you anywhere. Some power has gone to quite some lengths to wipe you from every database. It causes one to wonder who your employer might be?"

"I'm a courier," he said flatly.

"Ah, a courier. That's the first thing that makes sense in all this. They're such a nasty crew of lowlifes if ever there were."

He had been biting his tongue with his grandmother for some time, forcing himself not to think badly of her. She was protecting her family, reacting the way almost anyone would. He bit down hard again.

"You didn't check it in the right manner. There's no way you could have thought to do so. I'm well aware my DNA profile doesn't match anyone alive; I'm not alive yet. You wasted your time there. And a paternity test would be impossible without knowing against whom my DNA should be checked, wouldn't it? You'd have to have at least a clue concerning my parentage." He pointed at his mother and father. "Well, they're certainly alive and I've given you more than a clue."

Sophie was astonished.

"You're actually going to take this even further? To such lengths?" The extent of his purported madness or pathological deception was becoming clear to her now as she understood at once that he'd sink to profaning her religion to pull it off. "You're trying to say that your triskelion is actually *my* triskelion? That they're one and the same and you got it from me?"

Enguerrand leaned closer to her.

"How do you think I got these?" He pointed to his eyes. "When is the last time you saw someone with eyes like these? Ever? In your life?"

Now Sophie was the one biting her lip and saying nothing.

"My mother died of Lacaillian fever just after giving birth to me. I almost died as well." He now fixed Louis with his glaring cat-green eyes. "My father was a great man, the undisputed leader of the free-rangers of Arcadia and Vela Eridani, a man who never once went back on his word...not ever...not once."

Enguerrand rose. He brought this singularly unique conference to an abrupt end.

"For Vanessa Braverman's location I gave my word to double the speed of your vessels, Monsieur Duprey, and to enrich your coffers with three hekats of ambrosia. This I accomplished while you reneged. You then outrageously changed the protocols of our agreement and added the new demand that I identify myself. Doubtlessly, once you prove who I am, there won't be another obstacle put in the way of you making good."

He waved his arms around the Cage.

"I wish it could be done now, but obviously that's impossible. In my guesthouse quarters, I'll await the coordinates of the people I seek. When you know who I am and recover from the shock of it, you'll find me there."

Louis growled at him.

"Don't leave this homestead. You won't get far if you try."

Enguerrand growled back at him.

"As I told you when I arrived, I'm not leaving here without her whereabouts. Of that you can be certain."

As Enguerrand collected the rucksack filled with the delights his mother had prepared for him, Sophie reached over and stayed his hand. She wanted to make him understand something.

"I wanted to trust that you were a good man. You seem far too lucid for the appalling things that come out of your mouth though, so I'm at a loss to understand your aims. Whoever has put you up to this amazingly complicated charade, Enguerrand, you have to realize it's painfully obvious that you've somehow gotten yourself into something that can only end badly. If you needed help from us, you might have just asked. That would have been far better; there's no shame in seeking it."

The rest of what she said cut into him.

"I am shocked and angered that you've brought this malignancy into my house though, especially considering how much you were treated by us. You taught me something important however. I'm not such a good judge of character as I had imagined." His mother's reprimand was given out so emotionally that she wound up short of breath, pushing back strands of lustrous hair she'd shaken loose. "You seemed like a good man to me, Enguerrand. This has been very hard to witness."

He had to silently allow her rebuke without offering another word of defense; he'd already brought every weapon he had to bear. He accepted the reproach manfully, but this, from his mother, cut to the quick. He shocked her, and himself as well, with his response, taking her hand and drawing it to his lips, kissing gently, respectfully, certainly like no other kiss he would press on any other hand.

He had to tell her this, whether it violated every law of this universe and the one adjoining.

"Your son will be a fine man," he prophesized. "He'll have his flaws like anyone, but in the end, he'll be worthy."

Adrienne was disgusted.

"There he goes again with the tears; it's becoming positively ridiculous."

Enguerrand Duprey was in fact weeping again, but this time there was something final and conclusive pervading the tears.

It was the last time he would ever cry.

Enguerrand could hardly sit alone in the guesthouse with the emotional storm raging within his head and breast. He saddled a fine chestnut colored yearling and took the colt through its paces along the paths of the vineyard.

He was an excellent horseman which the mount knew instinctively. The evening drizzle had ceased and night had truly fallen. At night, the vineyard was the most serene and peaceful place of his boyhood. The smells and hoof beats and the constellations in the sky above engendered another indescribable and soul-wrenching déjà vu.

He had weathered so many that this one washed over him without his offering the slightest resistance. He was back where it was impossible to be at a time before his birth in a place that no longer existed interacting with his dead parents—and all transpiring in the halcyon days of the most inexpressibly beautiful planet in the entire Spiral Arm.

He collected his thoughts, going over everything he had said, assessing what he had done right and wrong, intelligently or foolishly, and wound up right back at the start.

He dismounted at one of the most charming locales on the estate, a marquee built at one of the highest crests among many that undulated along the rolling hillsides of the Duprey homestead; the view was spectacular.

The gazebo's trellises were swathed in a thick, pink cloak

of Zepherine Drouhin climbing roses, long blooming, thornless and profuse. Roses and vineyards had an antique nexus and even here dozens of light years from their ancient biome on Earth the tradition was respected. At the beginning and end of every row of grapevines a rose bush was planted. This had once been a primitive early warning system for vintners since grapes and roses are susceptible to the same kind of mildews, but now the custom was a ritual dedicated to visual poetry.

Enguerrand heard the riders before he saw them. Louis Duprey—with a half-dozen of his men—came thundering up to the gazebo and there was incongruity that arrived with them. Enguerrand did the mental math swiftly. There had only passed the scarcest duration to have accessed the genetic information and made the match.

It seemed strange that no procrastinating pause had intervened while his family recovered from the shock of discovering the true identity of the man they had been sheltering. And from the unfriendly faces his father's heavily-armed retinue wore, he could see immediately this was no cortege of honor meant to escort him back to the manor. Even through the fallen darkness he made out that their glowering looks told him this was a posse.

"*Qu'est-ce que c'est?*" he called to his father. "What is this?"

"Your arrest?" Louis shot back. "Would that suit you?"

"*Oh, la vache,*" Enguerrand actually half-laughed. "On what ridiculous charge?"

Louis stood in his stirrups, pulling on the reins.

"We're still in the process of determining that."

There was nothing humorous, Enguerrand realized, about the exigency that if he were held here on Arcadia past three periods, his wife and daughter would be put under the lash. If he died trying to escape the result might be the same.

Enguerrand beckoned to his father to join him on the rose-decked platform.

"Hear me out. Just you and I, man to man."

After searching Enguerrand yet again for weapons, Louis' entourage surrounded the pergola while the Dupreys faced off. Louis opened the exchange sarcastically.

"There's no tensilated Janssen cage here. Aren't you concerned," he looked up at the dark sky yet still streaked with the slightest tinges of marmalade orange, "that with us here in the open like this someone might be listening?" He then answered his own question. "Ah, but if anyone is it would surely be those who put you up to this, wouldn't it? To see how the ruse is going? To weigh what kind of fool Louis Duprey is?"

Enguerrand's look said he was completely, honestly, hopelessly at sea. Louis took it as but another insult upon his intelligence.

"Enough with this charade!" he exclaimed. "I haven't any idea what you thought it would accomplish, but your DNA doesn't match anyone. Not mine, not Sophie's, not anyone."

The blood drained from Enguerrand's face.

"That's not possible." he replied, in the same hurt tone children use to protest that the tooth fairy had to exist.

"Oh, yes, quite impossible," Louis mocked. "How could fate have cheated us so indiscriminately?"

Enguerrand paced back and forth, his boot heels reverberating off the wooden planks of the gazebo deck, back and forth, mumbling under his breath.

"That's not possible…"

"Here, let me help you out," Louis scoffed. "Maybe Sophie and I adopted you? Is that where this tale goes next?"

"I *am* your son!" Enguerrand insisted.

It had come down to this then. Not all-knowing Nexus, infallible nanites, not the unshakeable opinion of his immovable grandmother nor the genial warmth of his mother nor anything else was going to settle this. It was now just man to man. Enguerrand took his father's hand and placed it on his heart.

"I am Enguerrand Duprey, son of Louis Duprey, born and bred on Arcadia. I believe we possess souls that are guided by right. I am a free-ranger and I hold sacred that cause above anything and everything else and will gladly choose death before inoculation. I pledge myself to come to the aid of my fellow free-rangers, no matter the overwhelming opposition, no matter that my life should be forfeit. And, as a Duprey, my word is my bond. I will never give it—to free-ranger or anyone else—without upholding it to the letter."

Enguerrand's heart raced and Louis could feel it.

"You taught me that. I memorized that when I was six years old, before I even knew what the words meant." Louis hand pressed against his son's triskelion. "You gave me that when I was eleven. I swore to you I would never take it off, father, and I'll die before I ever do. For the love of all that is good, you must simply believe me."

"The same good," Louis reminded him sharply, "in which you only hours ago admitted to my mother you've no faith?"

Enguerrand apprehended that no power in heaven or Earth would help him now—save his own father. He would sink or swim right here, right now. He squeezed Louis' hand.

"*Père*, father, please…believe me…"

Even in the darkness Enguerrand could see the faintest change in his father's eyes.

"I am your prodigal son," he pressed, "only that I didn't squander any fortune and I haven't come back to ask for another chance at my inheritance. I'll take nothing more than your recognition and right now that's worth more than any birthright. Look deeply, father; don't you see some part of you in me?"

Louis harrumphed.

"Am I supposed to have taught you that parable too? Is this how it goes?"

"You did, in fact," Enguerrand told him honestly. "When I

complained once that I had no brother. That's when you told it to me, trying to make me see the fortunate side of being your only son."

Now he could see his father's eyes reacting again.

"Just what sort of preposterous game is this, Enguerrand?" Louis wasn't mocking; he seemed to be requesting the impossible, an explanation to make sense of everything. He was actually weakening though. "What are you doing?"

Enguerrand had a simple answer.

"I'm saving your grand-daughter."

He took his father's hand down from his breast and clasped it in a handshake.

"But, no matter if I'm your son, a madman, or anything else. We both know who you are, Louis Duprey. I have given a great advantage to the cause and I have earned what you owe me. I demand it now, at the risk of your honor."

Louis turned everything over, weighing it all, coming to a decision. Enguerrand's words had seemed to hit home—finally.

"I don't know who you are," Louis pronounced the words like a judge irritated by a quirk of the law but upholding it anyway, "but, fortunately for you, in this case that carries no weight." He was convincing himself, not Enguerrand, but he was surrendering. "Even if you delude yourself that you're my grandfather."

Louis turned away from his son and paid the debt obliquely, surrendering to the rules he couldn't bring himself to transgress.

"Sybaris." Louis said just the one word and as he spoke it the relief flooded through Enguerrand, causing his balled-up fists to go limp, unleashing the pent of anxiety and fearfulness of failure he'd been holding in. "The destination you seek is Sybaris."

Enguerrand didn't doubt for a moment Louis Duprey's word. His father was as proud a man as existed anywhere. No one played semantic games with fine print connected to his sincere oath. Enguerrand knew it had been everything such a man as his father could do to permit up to now such unseemly liberties to be taken with it by Adrienne in the first place. The continued pounding by Enguerrand had finally caused the citadel to collapse.

"Do what you're planning, only just go. May you be forgiven for whatever is to happen, and me as well for aiding you."

Louis added cautionary advice at no extra charge.

"You should heed this warning about where you're going, though." He paused for the appropriate gravity. "Vanessa Braverman," he broke off briefly and corrected himself with a curious and confused look on his face, "both of them, that is, they're at the most evil place in existence—Sybaris." The reference required a breathing space, and an interval for a ritual that many free-rangers observed when pronouncing the moniker of this most foul of all colonies. Louis Duprey spat off the side of the gazebo, literally cleansing his mouth after uttering the filthy, feculent place name. "Only heaven knows what would take anyone there, but you have my word, that is her— excuse me, their—current location."

Louis was less troubled about the well-known reputation of the destination and more concerned by the complete lack of anything at all resembling knowledge about Enguerrand, his true sympathies, his access to bewilderingly superior technology, and not least, whom or what he was desperately chasing and why.

But he was done beating his head on that brick wall and settled on another important point.

Whoever the young man was, he was sending him off to a locale unlike any other.

"If you have never been to Sybaris," Louis cautioned him, "you have no idea what you're getting into."

Here was another great event in the future about which Enguerrand could say nothing. He could only imagine how thrilled Louis would be to learn that Sybaris now didn't exist, that just like the original Sodom-like city in Magna Graecia from the annals of ancient Earth, too many horrified neighbors came together for the sole purpose of doing humanity's spring cleaning.

It had passed into the realm of dreams, just like everything before him now.

But this, the Duprey estate, all of this didn't exist either. Everyone in his presence now was dead, the place itself, the freehold, a casualty of war, just…gone. It took every ounce of willpower to fend off the sadness and prepare to leave his family undisturbed to the fate which had already played out.

He was a transgressor in a shadowland and they were shades of a great entropy that had swept past. It filled him with grief, but also with an even greater emotion: an innate and deep fear of the eternal underpinning with which he was tinkering.

"It's hard to define 'been there'," Enguerrand half joked, but really one of the few humans to appreciate the difficulty.

Louis raised an eye.

"Plenty of men have gone to Sybaris and wound up failing to return." Then he re-considered. "But anywhere for you is better than here. You're persona non grata and must leave this very instant."

Enguerrand didn't need him to explain. He realized his grandmother wanted his head.

"Our business is concluded then," Louis said perfunctorily and turned to leave.

Enguerrand wanted to thank him but spent his last words on something far more important.

"Madame Duprey?" he inquired, "she has changed her plans regarding Lacaillia?"

Louis fixed him with a murderous look.

"Leave Arcadia immediately and don't dare ever return here. My debt to you is paid."

Enguerrand wished these last words exchanged with his father had been others but came to realize the desires of netherworld entities like him counted for very little.

Chapter Eleven: Killing Schrödinger's Cat

It would seem our actions have lucky or unlucky stars to which they owe a great part of the blame or praise which is given them.
—Francois de La Rochefoucauld, Maxim No. 58

ENGUERRAND DUPREY MADE a dangerous intortion jump through the marrow of inner space. He floored it. The cruiser was pointed in the direction of the nastiest place in the universe and her horses whipped toward it until they frothed at the mouth.

Since *Ultramariner* lacked the one rotodynamic magneto, he'd jury-rigged a few things to put a patch over that deficit. Otto-matic was unimpressed with his human make-do. Enguerrand flew with a nervous Nellie back-seat driver.

"There is a 12.6541 percent chance of complete and total failure of the integrity of *Ultramariner* resulting in the loss of the ship if you continue at these speeds with the craft's drive compromised as it is."

Enguerrand enjoyed one of his mother's pastries while

studying half a dozen virtual screens, all concerning Sybaris. He wiped a few delicious crumbs from his lips, washed the tartlet down with a stunning Riesling and responded to the potential crisis.

"Shut up, Otto." He licked his lips to get the last drop of Arcadian nectar. "I'd throw you out to lighten the load if I thought it would speed things up."

For a moment he thought Otto-matic was actually going to disobey him, but it complied, zipping its mechanical mouth and hanging out a frowning pout to exhibit its dismay.

"What? Are you afraid of dying or something?" Otto recognized that as rhetorical; it was programmed to ignore those sorts of human queries if it deemed appropriate. "Unless you're offering to get outside and push to help get this hoop moving even faster, just shut up."

Where they were passing, of course, there was no outside or inside or any other side or perhaps more appropriately though impossible to truly fathom, there were an infinite number of sides joining in kaleidoscopic synapses which ran through something far, far less than nothing. It was an appropriate place though for the troublesome puzzle that was plaguing Enguerrand.

Enguerrand had been wrestling with something far, far more unnerving than even the potential catastrophe of rotodynamic failure hurtling through the marrow at several dozen times the speed of light. He realized now there were greater terrors than that and one of them had already reached out and dug its claws into *his* marrow, the essence of his very being.

He wished he had someone other than a mechanical with whom to discuss a cosmic matter that was pressing on every mental pressure point. But lots of couriers were used to being always outnumbered, over-matched, unappreciated. He made do with what he had.

"I want to ask you something, Otto."

Otto shocked him; maybe he was just the one to ask after all.

"I've been thinking about it, too, Mr. Duprey."

There was a pause as the man and the android shared a silent, confused look—confused for one of them at least.

"I'm sorry. I should have waited for the conventional specificity before replying."

"No," Enguerrand made a sweeping gesture with his hand, "by all means, proceed, Otto."

"Well," Otto began, "the matter of your DNA failing to match properly, indeed, is an issue that touches on a quite interesting topic." The mechanical didn't want to appear too presumptuous so he paused for the human to confirm what he already knew. "This paradox has been weighing on you?"

"Yes, Otto, it crossed my mind a few times," Enguerrand replied with mostly sarcasm. "How is it possible that I failed that test?"

"There is no such thing as possible or impossible in quantum indeterminacy," Otto reminded him. "So, we'll have to dispense with that. As you well know, a subatomic particle is either this or that, here or there, spin either up or down—but only after it is observed."

Enguerrand let out a very anxious puff of distressed breath; he probably wasn't going to like hearing the rest of this.

"What do you suppose matter in the universe is doing when the lights are off, when it's on its own, when no one is looking, when no tests are being performed, when there is no human observation? What are particles' status before they…are? If a photon, for example, is neither a wave nor a particle until it is forced to declare itself—by us—what is its condition before that exigency?"

Enguerrand had no idea. No one alive did.

"I don't know, Otto."

Otto smiled at Enguerrand.

"You forced a declaration, Mr. Duprey. You insisted on the most deterministic of tests. You put the collective wave-functions of the googleplex of particles that composes your entire body through such an assessment as to make every double-slit, entanglement or spin experiment seem as primitive as the first hominid's attempt to create fire by friction. You forced a group of observers to make sense of you—here and now—when there is no sense to be made of you and the matter that composes you here and now. Certainly you can't be nonplussed that something—anything—even occurred at all?"

Enguerrand had to agree; there weren't too many other plausible answers. But something else came with that solution.

"Then I've...recreated...myself? If I don't have my own DNA anymore, who or what am I? Am I still...Enguerrand Duprey?"

Otto laughed.

"Don't be silly." He saluted Enguerrand to drive the point home. "I recognize you utterly, from tip to toe, captain. You are the human in command of the *Ultramariner*."

Enguerrand wasn't laughing; he was thinking, deep in thought. There was one last thing.

"When we get back, who will I be? Will I have my DNA or...*my* DNA?"

Otto liked that query.

"That's an excellent question, Mr. Duprey. But, one unfortunately that I can't answer. You're asking me if that cat in the quantum mechanical box is dead or not." The robot perked right up though. "On the plus side, if it turns out that your scrambled DNA is what sticks into the future, well, that would mean that you may spend the future unscannable as well, yes?"

The amanuensis put its finger to its temple.

"Give that some thought. This may turn out to be a

fortuitous accident after all."

Enguerrand cursed that under his breath, then refocused his attention on what lay ahead of him. It would require all he could muster.

Much was inscribed about the human race in Sybaris. That it even had been built where it was said everything about the unbounded imagination and perspicacity of the invincible and unstoppable *Homo sapiens* that had spawned on Earth. It wasn't enough to be more powerful and fearless than bulls and bears, to possess more cleverness than owl, dolphin and great ape together. The truly unstoppable dynamic of this progeny from the menagerie of Sol's third planet was feline. Mankind was curious. Humans *must* explore and for that reason alone the conquest of the Milky Way, the seed of Mother Earth cast and sown, was foreordained.

Centuries ago, pioneers on the leading-edge could scarcely ignore the mystery of the orbit of the red and blue giants in the system where Sybaris would be built. There was nothing unusual about binary pairs; as a matter of fact, most star systems were multiple pairings. These two didn't just whirl about each other though. They behaved more like teacups on a tilt-a-whirl, following a figure-eight looping course.

As enchanting as this celestial dance was, the mesmerized explorers acknowledged physics forbade it to exist. *Three* stars, they knew in principal at least, could trace out a figure-eight orbit. The math was against even that though, maybe one per galaxy throughout the Universe.

Juggling two stars this way however was patently impossible, so the discerning primates looked closer. There was a third after all, an invisible one, a four solar mass black hole also taking its turn on the looped racetrack, the three bodies forever passing by and missing each other in a perfectly timed *pas de trois*.

Here, though, the intelligence, power, fearlessness and curiosity of the discoverers gave way to the piston that drove the entire engine: magic. It didn't take the stunned human observers long to realize they had uncovered a place like perhaps no other, a navel of the cosmos itself.

The shape was that of the symbols of infinity, the lemniscate, the omega, the ancient icon of ouroboros, the snake eating his own tail from age-old Egypt. The initial settlement was constructed orbiting the obvious of the trio: the black hole. This they christened the "center" because they occupied it and therefore could, in the position to receive blue luminosity on one side and red sunlight on the other. And there was a third genre of beamed emanations that bathed the Sybarites, this coming from the black hole's event horizon itself: Hawking radiation.

It really existed after all, this glow of a universe that pantheists claimed was the wispy signal of self-awareness.

The freest thinkers, the most open-minded, the iconoclasts, dissidents, mavericks, non-conformists, bohemians, and eccentrics were drawn to Sybaris. The code was a simple one: anything went.

At first a renaissance of the arts exploded—philosophy, religion, music, poetry—during Sybaris' youth. By middle age, the luster had faded. The Hawking radiation was just simply heat, like any warmth anywhere. It didn't confer immortality on the Sybarites or cause them to levitate.

As jaded boredom and depression finally took root after a few decades the highest ideals from its founding were at end jettisoned into the orbited black hole along with the toxic trash from the settlement.

The decline, when it slipped over the edge, plummeted rapidly into a degeneracy of virulent proportions. The only maxim kept inviolate from its founding was that anything went. Now, however, since they tired of waiting to sprout wings that never grew they opted instead for horns that came forth with a vengeance. Eventually no one wondered if Sybaris were the navel of the Cosmos; there were many indeed who speculated that it might be compared to another orifice.

Enguerrand called up all the information he could manage to soak up about his fast-approaching port-of-call. He couldn't shake the feeling of a pair of eyes peering over his shoulders, because there were.

Enguerrand finally asked.

"What, Otto?"

The reason was given a little sheepishly.

"I wish there was some means for me to help."

Enguerrand's blank stare caused him to repeat the offer in another way.

"I'm here to aid you in any way I can."

"Pilot the vessel," Enguerrand said flatly. "Get us to our destination and you'll be helping out just fine."

"Yes, I just wish there were more."

There was the hint of exasperation in his voice.

"More what?"

"Well, it must be quite an intimidating feeling for you, alone, unarmed, transiting to the most dangerous locale in the known universe, without the slightest inclination of what you'll face but certain that whatever it is will be quite probably the last..."

Enguerrand couldn't restrain interrupting him with a genuine laugh and thinking to help Otto laughed along with him. Enguerrand's comedic reaction clued in the android.

"It's the way I put that, isn't it?"

"Yeah, Otto," Enguerrand poured himself another draught of Arcadian malbec. "If your idea of helping me is attempting to scare me to death you're doing a bang-up job."

Otto did, nonetheless, focus on one word.

"You're scared, Mr. Duprey? To be a lone sojourner in such a place?"

Enguerrand Duprey had faced death already many, many times and been the agency to visit it upon others even more. There were no more swashbuckling pep talks to share before life and death confrontations, either with himself, fellow comrades-in-arms, or anyone else.

"There's no way to die other than alone, Otto."

Otto agreed.

"Yes, that's certainly a stoic's way for you to behave."

Enguerrand furrowed his brow and corrected him.

"What, *moi?*" Enguerrand pointed at himself. "What makes you think I was referring to myself?"

Otto smiled.

"Ah, yes, I see now. Others are going to die alone."

"If I have anything to say about it, yes, others die alone." He added the qualifier. "In my presence."

That really set off Otto.

"That says much about the human race, doesn't it, Mr. Duprey? That there could even be a place such as Sybaris is one thing; it's proof that humanity has an abiding partnership with the purely horrific."

Otto determined the human was interested; he continued.

"You're a man of morals though. You're not like the creatures with whom you'll soon be interacting on Sybaris. You believe in things that can't be seen or touched but are anathema to the dark, evil and chaotic and yet..."

"Yet what, Otto? Please, finish."

"And yet when it suits, even a good and decent man like you can indulge in spates of cruelty and indecency." Otto pointed at Enguerrand's pendant. "Will you be removing that icon when you disembark at Sybaris?"

Enguerrand grasped the point and bristled.

"You mean to assuage my conscience? So I don't have to

look in mirrors and see the image of a hypocrite? Is that what you mean?"

It was.

"Yes, something like that."

That set off Enguerrand.

"This image of my beliefs will come off from around my neck only when it's not breathing any longer and not a nanosecond before. As for the rest, my father explained this all to me. It's too bad you never had one."

"Yes," Otto couldn't dispute that. "You have me at a disadvantage."

Enguerrand pulled the triskelion from his breast, holding it as if to buttress his argument, tapping his talisman.

"I'm human, Otto—both good and bad, but mostly good. Both right and wrong, but mostly right. We're sane, functional, direct, good-natured superlative entities, who are sometimes insane, dysfunctional, indirect, ill-tempered and appalling. There's no crisis of conscience for me, nor any shame in being who I am. That's how we came to make you and not you to make us."

Otto had come to a conclusion.

"Maybe then it ought to be the residents of Sybaris who should fear you rather than you fearing them."

Enguerrand took a sip of his wine and thought it over.

"Maybe," he concurred.

Enguerrand and Otto beat the rather tame odds of pushing a quantum cruiser close to its limits with the rotodynamic magneto bypassed, breaking out of intortion close to the hard to delineate boundary between Creation and the Free Range, just a few thousand kilometers outside of Sybaris' orbit.

The real gambling would ensue now; not everyone who entered Sybaris also exited. The intended market of potential tourists was a thin one: those careless enough with their very lives to not be put off by the freely advertised caveat that seeing the sights on Sybaris was hardly something guaranteed to be survived.

It was the only deference to civilized mores that still held—one received a formal warning before entering Sybaris.

Chapter Twelve: City of Sin

It is well that we know not all our wishes.
—Francois de La Rochefoucauld, Maxim No. 295

CUSTOMS WAS THE last official hurdle between himself and Vanessa Braverman.

"We're being hailed," Otto advised.

"Put them through," Enguerrand directed.

An unusual hologram exteriorized instantly, the dimension and contours of the avatar meant to impress that the Sybarite government functionary cut a wide swath. The head was blockish, a passably squared cube, the vertices at the jaw and cranium virtually pointed and cornered. The strong face was wide and flat with a low nasal bridge and short nose.

His stark appearance was accentuated by the hairstyle. The left side of the scalp was shaved clean to the pate, all the rest from a line running down the center of the crown and combed to the right, pulled tight and bound, the jet-black queue laying on massive, muscled shoulders.

"State your business, *Ultramariner*," the intimidating customs officer demanded.

"Permission for entry," Enguerrand stated manifestly.

"Your dealings?"

"Simple tourism."

"One individual?"

"Just myself." Enguerrand's solitary status caused the eyes to open wider, a skeptical appraisal that the nerviness was quite obviously very ill-advised. It precipitated the next question too.

"What to declare that will be coming in with you? What weapons?"

It sounded vulnerable when Enguerrand pronounced it for the record.

"Just my person and unarmed."

"How many credits will you transfer for your expenses while on Sybaris?"

Enguerrand Duprey was unscannable. His monetary transactions would be tricky in the extreme—meaning impossible.

He spoke with sadness.

"There will be no transfer of credits," he said.

The Sybarite frontier guard had seen and heard many odd scenarios and problems at this post. Not many travelers, his reaction implied, showed up at Sybaris flat broke and requesting entry.

"No credits?" He repeated, growling.

"I'll be paying in kind," Enguerrand assured him. "Ambrosia, two hekats, triple A quality, to be converted into Sybarite credits upon arrival." He amended the declaration. "I'll be bringing in a third hekat for my own personal use, to remain in my possession."

That was more like it. Ambrosia, especially here, opened more doors more easily than credits any day.

"Accepted tender on Sybaris," the gatekeeper said happily, almost convinced immediately now of the applicant's *bona fides*, and beginning to warm to the idea that his job would be much easier with a no-frills, stripped-down entry.

"If it is just yourself, no other humans or mechanicals, our covenants are very simple." Scrupulous formality required corroboration. "No captives, contraband, sexual chattel to declare—nothing of that sort?"

These wouldn't have been deal-breakers. Only a few kinks in the red tape would have had to be ironed out in those cases.

"No," Enguerrand assured him. "I left all my concubines at home."

The revenuer didn't like that and gave him an officious reprimand.

"No jokes, please," he glowered. "You're making a customs declaration. All of your comments are taken literally and seriously."

"I understand," Enguerrand apologized.

"I doubt you do," the Sybarite remonstrated. "I'm going to do my best to fix that. I suggest you listen carefully." The legal system on Sybaris was simplicity itself, so primal and unfettered and direct that the whole of it could be explained in one fell swoop. "You're free to do anything you like on Sybaris. The concepts of legal or illegal, criminal or lawful, prohibited or permitted, innocent or guilty—none of that exists. On Sybaris one is at liberty to do what you will to yourself or anyone else, and that freedom devolves upon you as well with regards to others. The authorities consider that none of our business and we only advise all visitors to watch their steps while here."

The Sybarite's avatar nodded at Enguerrand.

"That is difficult to grasp. Do you fully understand?"

"That seems clear enough," Enguerrand signaled.

The duty officer held up a finger.

"There are just these two exceptions. Only the police are allowed to possess arms. There are no weapons of any kind allowed." Now he furrowed his thick brow to emphasize the cardinal rule on Sybaris. "And if we believed in crime there would be only one: nuisance. Don't make a nuisance of yourself…to the state. No one will outline or define it for you, but if you're foolish enough to bring yourself to the attention of Sybarite Security it all will be explained for you then. Since we have no crime on Sybaris, there are likewise no jails. Police, in dealing with those unhinged enough to interact with them, dispose of cases on the spot, either EXP or EXT. Minor nuisances are expelled with their credits and property forfeited. The other kind, EXT, extermination cases, well, their assets are likewise relinquished to the state."

The traffic warden placed his hands together using an inflection signaling that everything his perfunctory duties required had been satisfied.

"Don't make a nuisance of yourself. Whatever you're here to do, see to it in such a way that our police need not involve themselves; you won't enjoy dealing with them."

The Sybarite waited for a question or comment from Enguerrand. It didn't come so he concluded the interview.

"Aside from that, we hope you enjoy yourself in any way at all that you please." He was as hospitable as a ticket taker for a charity event at a service club. "Welcome to Sybaris."

Coming down one of the eight elevators that crisscrossed each other from hub to wheel, Enguerrand got a feel for Sybaris' size.

In simplest terms, it was built just as a giant quantum cruiser, only this enormous hoop was expansive enough that short cuts were necessary, through the octet of conveyors that ran through far-stretching tubular spokes.

The massive rim that was spun however was never meant to fly; it was a mind-boggling sixteen hundred Centauran leagues in circumference. Unlike an inflated tire tube though, the titanium and steel sides had been zipped up, the shape of an A-frame wheeled into a three-dimensional torus, the walls converging to dispense with a ceiling.

The elevator opened to debouch passengers, ready or not, straight onto the most unique promenade in the entire galaxy: Boardwalk on Sybaris, the longest moving walkway in existence.

Ancillary escalators, moving sidewalks, pneumatic tubes, and elevators fed off from either side, but for those wishing to "pass go" keeping to this line was advised.

At first glance these were the sights and sounds of the great Casino Concourse on Kappa Tucanae B, the same blisteringly garish and bright lights, the same clinkety-clank of hundreds of thousands of eye-catchers fighting for glimpses. Behind it all, in the background, was the cacophony of unnumbered grafts, cons and vices being hustled, the ones closest to him drowning the others. This wasn't Kappa Tucanae though.

"This is the place! Look no further, young man, and come right in." The denizens of Sybaris were on him from the first moment. "The first five minutes are completely free of charge."

A gaggle of ill-clothed children had already attached themselves to Enguerrand, each promising to be the best guide ever. Thankfully, the proprietor of the adjoining establishment came to the rescue, booting the urchins aside and shepherding him toward his place of business.

"I didn't get this spot right by the elevator for nothing, Astro," he confided to Enguerrand conspiratorially. "You won't be disappointed."

But as he revealed to Enguerrand what his services entailed Enguerrand pulled away with a look very different from disappointment. The costermonger could see he was losing this mark already and doubled down.

"No, no, Astro, don't be so quick to pass us by. What's the matter?"

The more he explained what was being offered, the steelier became Enguerrand's stiff-arm. It wasn't his arm under assault though from that moment on, but something much more vulnerable to attack: his eyes, ears, soul and his basic morality. Enguerrand, who'd been everywhere, across sixty parsecs of space, wasn't prepared for it, but then very few were.

A dull panic built and descended as he came to reckon that it would take quite a while to explore every repugnant, vile, perverted and shocking corner of Sybaris, and even then the odds were good that he'd have to start over again if he happened to look right when Vanessa Braverman might have passed by to his left.

She wasn't registering with Nexus at the moment, but she was a free-ranger whose location blips could only come when she interacted voluntarily, unzipping to pay for something to eat, drink or do.

The nonexistent trace pips meant that someone else in her company had to be pushing the credits through for whatever she needed. He didn't want to underestimate her and besides Brabec had said she was smart, smart, smart. His only choice was to stay on Boardwalk and ride it around and around Sybaris while he prayed for enough luck to bump into her.

Enguerrand needed more than luck though; stamina was put to a real test, too. Before long Enguerrand had an almost irrepressible desire to scrub his eyeballs and eardrums of the nonstop assault of defilement that poured onto him as he slopped his way through the sludge and putrefaction that was the sewer of Sybaris.

As Customs had made clear to him, there were no bounds to human imagination and desire here.

Such a gutter-trek made Enguerrand almost agree with his lifelong enemies of the Free Range, those dour souls in Creation who warned of what pure freedom would ultimately end up resembling. These two-legged things that spewed prurient filth on him, these Sybarites, unabashed, unashamed, with no single upright thought to rein in their feral bearing and animal braying—creatures such as these required and deserved moderating nanites, even if that expedient went against everything he was taught since birth.

He tried to banish that treasonous thought but his mind rebelled, holding onto it for dear life and careless of the politics.

Enguerrand still was nowhere near experiencing the true depth though of what Sybaris had in store; he'd only passed through the softcore sections of the spinning ring of perdition.

Yet even these quarters were no place for the timid. It wasn't that every fetish, need and desire was to be found on Sybaris, but that they were taken to such pathological extremes as well. To satisfy the weight of humanity's worst and forbidden imaginings nothing was beyond the pale for importation—live, dead, moribund, human, animal, mechanical—from everywhere but mostly shipped in from the overpopulated and constantly dying Home Sector.

Whatever permutations could be combined using the energies of the hidden, demonic, abased fantasies in the darkest corners of the human mind—this created a powerful evil.

Vanessa Braverman wasn't anywhere Enguerrand looked, but the places he investigated searching for her made his boyhood catechism's description of Hell, the ones to have caused young nightmares, come back to life. Enguerrand pressed on; he had no other choice.

Some hours later, demanding a moment of fresh air, he gave in and stepped off the crowded treadmills for a short breather.

The street vendors got to him first, reminding him of the black clouds of mosquitoes he'd tramped through hanging over the swamps of the moons of Geb in the Draconis system.

They peddled everything.

This batch however were mostly Hawking hawkers, offering pills either to counter the ill effects of the Hawking radiation that threatened from the event horizon of the black hole so near, or conversely to heighten and intensify the benefits of this rare and ethereal phenomenon.

Enguerrand wasn't buying either kind.

"It's just heat," he said beaten down, physically taxed by repelling the prior cohorts of hucksters that had kept up a constant assault.

Where he happened to exit the Boardwalk was at the Boötes Void concourse, aptly named. If one were for some reason searching for a moral equivalent of the third of a billion light-year swath of nothingness one need not travel the 700 million light-years to the void.

The colporteurs here seemed positively demonic enough to have come from such a place and even for Enguerrand who had been bred and raised amid the horrors of combat, were a daunting mob to attempt to keep at bay. Each of them from competing enterprises took their turns next.

What these salesmen were offering couldn't be found even on the contracts Mephistopheles himself crafted in exchange for people's souls. Enguerrand was struggling to accept that any human mind could conjure such deviancy much less peddle it.

They could see they had a novice on their hands and that got their blood up. One pitchman started to fill him in but was rudely interrupted by the next. The Sybarites argued the pros and cons of each other's services, making the details nauseatingly clear to Enguerrand, standing up the hair on the back of his neck.

"You'd expect me to do something like that?" Enguerrand asked in a voice that didn't seem like his, with the inflection of a boy, as if asking evil itself why it wished so badly to cause harm.

The salesmen called a temporary truce to take in the rube, their mouths agape at the boondocks provincialism of the creepily innocent hayseed. The Hawkings hawkers had already gave up on making a sale, so they let him have it by laughing in his face.

"What a lump."

"What are you looking for then, lummox?"

Most of the vendors attempted to stifle their mocking snorts, but one couldn't restrain himself. He made a sickeningly lurid, abysmally vulgar trilling noise in Enguerrand's direction. It came from the creature's throat.

Everyone laughed, but like the lowest-brows, bordering just above lunatic.

"Yes, so what is it you're looking for, wayfarer?" they wanted to know between insane belly laughs.

Without thinking, Enguerrand answered them as honestly as he'd ever replied in his life.

"My wife. I miss my wife right now. And my child. That's what; my wife and child."

That sucked the oxygen out of the conversation as quickly as blowing the latrine valve on a tiny C-class shuttle. Not another word was said as Enguerrand stepped back on to the Boardwalk and departed. From behind him though, even above the racket and tumult, he heard their parting shots.

"Did you hear what he said?" one of the sharpies voiced incredulously.

Another had heard indeed and spat his opinion disgustedly.

"Green-eyed freak."

Enguerrand took the elevator short cut to the section on the far side of Sybaris, passing "up" toward the spinning hub, through departments of reduced gravity the higher the car went.

These suburbs weren't useless at all and contrary to first thought, the rents here went for a premium. The Sybarites put the light-footed, cobwebby artificial gravity here to best use.

The bordellos were the principal feature of this arrondissement of the city, turning weaklings and pushovers into supermen who could twirl their lovers in the air. At the weightless hub, a radial roundhouse that turned around all three hundred and sixty degrees, the elevator car flipped floor to car and slipped back "down" the selected shaft, sliding open the door to an even deeper level of iniquity.

Stepping out now into one of the more dangerous quarters of Sybaris he'd left the milksop, candy districts of fetishists, con artists, gambling sharps, fortune tellers and hoaxers.

This place was very different; it was the hard core.

Anything could and did happen here and the very air itself hung with the smell and cold, dead, heaviness of torture, violation, humiliation, degradation and murder. The police were everywhere.

Enguerrand held his nose, gritted his teeth and opened his eyes—wide. He'd uncovered his way to her after all, and quickly. It didn't matter that he'd caught up with her in one of the lower levels of Gehenna, he'd actually found her.

Trying to buck up his interior warrior, Enguerrand congratulated himself to distance the fear that no matter was building, focusing on the one task before him now.

He'd have to convince Vanessa Braverman to take a short quantum cruise back with him, force her to do it, or kill her if she declined, and if not, die trying.

It was just that simple, he told himself.

Just take it one pace at a time, easy does it, just like he'd been doing. The next footstep forward was simply to get off the Boardwalk and past the Sybarite gendarmerie that swarmed everywhere.

These were without doubt the meanest cops in the galaxy and were most definitely best kept at a distance—especially by someone who would soon be making a nuisance of himself.

The treadmills moved him along, primitive and inefficient, yet the only expedient. This hunt was going to be gate by gate, concourse by concourse, face to face, and could very well prove fruitless.

Sybaris was a big place he admitted nervously to himself, and the crowds pushing past him constantly were human torrents. By the time he found her, she might be gone already. Vanessa Braverman might have slipped by him before now without him even realizing it. There was food and drink at the next turnstile exit rest stop and he stepped off the Boardwalk taking a seat still close enough to observe the flood of people gushing by him. It was time to reappraise.

"This isn't working," he muttered under his breath dejectedly to no one. A slender young Asian woman slid in next to him as if they were old friends and agreed with him.

"Of course, it's not working. But I can fix that."

Everything about her said she wasn't kidding. For one, the way she spoke was like no sideshow barker. This wasn't a spiel; it was personal and professional.

"I can fix it," she repeated the claim.

For another, he recognized the tattoos and markings that spiraled around her tawny neck to end with a bold irezumi occupying a good portion of her left cheek. If she weren't a true Shinobi it would be very unfortunate and very unhealthy for her to run into a real one.

"You made it pretty clear back there," she parted her lips and gave the final proof, a beautifully symmetric grin of filed teeth, the canines fused with diamond tips. "And it's written all over your face."

"What are you selling?" Enguerrand asked, for the first time on Sybaris possibly interested in the service.

"I'm selling what you're buying," she abbreviated confidently. "Who are you looking for? You mentioned a wife and a child?"

Enguerrand hesitated, obviously unsure as to her intentions. She wasn't going to be walked around in circles though.

"Look around you, pilot," she instructed the greenhorn.

"Can you think of something that isn't for sale *here?*" Her expression mocked the very idea. "I catch faces for a living; it's as simple as that. I could be doing something else," she pointed to the depraved purgatory surrounding them, "but I prefer face catching. So, I catch faces and you're looking for one. It's pretty simple."

Enguerrand took the lifeline.

"She's a free-ranger."

"Of course, she is." Her facial muscles flexed the way teachers respond to brainless outbursts from the back of the class. "I didn't think she'd be a Berenician duchess. She has a lower profile, right, nanite free?"

She treated him as if he were something of a rookie moron.

Enguerrand took his lumps.

"That's right."

She went for the close.

"A thousand credits."

Enguerrand thought it over and that irritated her.

"You're not back home, wherever that is; a lot of people here don't want to be seen. Do you have any idea how many optics streams around Sybaris I pay a tithe on to be able to match an image for you, lover boy? They're controlled and restricted here, the property of the state, and far from free. I'm connected at the highest levels; a thousand is cheap."

Enguerrand agreed, only more so.

"Let's make it five thousand; one thousand right now, four more when I leave Sybaris—alive."

That brought forth a wide, sultry smile.

"How long are you staying, sojourner?"

"Not long."

"Five thousand," she drank it in. "That's worth my time."

Enguerrand wasn't such a rube after all.

"It's also worth you staying away from her and not cheating another thousand by selling *my* face to her or anyone else.

Peddle my image, risk getting me killed, and you lose three thousand net."

"Smart," she conceded, "You attach the four thousand in escrow on your departure lading?"

"No, it's a gratuity. It's a way to keep you on my side. I'll pay it. Just don't double-cross me. Deal?" Enguerrand asked.

The Shinobi face-catcher thought it over and decided.

"Done, then." She reached out and offered her hand and with the other she signaled for service. "I'm buying, fly boy. I don't mind saying, you've made my day." They knew her here evidently and drinks appeared immediately. "So what do you do," she small-talked, "to accumulate such a pile of credits to throw away on a woman's face?"

"I'm a courier."

Enguerrand's profession almost caused her to spit out the first sip of her aperitif. After recovering, she gave herself over to unbridled laughter. This wasn't faked at all. She found his answer very, very comical.

"Oh, I'm sorry, but Hippolyta's Girdle! You should see your face," she tried to catch her breath. "You look like you're searching for an outlet!"

The poor, befuddled, out-classed, free-range courier smiled with her. Every free-ranger, certainly by adulthood, knew these slights by heart.

"Well, if I had known she was the lover of a free-range courier..." She cut to the chase. "You overpaid, Ace. That's all."

Even here, that said, among the voyeurs, sniffers, lickers, the frauds, quick-changers, perverts, and scum, even here there was room to look down on a courier, and his certainly penniless runaway free-range lover.

"But I'll tell you what," she leaned closer, more friendly. Her visage made clear she'd been used hard all her life, but there was still something human, something feminine remaining. "I like you, free-ranger. And since you've made your health my business, I will give you a tip of my own." She flashed him the Shinobi hand gesture for no charge. "On the cuff," she said, beckoning with the other for him to take a look at something on a personal screen she thought he ought to see.

The Shinobi face-catcher figured it couldn't hurt her chances of getting paid quintuple by giving her client the best chance of staying alive.

Faces. His face. Vanessa Braverman's face.

Someone else had been asking about Vanessa—and about *him*.

Enguerrand recognized Vanessa's face immediately, even though it was two and a half decades younger. And, there were other hunters.

Chapter Thirteen:
Doppelganger

There is only one sort of love, but there are a thousand different copies.
—Francois de La Rochefoucauld, Maxim No. 74

MANY WHO CAME to Sybaris didn't dare cross into these precincts, the nooks and crannies of this ward filled with attractions exponentially more evil and dangerous.

He made his way as quickly as he could, staring downward to avert his eyes from the cadres of police that gave him head to toe scrutiny. He was a lone adventurer and here in this place among this crowd that was as common as an echo on the endless steppes of Aequoria. A determined courier could be counted on to come through in the end though and Enguerrand Duprey, wife and child in the balance, wasn't turning back from this one.

It felt more leaden and preordained anticlimax—not great elation—when he fixed his sights dead on her at last and began shadowing as unobtrusively as possible.

Making it this close, he swore to himself he wouldn't be leaving here without her. But finding Vanessa Braverman was one thing; carrying her back twenty-five years into the future, quite another. There was little choice when it came to holding back. Once half a chance presented itself, he grabbed onto it with both hands—making his move right in front of her by seizing a shocked free-ranger, clamping his iron fists around the stunned man's neck and yanking him around like a marionette.

Enguerrand snarled the menace straight into Nils Rimbaut's ear, his clenched teeth so close that the stubble on his upper lip scraped Nils' lobe.

"I'll kill you, I swear it."

A portion of this was theater, part serious warning, but definitely meant for everyone in Club Gemini—including Vanessa Braverman—to witness.

Enguerrand gave a terrific yank on the twisted collar-noose to punctuate the thought.

"I see you again; I kill you."

It made sense that Enguerrand had his hands around this particular neck. He was throttling his father's right-hand man from the old days, the *chef* who would take over the reins of the cause after his father's death. Adrienne hadn't been a party to her son's recent bargain with Enguerrand, hadn't said anything about shutting *her* eyes.

Enguerrand realized his grandmother was a very strange woman, certainly eager to find answers about the remarkable, unscannable young man who more than piqued her interest, along with his just as bizarre prey who scanned twice to make up for the hunter's blank slate. She must have sent Nils Rimbaut to Sybaris as soon as Vanessa Braverman had been located.

He was a bad choice though. Rimbaut was no mole and here was completely out of his bluestocking turf. He was the phalange's brain trust, not its muscle, the revolutionary genius physicist of the free-range cause, someone who Enguerrand as a boy imagined lived in a laboratory.

The older version Enguerrand knew had often expressed

supposed regret that he hadn't gone the gallant way of his hero, Évariste Galois, the mathematics genius cut down in Old Modern Paris by a dueling bullet at the age of twenty, so many centuries ago. Here was his chance however to rectify that, since Enguerrand's vise-like, air-restricting clutches were obliging. Once released, his only thought was to flee.

Nils Rimbaut, last seen taking to his heels, made a terrible spy.

Their table was very close to the ruckus, so the incident played out in full view of Vanessa and her party. They and everyone else at Club Gemini watched it happen.

Enguerrand politely thought he owed her an explanation.

"Stalker," was the first word exchanged. "He was stalking you."

She was caught completely off-guard, just as anyone would have been, just as Enguerrand had anticipated. He took advantage of her flat feet.

Enguerrand pointed out the door.

"He was at the last place, at Polymorphia. Didn't you notice him?"

She hadn't, but she'd picked up on something nonetheless.

"And so were you?" Vanessa rebounded logically. "How do you know he wasn't stalking *you*?"

Enguerrand motioned his hand back and forth between them.

"That's an easy call," he complimented with the comparison.

It wasn't an unbelievable flirtation. Vanessa was garishly beautiful, without doubt a quite fetching woman, but in a mid-forty, partied hard and it shows sort of way. She was crossing that perilous border where a woman first encounters something never experienced before: not being sure if she is still the brightest flame in a roomful of moths. He could tell his dart grazed a soft spot. She wasn't as invulnerable as in younger and more confident times. She heard what she wanted these days.

"Either way, I'd like to apologize for the disturbance." It was only natural he should suggest making liquid amends. "This place seems a cut above the rest. Let me buy a round for your table?"

Club Gemini wasn't such a terrible venue, nestled into one of the rotundas given over to comparatively less ghastly pursuits, as appalling as it was being the galactic epicenter for incestuous liaisons. It was on the "Ground" deck occupying two thousand square gauges of highly desirable floor space since Club Gemini's exterior bulkhead was Sybaris' too. This prime location was a "sweet spot" compared to Sybarite real estate "higher" up. The gravitational load here was just right—bracing, not quite so strong as on Earth, perfect.

"My treat?" Enguerrand repeated the offer.

Vanessa had her arm around a younger woman, who was—herself—and was flanked by a deuce of extremely atypical men, a pair of brothers, a very unfriendly-looking twosome who could be judged hired bodyguards by a blind man looking on from orbit. They were seated at a raised dais flush with the observation port, soaking up anything that supposedly was evinced from the cosmic maw below.

Vanessa thought it over.

"You memorized everyone's faces at Polymorphia?"

She wasn't being friendly just yet.

It was the perfect place for the perfect line.

"I saw you there," he vouched. "Of course, I'm certain everyone had their eyes on you."

She liked that.

"Well, a girl can't have too many white knights," she said off-handedly, beckoning a "why not?" wave to him.

And so Enguerrand joined quite a crew for cocktails, trying not to upset the two menacing men at the table.

"No offense offered, gentlemen, if you don't mind? I'm

buying."

Neither paid him the slightest attention.

However, Vanessa took an immediate and leering interest in the man with the unique eyes. She'd done anything with everyone and was always running out of fresh test tubes in her erotic laboratory. She took a good look at Enguerrand.

"Wonder how I missed you with those eyes," she said. "You're hard to overlook."

Enguerrand gave a restrained smile at the compliment since he was trying to sort out who might be romantically interested in whom among the quartet, not wishing to raise any hackles. It was difficult to focus on that properly, though, since two of the potential participants were the same people and therefore there wasn't even a name for this particular fetish. That took him aback to say the least, tying his tongue. He was hardly interested in seducing Vanessa Braverman, but he would have to make it convincing. Fortunately, she was an easy conquest; her carnal drive was already engaged.

"What do you do, green eyes?" She flirted away. "What brings you to Sybaris?"

"I'm a courier," he said truthfully enough, "and I'm just passing through," he lied.

"A courier?" She liked that too, a lot. "That makes you the scum of the galaxy." She raised her glass to him. "Welcome to the club," she toasted.

Enguerrand pondered about what sort of club it was. Certainly, the services the two men rendered had to be physical only that Enguerrand reckoned they specialized in the painful rather than the pleasurable. Every facet about them was a warning.

These two were bred for mayhem, combat, strong-arming. Enguerrand had rubbed elbows with his share of cut-throats, but this duo rated as menacing as any in his experience. Two deep, slashing parallel scars ran from the far tips of each eyebrow to meet at the hairline—leaving garish and truly hideous chevron scars across their foreheads. Beneath these carved, bone-scraping stripes, their facial features showpieces of disharmony.

Their noses, cheekbones and jaws must have had great storms break on them leaving crushed and sunken regions of the face; one's chin was oriented off-center and hobnailed with bony knots. Such misshapen visages in and of themselves were imposing and threatening, all the more so though was a consideration of what devastating barrages must have rained down on those battered tableaus. The bone of both from skull to mandible was thick, granite, facial bedrock. To treat it so violently meant that ferocious blows must have landed repeatedly on these moonscapes. And here they were, worse for the wear, but still standing and commanding Enguerrand's attention.

As for the young woman, the nineteen-year-old Vanessa sat next to them and was a lofty hymn sung in the cathedral of beauty—everything in its proportions, her youth unscarred, the antithesis of the two men sitting at either side of her. The odd, taciturn, sad-eyed girl weaving back and forth in her seat from too much liquor, ambrosia and more, Enguerrand tried to ignore. That tack went off the rails when she summoned the effort to blurt out a complaint.

"Why didn't *they* see that? Why didn't they notice that guy following us?" She asked her older self, leaving off adding that was their job but recklessly implying it.

Her accusation created a very awkward silence. Enguerrand did his best to keep the repartee civil and friendly.

"Well, these two strappers might not have noticed such a pathetic little man," Enguerrand flattered, making excuses for them. And, conforming to their quite prodigious bulk he amended the drink order. "Let me make that doubles for you two," he offered.

The arithmetic should have pleased more than it did.

"Thank you, little man," the older brother obliged without emotion, using the very pejorative that Enguerrand hung around Nils Rimbaut's neck. As he spoke, Enguerrand made out the horizontal grooves creased across his front teeth, the furrows permanently dyed with pigments. Aside from their scars, filings, and many other clues to their bellicose profession there was one telltale mark which alone gave all the identification required.

Both men had black swans tattooed on their necks, the swans' cervixes tracing their jugulars, as per protocol. A black swan indicated something so rare that nobody could be bothered to prepare for it, but if encountered by fickle and variable fate, would prove a catastrophe without solution in any event. This was the insignia of the most ruthless mercenaries, desperados, scrappers or bodyguards could purchase.

"Enguerrand Duprey, *a votre service*," the little man corrected him, and a bit curtly.

But, from the way the insult rolled off the black swan's tongue, Enguerrand could tell that catch-all nomenclature was used for almost every stranger he addressed. Although the slightly smaller of the siblings, he was still a huge, beefy horse of a man. Everyone who crossed his path was a "little man."

He asked Vanessas their names.

"And you ladies? Whose company do I share?"

For Vanessa Braverman the matter of her given name wasn't something so simple.

"We're butterflies. Do you know what those are? They're beautiful, delicate, dragonflies from Earth. They start out as terra-bound caterpillars crawling in the dirt and are wondrously transformed in chrysalises—by pure magic—to escape as dazzling creatures on multicolored, gossamer wings." She glanced at her younger self. "Vanessa is a species of butterfly on Earth. They're precious and lovely, just like her."

"*Enchanté,* pleased to meet you," he said perfunctorily to the young butterfly, but he wasn't interested in her and it showed.

The younger ladybug was in fact going through a transformation in front of his eyes, this one requiring no cocoon and far from marvelous, quite easily and sordidly explained.

Ambrosia was nothing to play with, especially for neophytes. Too much, too soon, too often would produce the wreck that sat across from him; it had chewed her up and spit her out. She was as animated as a zombie, but an under the weather, worn-out, sluggish one at that. Enguerrand was pretty sure she had little inkling what was transpiring, still he went through the motions.

"*Enchanté, Mademoiselle.*"

He wanted to go so much further with this particular young woman, but had to leave it at that. They had a few things in common, but better not to start at all. There were only two people in the universe currently either both in the womb and yet club-hopping on Sybaris, or having an affair—with themselves.

So, they shared a bond.

Enguerrand was greatly relieved that the innocent version of Vanessa Braverman, the beautiful one with the gossamer wings, was too befuddled and sedated by the ambrosia to realize she'd just been greeted by the bounty hunter of her fugitive future self. She was a pitiable sight, barely covered in hyper-salacious lingerie that, along with the torpor, left a ridiculous impression.

A shiver went down Enguerrand's spine as he silently answered his own question, the one he'd mused aloud about her before.

"I wonder what happened to you, Vanessa Braverman?"

He knew now: *she* had happened to her. Her future self came back in time to corrupt her, armed with weapons against which there were no defenses. It was impossible to say no to herself with her future persona in front of her very eyes. This was her future. It had come knocking and had its deviant arms around her. There was obviously, he had to conclude, no resisting that; he felt more sympathy for her than for himself.

Then there was what the sluice in the future had flushed into the past, the middle-aged Vanessa. She compared herself to an evanescent and benign butterfly from distant Earth; Enguerrand had never been there but knew of some other of its insect phylum that made better comparisons: praying mantis, maggot, black widow, tsetse fly.

She was supposed to be the object of his desires, so he made his next advance.

"But I asked *your* name," the gallant wouldn't be denied.

"I'll tell you my name," Vanessa coyly acquiesced. "But first, you tell me where we are."

She gave a nod over her shoulder to the real time, non-holographic, plain-old observation port occupying the better portion of the bulkhead behind her. Whatever was happening out there was transpiring here and now.

Enguerrand thought he understood her and traced a figure eight in the air with his index finger.

"You mean that stuff?"

She leaned across the table, close enough now for Enguerrand to make out the lightning storms, mental blizzards, and brain-quakes that were taking Vanessa Braverman down from behind those eyes.

"Below us is the navel of the universe, where everything is born and dies, where all terms and words come from. Why don't you ask me the name of *that*?"

That took him by surprise.

"Black hole?" he guessed.

"Well of course it's that. But could you speak with any less imagination?" She quoted ancient knowledge. "In the beginning was the Word, and the Word was with God, and the Word was God."

It came out seamlessly, elegantly, poetically.

"Logos," she declared solemnly, "that's what's down there." Her Cheshire cat grin was the kind any cultist would instantly recognize. "The word is a term that can't be uttered, he whose name shall not be spoken, *Shem ha-Mephorash*."

Enguerrand didn't want to jump to any conclusions.

"Strange," he mumbled, under his breath, trying to say nothing.

"Strange?" She took offense but laughed to hide it. "Shorthand answers like that are simple-minded. You're not simple-minded, are you, Enguerrand? Please tell me you're not."

He instinctively defended himself.

"I do alright in the intelligence department. But, all that from a black hole? A religion can be made out of that?"

She took a long, slow sip of her drink, burning holes into Enguerrand with her stare.

"The average person has more blind faith in a science that answers nothing, rather than simply opening one's eyes to the obvious proofs everywhere of a cosmos that is alive." She gave a little smirk. "Let's hope you're not just average either, Enguerrand."

The near-topless genius sat saying nothing for a while, flanked by muscle-bound, hired strong-arms on one side, her dead-eyed, anchorless teenage self on the other. "It is a religion though," she pursed her lips provocatively. "And I can instruct you if you like."

Enguerrand was curious to hear her out.

"Please do."

"Do you like paradoxes or do they make you nervous and uncomfortable?"

"Uncomfortable," he replied.

David Nabhan

That was the right answer; it pleased her.

"Paradoxes are sirens screaming at us that we're looking at something incorrectly and the greatest paradox of them all, the one and only, the one from the beginning to forever, is existence." Her smile was charitable. "What is all this around us if not the greatest mystery of them all? Every paradox vanishes if we can make that one go away."

Enguerrand wanted to know.

"How is that done?"

She put her finger up to indicate how simple it all was.

"Accept that the universe only exists, only can exist, because and when it is observed. It *requires* us as observers. All contradictions, anomalies, and conundrums are only there if eyes are open to see and be shocked by them. It's the way the godhead advises its children of its existence."

Her smile was now even more tolerant and forgiving.

"This isn't a new idea; it's thousands of years old. But something that needs observers to exist, to live—must itself be alive. And it is alive. It is the Universe; it is itself God. And now I'll tell you who I am. I'm its priestess." She wasn't joking, not even slightly. "I'm its priestess and its prophetess."

It was a lofty title and Enguerrand was open-minded about it.

"It would be an amazing show to put on if there weren't an audience, I agree with you on that."

Enguerrand wasn't considering her rambling; he dealt instead with the unnerving performance of watching an egg hatch to produce the chicken that laid it.

If Vanessa Braverman's return to the past was the impetus for her to pivot from one life to another, there were segments of that loop that made no logical sense. The cause, from the future, couldn't be both the root and the result of itself. But that's exactly what it seemed to be; a time loop that somehow twisted upon itself, a Möbius strip rather than a loop.

"A priestess and a prophetess too," Enguerrand marveled. "That's impressive. Can you tell me then which of those Hawking radiation pills I should buy?"

She gave a patiently indulgent sigh.

"Yes, the radiation is certainly real, isn't it? Can you imagine something created by and then broadcast away from a...black hole?"

Brabec Van Maanen Alexis, Alpha C-15307 said Vanessa Braverman was brilliant. She definitely sounded like it, linking everything from Kabbalah and Bhagavad Gita to black holes and singularities. She enlightened him about the Hawking radiation too.

"It's a divine aura," she pronounced.

Black holes *did* emit a halo around them as they interacted with the nothingness of space adjacent to their event horizons. The void itself wasn't nothing after all, but instead a roiling effervescence throwing an uncountable number of pairs of virtual particles and anti-particles into and back out of existence, filling the vacuum of all space with infinitesimally short winks of creation and destruction. Such was the essence of nothingness that it should have an ethereal heartbeat of its own that was neither here nor there, neither virtual nor real.

"The crackling backdrop where the halo meets the event horizon of a black hole..." she shook her head from side to side, "...is where you can put your hand out and touch the real face of the universe."

The dancing virtual particles—created out of the void, one of matter, its partner of anti-matter—flit into existence and then whirl inexorably together to annihilate, leaving the matter and energy accounts of the universe undisturbed. Nothing is stolen here, only borrowed, and only for some trillionths of seconds. So, it's no harm, no foul—until the black hole enters the picture.

She held up her thumb and index finger and squeezed them

together tightly.

"But at an event horizon, the gravity is so intense that a centimeter closer matters, or even a millionth or billionth of that distance. In these incalculably perilous environs, not every virtual particle successfully reunites with its intended suicidal partner. Some of the uncountable sub-atomic ghost-particles stray microscopically too close to the razor's edge of the event horizon and are swept down into oblivion—leaving their partners in the choreography to find themselves jilted on the dance floor. For those stood-up motes, Nature has no choice but to bestow—reality. They go from insubstantial, virtual, wraithlike half-essences to the real thing, in the instant, and radiate away as Hawking radiation."

Now she used both hands, sending her fingers in all directions, exploding the particles away from her in all directions.

"The interesting part is what happens next." She leaned toward him and thought harder, exposing the fine lines and creases around her mouth and eyes. They were attractive in a way, the result of so many ecstatic grimaces from so many carnal encounters. "What happens next can't be explained: the black hole shrinks. Part of it evaporates. It loses mass. Just to the extent that matter is created out of nothing, against the rules due to its borders interacting inappropriately with the rest of the space around it and touching it, to that extent must the black hole surrender part of itself to pay for the infraction."

Enguerrand understood.

"Matter can neither be created nor destroyed."

"Exactly," she beamed. "And for every nanogram of matter that makes it into this universe illegally through the back door, just that much must exit through an even more obscure portal, this one at the heart of the singularity that caused the imbalance in the first place."

Enguerrand was deep in thought but nothing to do with

sub-atomic physics or event horizons. There was another equal enigma, and it sat right in front of him. How could Vanessa Braverman be both so smart—and yet the addled victim of herself? If her life had continued as it should have, she'd have been the kind of sane, healthy, schooled, intelligent woman to have delivered the narrative she just did. But if that were so, she'd have never gravitated to the sewers inhabited by the likes of Brabec Van Maanen Alexis, Alpha C-15307. If an electron could be two places at the same time, he had to wonder now if a person could be two people at the same life too.

"You still don't get it though, do you?"

Enguerrand had his hands and head full so she made it crystal clear.

"How does the black hole *know* to shrink? What tells it to do that? How is something in our universe communicated to something built on a singularity, and the information exchanged across the impassable barrier of an event horizon?"

She answered all those at once.

"It's alive. It's a being. In all these eons of existence, the Universe had to finally evolve beyond the Omega Point, its material complexity finally arriving at consciousness, a self-realized entity, one with the instincts to strike out involuntarily at those things that can't happen but yet do. It reacts to cuts and bruises. It tries to heal where it's breached. There's no other possible answer." She put both hands up as in blessing. "All things are born out of the void. How were angels created if not out of nothing?"

Enguerrand couldn't be faulted for thinking about the kind that was thrown out of paradise.

"Demons, too?" he asked.

"Demons, too," she agreed.

She gave him time to take it all in, and Enguerrand Duprey made use of it. He had to concede nothing was ruled out. Where he'd been, where he was and where he wished to get back to had made him far more persuadable.

"So, you believe the universe is actually...alive...in some way? It's an entity?" Enguerrand asked.

"Not in 'some way,' but in every way," she corrected. "It's animated, it's sultry, it wants love and it oozes voluptuousness." She took a slow, languid, prurient sip of her drink, finishing by swirling her tongue along the rim of the glass. "It's female. Its flirtations are mathematical, symmetry being at the heart of all the fundamental forces of the cosmos. It's what causes us to be attracted to balanced dance and why sensual movements are repetitive and proportional." She treated him to symmetrical gyrations of her own, smiling and winking at him as she performed for him. "Do you see what I mean?"

In Enguerrand's eyes, in the spot he was in, she moved as attractively as the helium-3 harvesters he'd seen scraping the regolith off the surface of a dozen moons.

"It's dripping with mathematics, just dripping. Can you taste it?"

Enguerrand took a healthy swallow of his drink, concentrating on what turned out to be a terrible rendition of a smitten look of desire. It was the best he could manage.

"I can taste it," he concurred vacuously.

Vanessa wanted him to savor it and started gyrating again.

"Varying even infinitesimally the mass or charge of any elemental particle, tweaking the slightest fluctuation in the strong, weak, electromagnetic or gravitational forces, giving the merest nudge to the dials that set the razor-thin boundaries of every single constant of the universe..." Now she doubled the tempo of her suggestive bumps and shakes then abruptly ceased and leaned-forward, wild-eyed. "...and everything goes away."

Focusing on Enguerrand's triskelion she made it personal.

"Am I telling you something you already know? Aren't you looking for something, green eyes? Haven't you been searching for it everywhere with no luck at all?"

That caught him off-guard—he answered honestly.

"I don't know what I'm looking for."

She gave him an annoyed look.

"Why look away from a universe where matter is both a particle and a wave also being part divine and human, part sentient and inanimate?"

"All wrapped up," Enguerrand asked, "in the black hole beneath us?"

She leaned forward and whispered an infinitely ponderous truth.

"That's the entrance to the kingdom of Heaven," nodding in the direction of the viewing lunette. "The portal goes two ways though," she warned. "You can get to Heaven or Hell through there." She held up two fingers, the arch-priestess giving absolution. "Both survive on our attention. Our observation makes it all real. Just like anything alive it needs to eat, and that's the food it craves." She raised an eyebrow. "And I can tell the cosmos is hungry right now."

He wanted to ask what the universe ate, but sat quietly instead and nursed his drink. Everything that needed to be discovered about Vanessa had been gleaned. She rated, he told himself, among the galaxy-class mental cases he'd run across in his voyages—from the Oort Cloud all the way out to the Big Black. However, what set her apart was she also was someone with enough deviancy to take incest to levels not even possible—not in this universe anyway. She had pulled it off.

It sent shivers down the spine of reality itself. He also surmised he had about as much chance of convincing her to peacefully accompany him back to Brabec as someone lost in the furnace-like deserts of Draconis Sigma-6 would have of finding a single drop of blessed water.

This wasn't going to be easy.

During his reverie, Vanessa and her black swans exchanged data via their third eyes. The swan next to her breathed a muted reminder in her ear.

"We're going to go feed the bear," she said abruptly, turning her glass up. "But you're welcome to tag along with us if you like."

She could see he didn't understand the Sybarite slang.

"I'd like to show you something you've never seen before."

He couldn't say no.

"I'd love to see it."

Chapter Fourteen: Event Horizon

Neither the sun nor death can be looked on without winking.
—Francois de La Rochefoucauld, Maxim No. 26

FEEDING THE BEAR was just another of many unique activities practiced only on Sybaris. Though almost everything within the amazing habitat was recycled, there was refuse produced that the city-state needed to jettison. There was no better place to dump it than down below in the handy cosmic garbage disposal without par, sent through a drain that compressed the waste into infinite density, squeezing it out of existence, gone, taking the smells and shadows of the rubbish with it.

Sybaris took advantage of her ready-made trash compactor and rid itself of its sanitation cargoes for decades by stuffing it down the throat of the black hole it orbited.

A look of surprise came over Enguerrand's face as the party approached their shuttle, a craft being loaded with refuse.

"That's our berth?"

191

Vanessa smiled and nodded.

"But these are all garbage scows?"

"Don't be such a stiff." Vanessa gave him a playful nudge with her elbow. "Garbage represents colossal credits here and no matter how you make it, the money itself doesn't smell."

She could tell by the look on his face he that didn't follow.

"This is the only place in the galaxy where you can take this kind of ride," she explained. "They will dump trash into the black hole and we get to watch. While lasers play on it, it gets spaghettified as we orbit just past the event horizon. Fantastic show; you'll love it."

As it went down the gullet of Sybaris' collapsed star, rubbish collection and disposal was the fodder of a fantastical entertainment and the tickets weren't cheap.

Vanessa pointed out the refitted shuttle, with customized features meant for use in no other port, now an improvised trash barge docked at the Hub, loaded and ready to depart.

"This one is ours and we're the only party," she beamed. "I bought up all the seats. It's just going to be us."

Enguerrand realized how she had become rich enough to pull off such extravagances—with Brabec Van Maanen Alexis, Alpha C-15307's ambrosia and credits. She enjoyed her time in a place that seemed to be constructed from the beginning with no one but her in mind.

She explained as intelligently as any docent.

"The shuttle makes a glancing orbital fly-by skirting the hole and at the closest pass to the event horizon the locks are opened and the garbage is released. As it falls in, gravity is much stronger at the bottoms of the containers than it is at the tops, even though only feet apart. The tidal forces are beyond tremendous and everything is stretched fantastically, pulled into two pieces and those into two more, and then those pulled apart and separated, until what was once a clump is a stream. It's an amazing sight—matter dropping into forever right in front of you."

Enguerrand shook his head in wonder; he understood now. "Let's go feed the bear."

They boarded the craft and strapped in; there'd be no artificial gravity on this jump. Ironically, this would be a weightless tour, more a speeding carnival ride flirting with a singularity that could squeeze a scale hard enough to register pounds equal to the number of the thoughts of God.

"You're a courier and been through the marrow many times," she said. "There's more than Hawking radiation coming out down there. Let's see if you can feel it."

As the shuttle slipped away from Sybaris, Vanessa and Vanessa were buckled next to each other, a frightening, crawly advertisement not only of the strangeness of *where* Enguerrand was but *when* he was too. But, he'd passed through a temporal wormhole, he had to keep telling himself. A superbly engineered miscue of space-time transported him here—to meet two of the inhabitants of this realm, also impossible foibles of nature. He forced himself not to look at the situation too closely.

The journey closer to the event horizon provoked an even more agitated soliloquy from the priestess and prophetess. Her tutorial on how the cosmos worked and why she had been chosen to deliver the knowledge now shifted into overdrive.

Enguerrand wasn't listening to a word of how the square root of two, the Fibonacci sequence, the diagonals of hypercubes and the homotopy of multidimensional spheres all added up, but then she was sure enough for both of them anyway. When the lasers switched on and the show was about to begin, she paused, but only for a moment.

When Vanessa spoke, her tone suddenly changed and quite perceptibly. She wasn't playing guide anymore; something else now crossed her mind. She glanced in her younger self's direction. Her words were delivered perversely, as a question, as a statement, as an accusation, as a leering invitation.

"You were curious about whether we are related. Why did you ask?"

"There's an amazing resemblance. And then, of course, the place we were in...the clientele there...you know." He politely left it unsaid that Club Gemini was the galactic mecca for the fetish of incest. If this was a reprimand for his alluding to her obvious deviancy he was apologizing. "I hope I haven't offended you."

Vanessa wasn't offended; she answered immediately. Her eyebrow went up a little and the corner of her mouth twitched, both betraying slight nerves.

"She's my twin. My twin," she repeated, "I'm just the much older one."

Enguerrand wasn't surprised how she turned the phrase inside out. What he heard next though, from the young girl— did do the trick.

"She's not my twin; she's me."

The younger Vanessa managed her first real sentence. It had fought its way through the transcendental haze, just managing to hold on to that very basic truth. If she'd confessed this to anyone else before now, none of whom paid real attention, Enguerrand Duprey was the first person who heard it and believed it, without reservation. He also felt a twinge of empathy for her.

"She's me. We're not twins—she's me."

The young woman wasn't making any sense, except the perfect kind.

He not only believed her, but couldn't hide it. The older twin seemed breezily unconcerned with that or anything else and not the slightest bothered by her twin's preternatural disclosure. The priestess and prophetess even evangelized the finer points for him.

"She and I, here and there, back and forth—those are just

illusion. She is me and she is you too. Cosmos is a living thing and it needs to be watched; it's the quintessential exhibitionist. We're all nothing more than its eyes." The rambling sermon was accompanied by the widest, proselytizing, welcoming smile. "Do you understand now?"

He did understand. He grasped that the two black swans, extremely dangerous qualities as they were, belonged in the realm of normal and customary threats. Vanessa Braverman, though—both of her—were stark raving mad. She was insane and that was going to be a problem.

"That makes as much sense as any other theory," Enguerrand accommodated.

Vanessa gave him a salacious leer and went back to the other great pursuit in her life.

"This excites me," she admitted. "You excite me." She had to know. "Do I stimulate you?"

The tongue-tied, yet supposedly infatuated paramour managed to get it out.

"Of course I want you."

The flame of his desire though seemed strangely not hot enough to warm a cup of Lacertan tepid tea.

Vanessa wasn't insulted—she laughed it off.

"I know more than you think I do." She wasn't leering anymore. "You can trust that."

Fortune not only favors the bold, but often times lends a hand to the crazy too, allowing Vanessa to switch personas easily now, out of the blue donning armor, ready for battle, her look, face, manner, bearing—everything—changed.

"That's what tells me something about you isn't right." Her first volley was meant to knock him off his feet. "You haven't agreed with a word I've said, have you? You must be very polite—or it might be something else."

She moved her eyes to the black swans who were starting and flexing as if waiting for a bell to sound in the ring. "And then, from the beginning, not many ignore daunting obstacles like these two—just to talk to me. Do you want me that badly? Weren't you afraid they might take offense?"

Not so fast, Enguerrand's surprised expression said, but it was contrived and looked it every bit.

"You're a very attractive woman," he lied in his defense.

"Yes, there's that too. You're an incredibly handsome young man, green eyes, and yet you're completely enamored with me instead of my much younger and much prettier sister. This must be my lucky day."

He went with a line crafted to cause female courtiers of the Sun King to swoon.

"*Les femmes ne savent pas la totalité de leur coquetterie,*" he quoted one of his father's favorite maxims. "Women know not the totality of their charms." Then he compounded the lie, "You're as much as any man could want."

His romantic arrows bounced harmlessly off her breastplate. This wasn't a question of love, but of probabilities.

"And you're just the kind of man Brabec Van Maanen Alexis, Alpha C-15307 would want: a free-ranger, and a courier at that. There's no one better to move quickly, silently, unseen."

The absurd denial just came out of Enguerrand's mouth on its own.

"Who?"

Vanessa shushed him, busy now he could tell from the mumbling factorial and permutation that slipped between her lips, doing some math in her head. She had a solution.

"Well, the odds are definitely against you, but there's an easy way to be sure one way or the other. Probability rules all. How old are you, Enguerrand Duprey? I'm guessing no older than twenty-five? Am I close?"

The shuttle had picked up enough momentum to skirt the roiling environs of the event horizon. This transparent-bottomed boat had a crystal clear molyserilium belly looking out to a now-open cargo bay. The trash on board was loosed and nudged into the mega-gravity well yawning just beneath the streaking vessel. Bursts of colorful lasers tracked the stream of matter being "fed to the hungry bear"—one of the most unique shows in the galaxy. No one on board was watching though.

"Let's unzip for each other, baby." Unfortunately, she didn't say it like a potential lover. "Don't you want to know me? I want to know you."

Silence is the surest course of one who distrusts himself, Louis Duprey had taught his son. Enguerrand was as completely unsure right now as he'd ever been in his life, in this time or in any other.

He kept his mouth shut.

"You're unscannable, aren't you? Nexus can't find you because it doesn't know you, isn't that so? Isn't that what I'm going to see when you unzip for me?"

Only the autopilot was still occupied with the entertainment, entering the crescendo section of the fly-by, now putting the lasers on strobe. The critical mass, however, was inside the craft, not outside, sufficient to set off an explosive chain reaction.

Enguerrand left the door open.

"You could always come back with me peaceably, you know."

"You're not unzipping?"

"No."

"And I'm not going anywhere with you." She nodded in the direction of the "bear." "You're going somewhere else anyway. Kill him."

Vanessa hadn't even time to get to the "him" in the two-word death warrant. Enguerrand had never secured the latch on his safety strap, fully realizing when he embarked that not everyone who boarded would be getting off. His apparent stupidity and vulnerability served its purpose. He'd chosen the battleground wisely; the combat would be settled in the last place where anyone or anything could interfere.

Surprise being the sharpest arrow in any warrior's quiver, the "little man" was on the black swan, the older one, with a terrifying quickness.

He not only didn't move like other men, but, much, much worse for his opponents, neither did other men's movements register with Enguerrand in normal speed. When his blood was up, when the fever was in self-preservation mode, those around him seemed to maneuver as if stuck in molasses, in slow motion, their every move telegraphed.

The unfortunate older brother, perhaps one of the best-trained killing machines cast in flesh and bone, was as fierce and deadly as a prehistoric short-faced bear—yet trapped in a primordial tar pit so far as Enguerrand's eyes perceived.

He moved in for the kill.

Enguerrand Duprey didn't sport tattoos to advertise his membership in any masculine order. His teeth were unfiled, his flesh unbranded, his face unscarred. The only marks of who he was he wore on his thumb, his third eye, and around his neck, his triskelion.

He was a free-ranger, a man who was nanite-free and pure human from soles to scalp. Moreover, he was an Arcadian, a horse-riding, cattle-wrestling, bleeding, sweating force sufficient to tame the most vibrant planet in the cosmos, but with only bare hands. A free-ranger didn't shrink from anything.

That pluck didn't come from nanites, machines, wires, or coils; it was in his blood. Among all the brash and fearsome fighters from all the worst purgatories of the Milky Way that swaggered around Sybaris, he was the most dangerous of them all—by far.

The black swan only started to make his first clumsy

attempt at defense, as dilatory and useless as if he were a giant, lethargic, oversize and terribly ugly—child.

Someone had to die, and here and now. If it were Enguerrand, he'd be leaving his wife and child to the mercy of a maniac with an inclination to put them under the lash. There was no excuse for dying under those circumstances and it would never happen in this time, his time, or any other.

Others around him, they were going to die. That resolve was on his feverish mind as he dug the fingers of his right hand around the windpipe, pushing in and distorting the black-inked image of the swan. Enguerrand unleashed his ultimate, irrepressible, unrelenting weapon: he tugged.

Enguerrand pulled back his fist, clenched around the black swan's throat. He jerked it faster than he should have been able, changing the inertia quicker than possible, the resulting kinetic assault putting horrifically energetic torque on some very vital parts, ripping the cricoid cartilage of the trachea. It gave way immediately, snapping under the larynx. The black swan was still alive, technically, but fluids filled his pharynx instead of air.

He wouldn't do any more breathing.

The other brother had only just struggled out of his shoulder harness with an unusual mixed look of surprise, fear, anger and revenge flushed on his face. Simultaneously, Enguerrand caught peripheral sight of a much more perilous danger on his flank. Vanessa Braverman had paid top credits for this expensive private excursion and she'd even been able to defray the exorbitant cost for a rare and pricey add-on to the lading at the last minute.

She *was* crazy, Enguerrand thought, glimpsing her pull something from its hiding place beneath her seat. Possession of a weapon in the hands of anyone but a Sybarite police officer was a capital offense. He twisted his floating body parallel with the translucent-bottomed floor and swung his boot into her face so hard he wasn't sure if it killed her or not, but she went out, as quick as Mercury.

In weightlessness, though, the third law of motion pushed his body into reverse, the equal and opposite reaction, like it or not, it sent him straight into the screaming, oncoming second black swan.

Enguerrand put his fist into a hyper-speed jab, breaking his hand on the looming jaw and sending teeth and blood swooshing out of the shell-shocked mouth. The momentary stun was fatal since it was a sufficient lapse for Enguerrand to envelop his whole body, cat-like, around his opponent's head. With a broken hand the death grip and swift flexion took a bit longer and wasn't as efficient; but the result was lethal nonetheless. The grisly match came to an end with two dead, one unconscious, and one injured with a broken hand.

There was only one other adversary. The blood-pounding kick had rendered Vanessa instantly limp. Her weapon floated lackadaisically during the mêlée, gently wafting on eddies in the cabin.

The ambrosia-addled younger Vanessa had it now.

For the first time, with the young woman staring directly and purposefully into his eyes, he could see vestiges of a personality behind the eyes. It was someone who struggled terribly with a reality descending on her from the most outrageous and unexpected place, someone who had already decided that whatever it was that had selected her for such mistreatment wasn't going to be allowed the deference of watching her suffer the torment an instant longer.

She asked him politely.

"Is your name really Enguerrand Duprey?"

He saw no reason to lie to the poor girl.

"Yes, it is." He almost attempted to tell her that he meant her no harm, to try to put her at her ease—especially with the powerful implement she was fondling. The carnage around him screamed otherwise though. "That's who I am."

He left it at that.

"I believe you." She shook her head. "I just wanted to know the name of the person I was going to die with."

Free-rangers were said to have a sort of sixth sense to make up for the nanites they lacked. But Enguerrand didn't need his now; he'd long since entered lethal combat mode. Inner sirens screamed only one thing: get a head-start, and *now*.

"It's time for us to go, Enguerrand Duprey."

That was the last thing she said before pulling the trigger. She wasn't aiming at him though; the translucent molyserilium viewing deck took the blow. It shattered immediately, disastrously, pneumatically. Instantly, the pressurized cabin air pushed the splintered remnants of the floor into the infinitely greedy vacuum of space and rushed out itself through the gaping wound. It swept Vanessa Braverman out into the void, along with everyone and everything else not battened down within.

Enguerrand fought the torrent like a spider refusing to be flushed down a culvert, clinging to the bulkheads, clambering against anything solid, his fever-fueled muscles pressed to the limit and beyond, pushing himself forward by any handhold or foot brace, so petrified of losing this race that the pain in his fractured hand vanished under the weight of pure, unadulterated fear.

The airlock between the passengers' galley and the cargo hold was supposed to be his coffin, where his broken body was intended to be stuffed in and jettisoned out into the abyss. It turned out to be his lifeboat instead; he clawed his way inside and engaged the emergency lock.

Enguerrand caught his breath as the chamber pressurized, filling his lungs with glorious and sublime air, trembling but coming back to himself, wiping away the red blood squeezed into rivulets from his green eyes.

He had accomplished what he'd come to do. A great weight lifted from his shoulders and he wanted nothing more than to slump down and give in to it. He would have, but there could be no slumping in zero gravity; that would have to wait.

The unfortunate human detritus sent into the black hole—stretched, pulled, and extruded into hideous, kilometers-long noodles—had at least saved the indignity of having the macabre display turned into entertainment.

The autopilot, noting that part of the craft was missing and all of its passengers had disappeared save one, turned off the dazzling lasers.

It did something else, too.

It informed the authorities on Sybaris.

A nuisance had transpired out here, a nuisance of the first degree.

One prodigious burden was indeed removed from Enguerrand's back and consigned to a region from whence it could never return, since it was no real place at all, outside of time and space, even beyond the pale of any physical law. In its stead though, another pressing matter waited for Enguerrand when he docked at Sybaris, and it was real enough.

Enguerrand had to exit through the cargo hold as the passenger bay on the gashed craft couldn't be pressurized, freezing the airlocks in place. The welcoming committee was an intimidating and uncomfortably large number of policemen waiting for him, a dozen officers at least. The constable in charge wore a frown that could melt stone—from the neighboring star system.

He greeted Enguerrand with a very direct question.

"Jupiter's beard and Saturn's rings! What's gone on here, outlander?!"

The Sybarites weren't so concerned with human life; actually, they weren't concerned with it at all. Their property, their infrastructure, their enterprises and economy—here was where their interests lay. Enguerrand intelligently addressed the only facet that mattered.

"I'll be more than happy to pay for all the damages." He threw up his hands and matched the confused look of the constable. "I have no idea how to explain this other than a group of unhinged Hawking radiation cultists tried to murder me, and when that failed, committed suicide. I was just in the wrong place at the wrong time." He quickly went back to the only thing on which he wished to focus. "Whatever the cost, I have the credits here on deposit to make good the damage."

The constable turned up his nose at the mitigation.

"This isn't a body shop. You're on Sybaris, free-ranger. We don't repair ships; we see to nuisances. You savvy that?"

Dupris did savvy.

"Let me put it another way. I realize this is an inconvenience." Enguerrand, of course, didn't like the term "nuisance," and was understandably desperate to soften it with a less deadly-sounding term. "The amount of credits on my ledger is quite substantial." He didn't have trouble making the officer believe the next. "I've had my time here. I want nothing more than to make this right and to be on my way."

Something dawned on the officer as Enguerrand was making his case.

"Who are you traveling with?"

Enguerrand told himself it boded well that for some hardly educible, yet blessedly fortuitous reason the officer was at least mildly interested enough to attempt to round up all the relevant parties before dispensing with summary justice.

"Where are your companions?"

Enguerrand had no wing-man.

"I'm traveling alone."

That snippet of information worked instant magic on the Sybarite gendarmes—a ripple of guffaws, disbelieving hoots, and slang expressions not heard anywhere but here but whose meaning was plainly apparent undulated through the body of police. It even produced something resembling a smirk on the constable's deadpan and stone-cold face.

Enguerrand latched onto the opening tossed his way and hung on for dear life in the most literal sense. It worked so well the first time he put it to use again.

"I'm traveling alone."

The senior patrolman was done smiling, although still dismayed by Enguerrand's solo status.

"We get plenty of visitors here in real need of couch time with a mental professional, but…"

He didn't need to finish the thought. His fellow bluecoats chimed in about the suicidal lunacy of slumming around especially these parts of Sybaris on one's own.

The officer gave a gruff nod in the direction of the wrecked garbage scow.

"If you managed that by yourself, it's a good thing there aren't more of you."

And, almost as an afterthought, for whatever investigatory purpose there was, the Sybarite lawman—in the one place in the Milky Way that sneered at law—made a caricature inquest.

"There were four people beside yourself on board." He furrowed his brow. "Two of them," he made an audible growl to punctuate such a footnote worth mentioning, "two of them were black swans."

Enguerrand stood mute, not daring to say anything other than to give the simplest replies. The next question came wrapped in another very audible growl.

"What happened to them?"

"Gone," is all Enguerrand elucidated.

That forced yet another proto-smile onto the granite face. "Gone, huh? Funny you should mention that place, that's exactly where every EXT case winds up around here."

The impending death sentence was hardly uttered when it was instantly quashed by a reprieve. Enguerrand glimpsed her approaching out of the corner of his eye, the most beautiful sight he'd seen coming his way since catching sight of a cadre of his gung-ho free-range comrades streaking to his rescue in the catastrophic disaster of the Battle of the Velorum Gas Giants.

She was accompanied by someone whom the cohort of police recognized instantly as well. He was one of the twelve archons, the dozen arch-demons who governed Sybaris. The policemen's snickers, snorts and slack posture ceased instantly, replaced by attentive silence.

"This doesn't look to me like an EXT case," the Sybarite magistrate said airily to no one in particular, perhaps even speaking to the Shinobi face-catcher at his side, the Shinobi who buttered his bread by paying so handsomely for access to the visuals data stream he peddled.

"I told you I was going to take an interest in your health, fly-boy," she gave Enguerrand a wink, pointing at the now mild-mannered knot of Sybarite police. "How are you supposed to pay me if you go and get yourself killed?"

Before Enguerrand could answer she turned to the policeman in charge, incredulous.

"Wait, do I have this straight; they're saying he killed two black swans? *Two?*" She turned back to Enguerrand and gave him a seriously effected, deeply deferential bow. "I knew there was something about you, pilot."

The high councilor, her official liaison in the face-catching business, put a more acceptable face of his own on it.

"Those weren't the last two black swans on Sybaris."

It was in his interest to make the least of this; the other two individuals turned into event horizon spaghetti—the Vanessas—weren't even mentioned. Enguerrand was happy with the strangely abbreviated casualty list and intelligently said not a word.

The Sybarite politico dispensed with the case on the spot making short work of it.

"This seems more an EXP case, with the free-ranger forfeiting all his credits." He nodded in the direction of the Shinobi, "After an outstanding debt is covered."

"Four thousand credits," she reminded him, and quite curtly.

"Four thousand credits," he agreed, saying the words aloud, "the rest to accrue to the state coffers, and the nuisance-monger expelled immediately."

Everyone nodded their heads in agreement.

"You won't be coming back here, free-ranger," the commissar told Enguerrand. "Not ever."

No one nodded in agreement with as much fervor as Enguerrand. This expulsion from Sybaris was to be the most compliant order ever sworn out; where Enguerrand was headed there *was* no Sybaris.

To make certain there was no misunderstanding and no hard feelings, Enguerrand handed over to the constable all the rest of his once-staggering stockpile of ambrosia, down to the last Myrmidonian gram.

"I won't be needing this."

Credits and ambrosia were the only things that tilted the scales of Sybarite justice, if ever.

There was just the slightest reluctance on the constable's part to have his bailiwick completely invaded by the powers that be and their Shinobi partners in graft.

"Perhaps it's too hasty to call this a nuisance," the constable grudgingly concluded.

He pretended to have a say in it and changed his verbiage if not the outcome.

"It's more a case of wrong place and wrong time. We'll use your term, free-ranger. We'll call it an inconvenience." He turned to his adjutant, feigning to be giving the order. "No EXT; this fellow traveler is simply leaving, EXP. Escort him."

Enguerrand was pleased not to have left stiffing the

Shinobi, but where he was going, there was little chance he'd bump into her again. Still, had the face-catcher tracked him down in the future, he thought, sharing a joke with himself, the interest alone, twenty five years of it, would bankrupt him.

He didn't say a word to her, only flashing the Shinobi hand-signal for things that are so deeply owed but can't be expressed.

She had saved his life—and that of his wife and child.

The last thing he did before leaving was to give a thought to taking off his shoes and leaving them at embarkation. He almost left Sybaris barefoot—worried there was no way to scrape what he had walked through off the soles of his boots.

Back on board *Ultramariner* Otto-matic was Otto-ecstatic.

"Well done, Enguerrand Duprey!" It had already pulled what it needed from his human charge's third eye to account for the congratulations. "I had my doubts about you, I must say. But, well done!"

Enguerrand thought that was a strange comment from a droid, but let it go.

"Back track us; lay in a course for the pulsar portal." Enguerrand was in no mood for conversation. "Get us out of here."

Otto respected Enguerrand's lack of camaraderie; he had to.

"Aye, Captain. Laying in a course as ordered. In three...two...one..."

Ultramariner made her jump into the quantum foam, passing through the marrow only a bit herky-jerky, sputtering along with a missing rotodynamic magneto, on a bearing into the Big Black, into nowhere on any chart, headed for an as yet undiscovered gateway and bound for twenty-five years in the future.

On their way Otto saw to dressing the only casualty suffered: one broken hand. It was Z-rayed, set, and injected with bone sealants that flowed straight to the fracture and formed rigid splints—from the inside.

"If you'll please just hold your hand still, this will only take a few minutes."

Otto bathed the break with UVC ultraviolet to harden the stanchion. During the procedure the android couldn't take its lenses off Enguerrand for some puzzling reason, made all the more peculiar by its request.

"Could I ask you something?" This was a rarity; Enguerrand not often heard a mechanical express any real interest in what a human had to share. "Did you make her think you didn't know that she knew? Was that your strategy?"

"I knew that she thought that she knew," Enguerrand gave out, "but just not that she knew that I knew she knew."

"Interesting," Otto understood perfectly.

"The true way to be deceived is to think oneself more knowing than others," Enguerrand quoted.

"Ah, yes," Otto accurately cited the author of the passage, "the duke?"

Enguerrand corrected him, "No, my father."

Enguerrand looked intently at the automated corpsman reconstructing his hand; it would be made better and stronger than it had been before. Enguerrand almost wanted to know what "interesting" felt like for an entity that ran on variegated electrical potential but he didn't ask.

During the silence that followed while his hand was being mended Enguerrand could see Otto was plainly bursting at the seams to inquire something more of him.

"Get it out, Otto. Speak up—what?"

"Well, I was only wondering what you feel now having…"

It was a shocking question for a machine to ask a man and even more shocking for the machine to be now at a loss for words.

"As a free-ranger, a religionist, as a man who believes in

right and wrong, and sin and grace, and blessings and perdition, you must respond differently to great emotional events in your life."

The android paused again.

Interjecting, Enguerrand defended himself.

"There are still a few commandments I haven't broken, Otto."

"Oh, I meant nothing untoward. And, yes, I was able to determine your integrity from the first. That's not what I was implying at all."

"Then what?" Enguerrand snapped.

"Well, but for you, four people would still be alive back on Sybaris. Does that not equal a transgression, and quite a serious one?"

Enguerrand shook his head in the negative—adamantly.

"You have everything wrong, and since you're the diodes and quantum processors making this ship go, that makes me a little nervous." Enguerrand corrected him, "There were three people who died at Sybaris, not four. And I was in the act of defending myself."

Otto smiled sheepishly.

"That's right, what an odd blunder. Three people, not four." Then Otto furrowed his brow. "Of course, it all depends on how one counts the carnage. But, yes, either three or four."

Enguerrand pronounced the verdict upon himself.

"It was an act of self-defense, not murder,"

"So no qualms then? No pangs of guilt?"

Enguerrand had to confess that his soul wasn't completely unscathed. He spit the words out quickly and then enforced a long silence.

"I feel bad for Vanessa."

Otto had the audacity to break it finally.

"Which one?"

"Both," Enguerrand replied.

Chapter Fifteen: The Decay of a Proton

One cannot answer for his courage when he has never been in danger.
—Francois de La Rochefoucauld, Maxim No. 359

THE MACHINE PERCEIVED it first.

Ultramariner continued her jump through the quantum slipstream—making for the pulsar portal with neither man nor machine saying anything further. But then Otto detected something amiss; Enguerrand could sense it by some subtle unsettledness coming over the amanuensis' face, an unease in the eyes.

Enguerrand was just at the point of asking if something was wrong when he too realized full well that things were far from normal. A hardly discernible blue haze began to form within the control cabin of the cruiser, a crackling, statically-charged effervescent blue—but not really blue, it was a new color Enguerrand had seen before.

Otto hadn't though, and with hypersensitive detection abilities to parse any light of any color, visible or not, at any

210

range of the spectrum from gamma rays to super-attenuated VLF waves the shock of not being able to immediately identify this particular energy now gaining intensity and filling the ship like a bolt of blue ball lightning was enough to cause the machine to actually stoop to query the human.

Otto let the words slip from his mouth.

"What is that? What's going on?"

The human and android both watched in a combination of stunned silent shock, terror and amazement as an entity took form within the confines of *Ultramariner*. It had to be an entity because it could be nothing else; it exuded purpose, direction, lifeforce.

Something boarded their vessel as it hurtled through the marrow. Otto's mouth flew open, his jaw dropping.

"What under all of Andromeda's suns *is* that?

Enguerrand was incapable of answering. His fright came all the way around, cycling past the dread of helplessness and now settling on a resigned limbo. He could neither move nor speak.

Otto was responsible to his human captain and besides couldn't know any emotion, including terror.

He stepped into the breach without hesitation.

"Identify yourself!" Otto demanded curtly in New English. "Identify yourself immediately and state your business."

The lifeform didn't speak New English—it didn't speak at all.

It didn't need to. Just presenting itself said more than everything ever said in New English and every of the thousands of languages all together. To look upon it was to know that few eyes had dared view it and yet gone on seeing. Yet, in fact, there was no way to properly take it in aside from only the very scant part of it that made an impression in the third dimensional universe of Enguerrand and Otto.

All the rest of the corpus of this Karnifex occupied space in the shades of the multiverse, moving in directions and into places impossible to even imagine to imagine.

It was an infinite-dimensional being, and the indentations and footfalls it made in the paltry three in which it currently deigned to transgress were as incomplete and flimsy a real description of the indescribable as would be a sphere passing through the environs of a two-dimensional world. All that could be perceived of it by 2-D beings would be the swatch of it that fit—the infinitely thin slice of it that lesser-dimensionals would take in as a simple circle.

What couldn't be seen of it somehow was made known to be there nonetheless, echoed beyond the slice of the Karnifex that could be made out in this world, in Enguerrand's universe. The hint of it alone was more terrifying than a flame first seen by entities made of tissue paper, the concept of burning yet unknown but the first-hand knowledge of it when finally gleaned instinctively horrifying.

Machines, however, thankfully are crafted without the single greatest Achilles heel: fear.

"Identify yourself!" Otto demanded again, this time even more aggressively and foolishly taking a single hostile step in the Karnifex' direction.

A shaft of energy shot out from the Karnifex, enveloped Otto, and turned him "off" as if pulling the kind of old-fashioned plug Brabac used to mock free-rangers. Otto was as challenging now as a sack of flour or a chaise lounge. Enguerrand was absolutely alone as the Karnifex sidled closer. He found himself only arm's length away from the most omnipotent, unstoppable, inexorable entity in the universe—or any other.

Enguerrand awoke to the ministrations of Otto, the amanuensis having refrigerated his hands to provide a cold compress against Enguerrands' flushed cheeks.

"We're not dead," Enguerrand declared.

"No," Otto agreed, "we're alive."

Enguerrand pulled himself to his feet, blinking his eyes, shaking off the stupor.

"During your short unconsciousness, I reprised all the data concerning that…" Otto was reluctant to call it by a name. "…about that phenomenon." He shook his head with a false determination. "You were mumbling in your stupor about Karnifexes and taking away people who don't belong. Karnifexes don't exist, Mr. Duprey. They're mythical creatures, space lore, nothing more."

As difficult as it was to control his trembling lips, Enguerrand managed a defeated smirk along with gallows humor perfected over the course of dozens of routs and defeats.

"That mythical creature sure knocked you for a loop. Imagine what he might have done with you had he been real."

Otto had obviously been thinking about that.

"We encountered something real." Otto was going to shove the Karnifex back from where it came. "And there's no doubt that the phenomenon could be an occurrence of the most singularly rare nature having transpired only once, perhaps never before and never again." Otto had a good analogy at the ready. "Like the decay of a proton. It should take trillions of years to see it happen but there's nothing to say that one of the one hundred thousand quadrillion vigintillion protons should cheat the bell curve of its half-life and be the outlier that should fall apart right now, right in front of our eyes.

Enguerrand's smirk evaporated, replaced by a blank stare.

"That thing is after me, Otto."

Otto was certain that wasn't the case, or at least pretended to be.

"If that were so, you'd be…" he paused. "Well, you'd be *gone*, wouldn't you?"

Enguerrand was just as certain.

"It's waiting for me to accomplish something. It's prodding me, urging me to…do…something."

Otto mulled that over.

"And then it will, in your words, take those away who don't belong? Is that what you're saying?"

Astoundingly, even in these circumstances, Enguerrand's smirk returned. Otto had to count him as the bravest, most unruffled, imperturbable, fearless human he'd ever met.

"I will have to figure out what it wants me to do." He said it like someone laying his head on the chopping block before the axe man, the last reconciled words timidly whispered in one world before passing to the next. "And then not do it."

Not another word was spoken by either—for the next two and half decades.

Chapter Sixteen: Tempus Fugit

Fortune turns all things to the advantage of those on whom she smiles.
—Francois de La Rochefoucauld, Maxim No. 60

WAITING ON THE other side of the pulsar portal was something almost as unexpected as a Karnifex. As soon as the craft regained control, escaping from the cosmic slipstream gushing from the wormhole, Enguerrand Duprey realized something important was missing. A long, stunned silence ensued, finally broken by an absurdly simple question.

"Where's the station, Otto?"

The reply was one usually not heard from an autopilot, amanuensis, or Nexus itself—they knew everything.

"I don't know," Otto revealed.

Brabec Van Maanen Alexis, Alpha C-15307's station was not where it should be. It was simply gone—along with the slightest trace of it.

"What do you mean you don't know? How could you not know?"

Otto confirmed it.

"I know as much about this as you do."

Enguerrand did the mental math.

"Well, that's nothing."

"I can only surmise," Otto guessed, "that something must have changed out here in the last twenty-five years."

"Hail the station," Enguerrand ordered nervously. "Wherever it is. Send a transmission."

"Hailing," Otto replied, and then confirmed: "Nothing."

"Hail it again," Enguerrand ordered, frustrated. "Try again."

Otto shrugged. "Hailing," and then confirmed again. "Nothing."

As far into the Big Black as *Ultramariner* was, there was no data stream. Enguerrand was in the dark out here, in every way.

"Has Brabec released my family?" Enguerrand pressed. "Is this over?"

"That's a possibility," Otto calculated. "Would you like the probabilities of that being the case?"

He did not.

"I want to know where my wife and child are! We'll need Nexus to figure this out. What's the nearest star system?"

Otto informed him that Epsilon Fornacis was the outer edge of human engineering's electromagnetic tessellation. Enguerrand made the only call he could.

"Epsilon Fornacis, let's go," he ordered.

Otto hesitated. There was no protocol for this.

"Are you sure?"

"Of course, I'm not sure. Epsilon Fornacis—now."

The jump toward the yellow giant was a tense and silent one. But, no sooner was the furthest tissue of the umbrella of civilization pierced than Otto-matic, as autopilot, brought something of note to the human pilot.

"Excuse me," a start so normal, "our course is taking us

toward an anomaly of staggering proportions," to a finish so disturbing.

Enguerrand, of course, didn't understand.

"Say again?"

Otto was specific.

"The aberration concerns the number of craft jumping in our immediate vicinity—and their direction."

"What about them?" Enguerrand asked nervously.

"There are tens of thousands in our sector and also in those abutting it, as far as can be scanned, all moving—out."

Enguerrand was dumbfounded; he just stared at Otto. The autopilot deduced from the silent gape that he needed to hear it again, put another way.

"There are thousands of ships streaming past us. They're all coming from 'inside' and headed 'outside.' Every one of them." Otto finally decided to editorialize. "What is more worrisome is that they don't seem to have destinations in mind. None of them. They're just moving out, away, and at quite extreme speeds."

Otto put a finger up.

"Correction. Data streaming from the Far Side makes that hundreds of thousands of ships, everywhere, all with random polar coordinate headings, but all outbound." Otto put yet another finger up, raising the alarm. "I apologize for the rough numbers. Nexus seems to be compromised; we're not getting a clean data stream."

Enguerrand gave the only appraisal he could.

"That's not possible."

"Which," Otto tried to clarify, "the traffic advisory or the failure notice for Nexus?"

"Both!" Enguerrand shouted. "Is there not a *single* ship headed in?"

"Excluding us?"

"Of course, excluding us, you sack of nuts and bolts! I

know which way we're going!"

"None, then," Otto took his lumps.

Brabec's missing station took a back seat to this.

"War?" Enguerrand asked in a hushed and confused voice. "It has to be war..."

"It could be war, yes," Otto agreed. "Or some other natural calamity. Perhaps a gamma ray burst, or colliding black holes, or something as yet unknown." One thing was certain though. "If it's war," this possibility could be quantified. "It would be of a size and nature never before seen."

Otto stopped short; other results were in.

"I have an addendum on Nexus: it's confirmed. Nexus is failing; vast sections from Core quadrants are totally incapacitated." The machine turned to the man and requested the input. "Our heading, Mr. Duprey?"

The order was simple.

"Hit the brakes, Otto."

"Aye, Captain," the autopilot complied. "Taking us to adrift in three...two...one."

Nexus was indeed flickering out and uncountable fleets of ships were being driven past *Ultramariner* in what was quite obviously a headlong panic. The pieces were put together from information that could still be accessed; Otto managed to pull in the keystone.

"This is a Class 1, Level A Emergency Transmission. It's being repeated on—wait—correction. This is now being relayed as all-channel. I repeat, this is all-channel, in all domains."

A grainy, pixilated avatar now stood on the communications stage. The man was completely done up in his finest military dress, including gold-braided epaulettes, ceremonial sash, many badges and ribbons of distinction proudly displayed. He was a free-ranger; anyone could see that from the uniform and the beret. There was more to recognize though.

Enguerrand Duprey was acquainted with this individual.

"Isn't that the man you threatened to kill on Sybaris?"

Otto, of course, knew that it was. He was making a conversation out of it, the way he knew humans preferred and enjoyed.

"That was twenty-five years ago," Enguerrand reminded him, very quietly, deliberately, not focusing on the identity or whatever grudge should have sprung from a hatchet buried so long ago.

Otto knew humans appreciated irony, just hadn't absolutely mastered how and when to use it with each individual so different; it was quite a math problem and the combinations fairly complicated. A personality like Enguerrand's made the job harder, but this time the jibe came out well delivered.

"From the look on his face one could surmise that he never got over it."

Enguerrand had never really liked his father's second in command, and before had never known why. He had a reason now with the best grounds there ever were or would be. It was Nils Rimbaut.

Looking closer he could see something else about him straight. Rimbaut's eyes had the same dead, forlorn, absolutely insane reflection he'd seen up close in Vanessa Braverman's. He had something to say, and it was all-channels with communications failing, wearing a look that warned that no one anywhere was going to like this. The image hit Enguerrand like slamming into degenerate matter, pure neutrons, face-first.

Here was Louis Duprey's *bras droit*, his right-hand man, making the speech of a lifetime, of an age, a speech for all the ages, and those never to come.

"Thousands of years ago on ancient Earth when it was beautiful, sacred and human, a brave group of Jewish defenders fought to the end at a place called Masada. Their citadel was atop a mountain impossible to scale, surrounded by a desert without provisions, but assaulted by an invincible army. The attacking Roman legions were used to moving mountains and this was just the next of many. When a monumental earthen ramp, by the shovelful, by cartfuls, had been thrown up to the ramparts, the unassailable fortress became an inescapable deathtrap. The evening before the final onslaught, the defenders came to a heroic decision. Every husband and father atop Masada slew his wife and children and lots were drawn to select ten men to dispatch the grieving warriors who welcomed their own deaths. The last ten *sicarii* drew lots again among themselves to appoint their own executioner, who in the end himself committed suicide."

This wasn't the kind of tale Enguerrand wanted to hear coming out of a madman's mouth—especially being broadcast across great swaths of the galaxy on a Nexus that was crumbling before his eyes. An uncountable armada stampeding didn't help either.

He didn't want to hear it but had no choice other than to listen. It looked like—in an inexplicable madness unleashed—Nils Rimbaut had every soul in Creation and the Free Range as a captive audience.

Enguerrand listened with everyone else.

"The only thing that makes us human is our freedom. Without that quality what we breathe isn't air, what flows in our veins isn't blood, and what we think in our minds aren't thoughts. This has been known since we rose from our knees and began walking upright. At Masada, and Thermopylae, at Stalingrad and at Sigma Coronae B, heroes have shown us time and again that death is preferable to dishonor, so the victor is denied the spoils even in defeat."

Otto-matic, no matter exponentially faster, smarter, and clearer, wasn't built for any of this to begin with. That together with Nexus crashing wasn't doing Otto any favors. The machine stepped forward and proved it by essentially saying something stupid. The mechanical picked this moment to right this wrong and reinforce the human as mistaken.

"It was a bad idea to trade that rotodynamic magneto back there with them," Otto chided. "I told you that wasn't at all a good idea."

Enguerrand dealt with the shock and silently let the rebuke pass. Rimbaut pronounced the verdict sadly.

"We free-rangers have lost, but our defeat is too costly for humankind to endure though. The very soul of our species was at stake in the balance, and we free-rangers, the last firewall standing between mankind as peoples or humanity converted to a virus—to our miserable shame—we lost this great struggle."

Otto's suggestion started to make sense. This psychotic version of Nils Rimbaut might have been the stumbling, catastrophic result set in motion by Enguerrand, somehow, someway, through a series of events he was desperately trying to link together properly. It wasn't pleasant musings, at all.

"We can still salvage our honor, however, still exit the stage with something our enemies will never take from us: our dignity. Our victory is that human beings will never be converted into a horde of ants to over-run the Milky Way. We will have saved thousands of future generations, trillions of people, from this horrific fate."

He chanted the free-rangers' battle slogan.

"We choose death before inoculation. And with our dying thrusts, we take all the enemies of liberty with us, dragged down to accompany us into the abyss."

Rimbaut stood ramrod straight now and delivered the *coup de main*.

"I, Nils Rimbaut, have created and detonated a device I've christened 'Masada.' It's appropriately the last word that will ever be uttered or heard by human tongues and ears. A vacuum phase transition has been touched off, ignited at the epicenter of the victorious traitors to the human race—in the Home Sector itself. By the time you hear these words, Earth and everything in its vicinity will cease to exist. Every second that passes will push the crashing wave of the collapsing false vacuum outward, swallowing creation itself. It will arrive at your location, no matter where you are, no matter who you are. Let us gather our families and prepare to meet the end—as humans, and on our feet."

Rimbaut saluted smartly.

"*Que Dieu ait pitié de nous tous.*"

May God have mercy on all of us.

Enguerrand had to absorb the words on his own. There was no one with whom he could share an overwhelming stupefaction that slipped over him and squeezed like the gravity on the mega-planets circling Iota Persei.

For some period, Enguerrand couldn't bring forth a single sound—much less a coherent notion. A suicide note had not just been read to him, but for every person in the Home Sector and Creation combined.

The primary thought kindled in his mind was a terribly mischievous and inappropriate one that sneaked across the synapses of its own accord, shocking his conscious psyche. It had been said for millennia that even if mankind were to do its worst, nothing could cheat the cockroaches of their eternal birthright. They were the uncontested heirs-apparent of the Earth—except—apparently, not.

Otto-matic's observation was hardly a morale-booster, nor the comment he voiced openly.

"You made a mess of things back there, Mr. Duprey."

The aspect chosen for his facial expression wasn't bracing; Otto chose an appearance that looked like a Denebolan mink panicked into frozen mode. The machine did quick calculations whose results didn't look good. It was already dusting off funerary mode.

The human hadn't come close to surrender yet—that

being a great strength of his kind—and rebounded naturally, come what may, only thinking now of how to defend himself, in preservation mode, not funerary, not yet.

Enguerrand said the name of the crisis aloud, trying to maintain calm.

"A vacuum phase transition—if such a thing has been triggered, can it be reversed, stopped, slowed down? Anything?"

Otto-matic was already gearing into its pre-programmed protocol of attempting to sidle doomed human crews into the first stages of acceptance of approaching and unavoidable termination, his cheeks only lacking tears. Enguerrand didn't appreciate the facial articulation or the slightest implication of making ready to throw in the towel, either one.

Before Otto could turn the sprinklers on Enguerrand exploded.

"Wipe that off your face!" Enguerrand shouted. "Answer me!"

Otto realized the *Ultramariner's* captain wasn't considering in the least a last moment in religious communion with the deity of choice. He dutifully complied and responded immediately.

"You're calling for data regarding a phenomenon not known to be possible to engender or not, until now. There is no body of information that would verifiably satisfy your request, even if access to Nexus were possible."

"Make a guess, Otto. I'll take anything."

"Stop a phase transition once it has cascaded forward?" Otto rubbed his chin as if his resisters were heating up over this particular insolubility. "One should find it easier to decrease entropy or make positive give up attracting negative. There's no putting that back in the bottle, no stopping this. There's only running from it."

Enguerrand shook his head "no" even as Otto was speaking.

"For God's sake, pull your weight! Make a guess!"

The hyper-intelligent android was stumped but went along.

"All right," Otto-matic acquiesced, "as long as it's understood that the reference pool is now the limited data in my own banks." He paused before going on, as if collecting his thoughts. Enguerrand had never seen an amanuensis at sea; it was bone-chillingly terrifying to witness it here and now. "Give me a moment."

Everyone who transited space, and most certainly couriers who topped the list, knew that the vacuum, the nothingness through which they sped was charged with innate and irrepressible energy.

Quantum cruisers utilized it to make jumps that made short work of dozens of light-years. Nothing was not only something, it was a crackling, roiling, turbid, dynamo. Nothing was what helped make star systems go round, the bottomless energy larder that powered much of anything that moved, the unfettered power that willed particles into and out of existence the way a steam kettle rattles its cover.

That it was still called the "void" was a silly anachronism. It was wondered, however, if there were a real nothing below the apparent one; it only made sense that there should be. If space in the universe were the face of a "false vacuum," there had to be a genuine vacuum, an authentic nothingness below it and one upon which the higher vacuum could fall precipitously if it were but nudged.

"Nils Rimbaut must have found a way to provide that spark, like putting a flame to dry tinder. The rest is the pure and simple physics of the reaction finding its lowest energy state—burning itself out until there's nothing left to fuel it."

Enguerrand had an idea what "nothing left" meant, but wanted confirmation.

"How far will this thing go?"

"As far as a stone will go once it's pushed over a precipice.

Nothing will get in its way until it hits bottom."

"And just where is 'bottom'?"

Otto actually smiled.

"Space-time has no bottom."

"That maniac has destroyed the galaxy? There's going to be no more Milky Way? Is that what you're saying?"

"No, not exactly," Otto clarified. "It won't stop once it's established a new and lower rest phase for the vacuum of space within the Milky Way. There's no stop sign at the terminus of our galaxy, Mr. Duprey. Why on Earth would you assume that it would cease there?"

Enguerrand clarified himself.

"Then what you're saying is that lunatic has destroyed...the entire universe?"

Otto didn't seem too overwhelmed by that, even as it dissected the end of itself—and everything.

"Well, it really depends on what your definition of destruction is. There will simply be a new nothing, and that nothing will be even emptier than the nothing that existed before. You understand?"

Enguerrand did comprehend.

"And the stuff that is embedded in the old nothing? What happens to it when the new nothing rolls up on it?"

"Well, of course," Otto answered this simple question, "it will have to go away too."

Into what realm all the matter in the universe would be swept was in the undetermined category.

Enguerrand now focused on the most practical and pressing matter.

"How fast is that thing moving?"

This seemed to interest Otto more than the other queries, and he'd come up with some conclusions finally.

"Excellent question." Otto had been working on this and had some rough answers. "There seems to be some remarkable irregularities in that regard. Certainly, it would start out at the speed of light, and according to what theorists imagined, expand out at that rate forever, into infinity." Otto frowned at the next thought. "That doesn't seem to be what's transpiring though. Judging from the areas that we can reasonably assume have already been subsumed by the transition, it must be accelerating. Juxtaposing the intervals between interface failures of succeeding sectors, adjusting for light lag, and considering the registry of the cruisers that have raced past us, it doesn't seem to be moving at light speed. A reasonably accurate estimate would place the demarcation line of destruction at approximately the fifty-light-year range from Earth."

It shocked.

"That much already gone?" Enguerrand whispered in his mother tongue. "*Est-ce que beaucoup déjà allé?*"

Otto-matic detected very obvious signals of emotional distress in the pitch of the human voice and reacted accordingly.

"I'm sorry for your loss," the robot consoled.

"But how can it be moving so fast?" It was more than just a technical query; Enguerrand was next in its path.

"There's no violation here, if that's what you're wondering," Otto had the explanation. "There are certain natural phenomena that can and have moved much faster than light. Only things embedded in space are prevented from surpassing light speed—certainly not space itself. It has moved millions, billions of times faster than light, when it expanded during the inflationary period for example, right after the Big Bang. Entangled particles exchange information faster than that, even now. This isn't material but rather an integral feature of space itself. A phase transition is a conversion of nothing into something even flimsier and flatter, like trying to clock the speed of water turning into ice across an infinite ocean. When finished, space will simply be emptier than the nothing we know

now."

Even this superlative feat of human cleverness had to marvel at something else though.

"Nils Rimbaut must be singled out for such an incomparable accomplishment. It would be of great interest to be apprised of the manner in which he was able to set this in motion."

"Yes," Enguerrand had to concur, "the brainiest guy in the room. They all said he'd set the world on fire, but I don't think anyone had this in mind."

Enguerrand had never understood his own cool feelings for his father's old ally. That mystery was now solved, though.

Enguerrand did his best to mask his fright, for dignity's sake, but he was only human.

"To have that wash over us...what would it be like?"

The captain wasn't giving in to capitulation, but he was scared. There was no reason to insult that, so Otto just gave it to the free-ranger straight.

"There'd be no 'be'—that's what."

That was enough philosophizing for Enguerrand; it was time to do something.

"Can we outrun it? If we retrace our steps at full speed, can we stay ahead of it?"

Otto went back to his original complaint.

"You really shouldn't have dismantled the rotodynamic magneto. That's going to make things close."

Enguerrand cursed the magneto under his breath.

"I don't care how close. Will we make it in front of that thing for a while?"

Otto's body language took on slightly unusual nuances for a quantum processor housed within state of the art meta-materials, electronic textiles, amorphous metals and polyethylene super-foams. It wasn't clicking on all cylinders though; its comforting coexistence with all-knowing, all-powerful, all-pervasive Nexus was gone.

"I really don't know," Otto shrugged. "Your instructions?"

Enguerrand made the easiest call in the history of human events.

"Step on it."

"Roger," Otto confirmed. "Into retrograde, stepping on it in three...two...one."

Enguerrand's contingency plan to avoid being swallowed by space started at the best place, the beginning. He'd come to some conclusions about the genesis of the terror coming up on them as they jumped back toward the portal.

"That spare part I left did indeed cause some problems," the human conceded to the mechanical. "Exposing myself to Nils Rimbaut as the man to have delivered it turned things one way and not another."

Otto had been processing the topic and had a ready opinion.

"As a witness to the time loop, meeting you as an adult coming out of it, hexagonal gradient class magneto from the future in hand, and then seeing you grow into the same man who threatened to kill him decades earlier, well..."

"...may have given him some strange ideas?" Enguerrand finished. "And with the defeat of the free-rangers' cause, this induced the mind of the ultimate suicide bomber to snap? Is that plausible?"

Otto didn't hesitate for an instant.

"Highly plausible." He kept close watch on the extreme fear, anxiety and depression overtaking his human commander. Part of his primal functions—should he need to engage in what would be his last duty—would be making Enguerrand's death as quick, painless and free from terror as possible. However, this human seemed incapable of throwing in the towel.

"Assuming I caused this," Enguerrand paused and thought,

long and hard. "Assuming I planted the seed twenty-five years ago to have caused this…" He dropped the other shoe, "What are the probabilities that the trigger should have been pulled right now? Not a period ago, not last year, not tomorrow, but just at the moment of our return?"

Otto gave an expression of what true and genuine android shock might finally look like if it could be pre-programmed into the tableau of all the other grimaces, frowns, smiles and swoons it could call up. He too now thought long and hard—even harder since he was without Nexus and on his own.

"I understand your question, Mr. Duprey." He said it slowly, deliberately. But then he repeated it as if he was hedging for time and that he truly didn't. "I understand your question."

Whatever train of thought the amanuensis attempted to hitch together, the couplers weren't exactly lining up. In this vulnerable state, Otto was thwarted from the task of gathering his thermionic thoughts. On the other hand, his captain was transmogrifying before him as well.

He'd never seen a human in this state.

"Are you alright, Mr. Duprey?"

Enguerrand Duprey had never been alright. Lacaillian fever had tried to snuff his life while still in the womb, and since beating those terrible odds and seeing the light of day, the blows had never stopped coming. He was born into a time of struggle, warfare, death, loss, destruction.

Everyone he'd ever known was dead—save for his wife and child. He was far from alright, but not yet forced onto his knees. In fact, at that moment he was a fearsome, super-energized, crackling, dynamo of biological luminescence.

His eyes were two brilliantly glowing emerald green orbs, pulsing with the most mental energy he'd ever internally generated.

Even an Otto-matic or any amanuensis anywhere, would

be wise to take very close notice.

"You didn't answer," the metamorphosing biological demanded again, energy bursting at the limits, yet sequestered within those simple three words. With this particularly unique human being, on this particular journey toward certain oblivion, Otto opted for silence.

Enguerrand switched to French. This was going to be the argument of his life, one to rival Rimbaut's, but not issued to the whole of humanity, but to the resonator of a single quasi-sentient, electronic device. He'd be using French.

"*Où allez-vous*, Otto? Where are you going, Otto?"

He seemed to catch the apparatus even more off-guard, if that were possible.

"Per your instructions, we're in retrograde, at full speed."

He almost inquired again if Enguerrand were himself or not, but realized better and quashed it.

"Yes, yes, I know. But what is our destination?"

"Brabec Van Maanen Alexis, Alpha C-15307's station," Otto named the obvious terminal. "You ordered us to return."

"We've just been at those coordinates. Brabec Van Maanen Alexis, Alpha C-15307's station isn't there. It isn't there because it doesn't exist." Enguerrand gave the only explanation there was. "It doesn't exist because it never was built. It was never built because Brabec hasn't discovered the pulsar portal— in this universe, in this version of reality, in this copy cosmos we made."

"We?" Otto didn't appreciate the pronoun.

Enguerrand didn't appreciate the snide accusation. "*Sacre bleu*, but you're a stupid robot, aren't you?"

"I beg your pardon?" Otto protested.

"Open your receptors and turn your volume down."

The man was going to school the machine and if the competition seemed unfair it was only by virtue of ignoring which had created the other. And, Enguerrand was pure biological, nanite-free, a free-ranger from his chromosomes to his fingernails.

"Where are the creators of the pulsar portal? How old would a civilization have to be to build such an unthinkably advanced engineering feat—a million years old, or older? Where are they? Who would build such a thing and then misplace it?"

"Unknown," Otto droned.

"Unknown? Just that?" Enguerrand pointed behind himself as if that were the direction of the Home Sector. "Much like the unknown rushing toward us at this very moment?"

"Much like that," Otto intoned.

"Well, thankfully there's one of us on board who thinks a bit beyond that," Enguerrand scolded. "Your circuits might be satisfied to leave the end of the world in the interesting head-scratcher department, which in itself is proof positive of a terrible defect in your design."

"The only flaw in myself or *Ultramariner*," Otto countered, "concerns a missing part."

"You are a quite ignorant robot; that's the only way to put it. No lump of metal and wire, no magneto caused this, it was destined to happen. That portal is something that couldn't be built, yet was. It's an open wound connecting two parts of space-time that can only produce self-healing catastrophes so as to prevent its use. It engenders curative disasters. That's what must have happened to the civilization that built it. Attempting to use the portal can only bring about terrible rifts between cause and effect. And a universe that can't rely on cause to precede effect is an injured universe. They were swept away by their invention, by who knows what terrible annihilation that befell them. Just this dangerous, forbidden relic of their existence is left as their tombstone."

"Ours," Enguerrand emphasized, "will be an even more ignominious exit.

"We're going down the drain itself and taking the bathwater with us. We won't even leave a stain on the enamel. That's hardly the fault of a single magneto. The minute the portal was discovered by Brabec, the goose was cooked. It is the ultimate self-destruct button, capable of scuttling a cosmos. It should have been put off limits, quarantined, sealed off in perpetuity or at least until the far future when our engineers should find a way to dismantle or destroy it."

The human had taken quite a few blows without complaining. It was the robot's turn now.

"That didn't happen though, did it? A worthless, selfish, villain found it instead and, with your help, put it to use fixing bets and scheming the market. This had to be the outcome, sooner or later. Even Brabec feared what he was playing with. Leaving anyone back there in the past, he knew was a terrific risk. And worse than almost anyone, would be someone like Vanessa Braverman, who could and would do anything she pleased, who might be able to end his life before they'd even met, who he realized was very, very bad for business."

Otto had indeed been listening attentively.

"Are you proposing something? Some course of action, Mr. Duprey?"

"*Mon Dieu*, of course I am! I'm going to turn this around. This version of events is going to be re-booted. I don't like this variant; this one simply won't do. I'll take my chances on anything other than this."

"What exactly *are* you suggesting, Mr. Duprey?"

Enguerrand managed to smother the last vestige of fear, uncertainty, despair and shock, and instead put on a face cast in case-hardened steel.

"Not 'Mr. Duprey.' I prefer 'captain.' And I'm not suggesting; I'm ordering. Your previous protocol is at an end. It's not possible to return me to Brabec Van Maanen Alexis, Alpha C-15307's station. It doesn't exist. Brabec himself may not either, along with my wife and child, or if they do will be impossible to find with Nexus down, in that stampede running for their lives and stopping for nothing."

Otto made to say something; Enguerrand waved it off.

"This is a Class 1, Level A Emergency. I'm the only human on board and that makes me the ranking officer. That is the only protocol you have."

Otto-matic made a remarkable comment, almost in the realm of a joke.

"Still, I told you leaving that magneto was a bad idea."

Superluminal death of the surest kind was barreling down on him so Enguerrand acknowledged the age-old, erring hallmark of his race since time didn't permit a real debate on the matter.

"Granted, you can blame it on the human if you like," then reiterating the sea changing transition that had taken place within *Ultramariner* rather than without, "but your prior protocols are finished. We're in a far different place, and I'm the human on board."

"And I'm the monster?"

To compel the autopilot to hand over the craft, against its will, to physically take the helm of *Ultramariner*, to push an Otto-matic aside and have one's way with a quantum cruiser would require a full squadron of extremely heavily armed men—without saying which way it would go.

"I called you that twenty-five years ago. Maybe it's time for you to let it go."

Otto-matic responded with the three most dulcet words Enguerrand could imagine hearing, three words which formulated the most generous reprieve ever given to the human race, yet voiced by something that was created, not born.

"*Oui, mon capitaine.*"

As Enguerrand pushed *Ultramariner* to absolute, seam-bursting full speed, dueling catastrophes traded places as the means by which the mechanically compromised craft and its occupants should meet their disastrous end.

"This velocity can't be maintained," Otto declared bluntly. "The probability of dissolution of structural integrity is..."

Enguerrand wasn't interested or willing to entertain slowing down in the slightest.

"Belay that." The human was less nervous and more centered than the autopilot. Something darker than pitch black, less weighty than nothing, more terminal than non-existence was licking at their heels at ever-increasing multiples of the speed of light. Enguerrand made up his mind to die if it should come to it, by being flung into the marrow as his vessel ruptured around him. That was preferable to being swallowed by the horror that now was only a few thousand kilometers astern—and gaining with pulse-pounding rapidity.

"Maintain our current speed," Enguerrand ordered, his tone as impossible to budge as death itself. Yet, even as the captain gave the order the ship itself seemed to demur. The bulkheads of *Ultramariner* actually started to pixilate.

"She's coming apart," Otto replied.

This was a rare phrase indeed to be heard coming from an Otto-matic. There couldn't be any more attention-getting commentary issued. Otto realized he'd been heard quite plainly and yet ignored. Since there was nothing more cautionary to be said in any of the hundreds of languages at his disposal he simply repeated it, in French.

"Elle se sépare."

"Maintain...maintain...maintain..." Enguerrand had nothing else to say.

Now the craft's pixilation reached a throbbing, heart-stopping rhythm, the walls of the vessel seeming to flit into an out of focus like a strobe light. They were on the razor's edge and just a little bit beyond.

"She's coming apart, Captain."

"*Maintenir, Otto, maintenir.* She will *not* come apart." He turned to Otto-matic and gave the amanuensis the most primal lesson in human decision-making, the kind delivered through clenched teeth. "She can't."

At the last moment a prayer slipped through Enguerrand's lips; it was like no other entreaty he'd uttered toward heaven ever.

"*Aidez moi, Dieu.* Help me, God."

Those words were the last pronounced by anyone, anywhere, in a universe that was being yanked out of existence.

It was a close call—a very close call. Scant moments after *Ultramariner* pulled clear of the pulsar portal in the past, the leading edge of the onrushing conflagration consuming the very stuff of reality, swallowed the very existence of where they had just escaped.

It snatched their very footprints into oblivion with all the rest, pulling everything up by the root and flushing it into nothingness...the real kind.

There would be no going back; back had ceased to exist.

Chapter Seventeen: Spare Last Chance

The accent of our native country dwells in the heart and mind as well as on the tongue.
—Francois de La Rochefoucauld, Maxim No. 342

ENGUERRAND RECOGNIZED THE footsteps crushing the soft and fertile loam of Arcadia, a sound deeply ingrained from his boyhood—the bootsteps of his father. Louis Duprey came striding out of the orchard of tall, noble Talarmarine trees, catching sight of his son in the clearing.

Louis called out to him as he approached.

"You found your Vanessa Braverman."

It was apparent Louis was hardly pleased to see Enguerrand alive, in one piece, and in front of him again. Then Louis added that he was aware of her fate as well—he calmly narrated the offence. "You murdered them, with me as your accomplice.

"*Oui*," Enguerrand nodded, "I found Vanessa Braverman, but neither you nor I killed her, I swear to you." He added an even more unintelligible qualifier. "But, yes, I succeeded; it was fated that I should."

About his sanity, there was none left. As for Vanessa, she hardly left his thoughts, giving him answers to all the insoluble mysteries with the power to drive anyone mad. He realized Vanessa wasn't totally unhinged, this priestess and prophetess believed in miracles he too had witnessed.

She'd managed to explain the fate of the builders of the pulsar portal and the nature of their offense. Where they had failed, a madwoman from Sybaris succeeded in understanding. She demanded a universe that was observed, but spectators like Adam and Eve had best obey the decree against transgressing onto the realm of God, because that's where chaos lived.

This was a profoundly reassuring feeling for Enguerrand—worth all the travail a thousand times over. He wanted to share that with his father.

"We live in a universe that necessitates marvel, a universe created by a Supreme Being that would cheat to protect that, a universe that selected…me…and you…to tip the scales just so, just now. You're soon to see that."

Nils Rimbaut had condemned the conversion of humanity into a horde of ants and tripped the gallows rather than allow the crime to be committed. Enguerrand was certain there was a far greater hand behind that now; reality itself cringed at the notion. It was all perfectly orchestrated, even to requiring a Brabec too smart, too self-interested, too wary to go himself, but ruthless enough to shove others through the portal for his gain, the perfect tool to bring about the end of one reality and the birth of another.

Enguerrand pondered what had happened to all the others before him who had made the journey; he doubted it had ended well. But only he now carried the last embers and he alone, to fan into fires to forge former defeats to rise like phoenixes from the ashes into great victories. A universe old enough to have evolved to feel the cumulative miracle of its creations was mature enough to protect it. There were indeed Thinwalkers after all—and one need not look for them in any other dimension. He himself was one, having tread in the thinnest of places that could or couldn't be imagined, the sliver of ether between dual realities and non-existence.

"But, you're right. I'm not so sure about my sanity." He readily admitted, "no one can lay his hands on what I've touched without coming back differently. I'm not the same man."

Something even more powerful than a super-advanced civilization had reached out and easily swatted their race out of existence—the same power that even now erased the next wave of interlopers in the dimension Enguerrand had just escaped.

The commandment could not be disobeyed: humanity may not create the stuff of event, touch the arrow of time, may not live forward and backward simultaneously. Only gods could dwell in those places; in this universe there was no room for more.

Its servant, Nature, struck back hard and mercilessly to prevent entry into this jealously guarded domain. He had no other choice but to acknowledge he'd felt the impossible-to-disobey power. He was the catalyst. In trying to save his wife and daughter, he brought about their deaths, along with everything else that either breathed or didn't. Cosmos didn't play fairly, which is how it always managed to win.

He'd been singled out and that presupposed a selector. And, he now believed, like Vanessa, there was something the Godhead and universe needed, something springing from its observant children: wonder.

"I failed my wife and daughter," Enguerrand continued, making the admission to his father but more confessing to himself.

A look of unbearable concern came over Enguerrand's face. "My daughter is in a place that can't exist—less real than between here and nowhere. She fell through the cracks. She never existed, though she used to." He paused and added something positive. "But, she'll exist again soon if I've managed to put everything right. She'll exist again soon, I hope."

Louis began to ask himself if the man before him had truly lost his mind. He couldn't restrain himself from taking steps forward to survey Enguerrand closely. Looking into his eyes he recognized that something was terribly, terribly wrong with the young man.

"What are you saying? You're not making any sense." He would suffer no more of this. "You obviously have a death-wish that itches, Enguerrand, and you've come to the right place to have it scratched. We can and will oblige you."

Enguerrand wasn't listening; the threat washed right over him.

"And my wife? She'll never be in my arms again." Enguerrand said it broken-hearted, driven past endurance, defeated. "She will be born two years from now. The tumblers have come to rest and our lives will be forever out of sync." Enguerrand gave Louis an undeniably insane smirk. "But your son will win her heart. The other me will have every chance I had and then some."

The young man was in great distress, but so was Louis. He was simultaneously terrified, furious and grief-stricken, and with good cause. For once, he had no idea what to do.

Louis managed to say the awful words with great control, as well as uttering the death sentence that followed.

"Just as you said, my wife is dying and my unborn son may be lost as well. Your words incriminate you."

Enguerrand wasn't alarmed in the least and, far from fearing his father, only wished to console him.

"You need not worry for your son, Monsieur Duprey. Your son is in no danger."

Louis didn't respond well to yet another prophesy.

He spoke as insistently, menacingly and stonily as any

sentence he'd ever uttered.

"This is your final opportunity. Tell me who you are."

"Me?" Enguerrand gave Louis a broad, irrefutably unhinged grin. "Have you heard of Thinwalkers, Monsieur Duprey? They pop out of nowhere, from nothing, when the universe wills them into being—when something need be done that physics won't permit. Do you believe in such things?"

Enguerrand Duprey looked as unbalanced as he sounded. He'd been back and forth across never to nowhere, twice. And, he wasn't all right. He was certain that he was, some good part of him, deranged. That, of course, was the only rational conclusion he could come to.

His sanity was a small price to pay. He was certain the universe had taken the side of the free-rangers, and that it was going to repeat this coda of the symphony of life as many times as required until the dice landed on the correct outcome.

Nils Rimbaut couldn't abide a universe peopled with insects, but a greater force abhorred it even more. That force chose wisely when it selected Enguerrand Duprey as its foil, as the instrument to repeat the refrain. He was no hero, but no coward either. More than that, he was a free-ranger and a courier. But when he apprehended the nature of the awful burden on his shoulders, he showed that he was capable, after all, of capitulation. He had no other choice than to surrender his senses.

"Do you? Do you believe?"

Louis Duprey gave his son an exceedingly disapproving frown. It said that he most certainly did not give credence to such beings as Thinwalkers and wouldn't deign to even comment on such tripe.

He became unsettled, however, by Enguerrand's obvious disregard for the danger he was in. He threatened him explicitly again.

"I warned you never to return to Arcadia. Coming back

playing the madman changes nothing."

Enguerrand didn't dispute that.

"I'm a little crazy, I'm afraid to tell you, Monsieur Duprey. I'm not myself at all."

Indeed, he wasn't himself anymore. Enguerrand Duprey was a different man than he was three periods prior; there were other parts beside his hand that were broken. He saved his future would-be wife, but she was lost to him forever. She wasn't even born yet while he was a twenty-five-year-old man who'd move back and forth through time no more.

She was as dead to him now as the wife he'd left on the other side of the portal. The fate of his daughter produced an even more profound and disturbing scar. His own daughter had been forced over the same abyss that didn't even exist now in some terrible place among never and maybe and forever, consigned to the fissures of the shifting monoliths of space-time.

Whether she ever were to be re-born, if he'd abandoned her not once but twice now, into what limbo the spirit of that entity slipped, all of that was unknown and a sadness too great to contemplate.

So, he didn't—and it cost him his lucidity.

He'd traded his mind for something even more precious— a second chance. The great battles his father would wage for the free-rangers' cause would be re-contested again, but this time he'd be at his father's side, not at his knees.

This time, the outcome could be in real doubt for Louis Duprey's adversaries. His son would come armed with an incomparable, indefensible weapon: he'd seen the future. Enguerrand would deliver counsel that could never fail, subterfuge immune to discovery, counter attacks for assaults not yet planned. He'd bartered his mind, heart and soul for those advantages, and they hadn't come cheaply.

"But, you should believe in Thinwalkers, Monsieur Duprey," Enguerrand advised his father, "since you gave birth to one." A trembling smile of great burden accompanied what he said next. "I never told you, father, but I *did* see an impossible ray of blue light, streaking across the entire sky, from one end of the celestial horizon to the other." He nodded his head and spoke very quietly. "I think I know what it means now."

Much of Louis' anger now transmuted at once, even as he unsuccessfully tried to hold onto it. More powerful was the complete assurance that the man before him was in the deepest pit of mental psychosis; the emotion that filled Louis now more than anything was a combination of anxiety, bewilderment, and hesitancy.

"Where I've been is someplace too far to come back unchanged, the lesson I learned taught to no other man." Enguerrand tugged his blouse open, putting the Duprey heirloom on display. "I'm sorry you heard me blaspheme in front of you when grandmother asked me if I still had my faith in the good and righteous or not. There has never been such a believer as I now."

Louis fell back a step, now completely unnerved by the conversation. Enguerrand took advantage, the son rushing to the father, clasping his arms around him and squeezing with all his might.

"*Je ne suis pas moi-même, et je ai besoin ton aide, père,*" the son said in a voice tired, empty and spent. Enguerrand was almost sobbing the plea. "I'm not myself and I need your help, father."

Louis tensed up, looking his son straight in the eyes as Enguerrand held him, close enough to feel the puff of his breath as Enguerrand sighed. He wasn't convinced though, and nothing would persuade him, nothing at all, nothing in the world.

He would be swayed though, and only seconds later—the proof coming from outside the world. For just as impetuously as Enguerrand had rushed toward him he stepped back now, with the strangest look of assurance and submission. He knew; he could feel it coming. Everything about him changed instantly.

Enguerrand spoke in a whisper, but Louis heard every single word.

"*Au revoir, père. J'ai fait ce que j'étais censé faire. J'ai accompli la tâche devant moi par Dieu lui-même.*"

"Goodbye, father. I've done what I was supposed to do. I accomplished the task put before me. I met the test, I didn't fail."

Now an eternally serene calm descended on him, completely unafraid and blissfully awaiting the entity whose arrival he perceived was imminent.

"I have to go away because I no longer belong here."

Louis had no time to wonder what the words meant. A ferociously resplendent blue—yet not quite blue—shaft of super-energized light bursting from oblivion, from the center of the galaxy, from another dimension, from all of those places and none too, erupted from nowhere and everywhere at once; it enveloped Enguerrand and took him away.

The sheer power of the act knocked Louis off his feet and tossed him a dozen meters through the air as if he were a fly being flicked away by the swish of a stallion's tail, great and noble animals extinct on Earth, but still found in Louis' stables on Arcadia.

When Louis was able to drag himself to his feet, rubbing his eyes and his broken collar bone, he stumbled to the spot where the man he was determined to execute had last embraced him. There was nothing there, nothing at all, save the realization that Enguerrand Duprey was indeed his son, and that he was...gone.

Chapter Eighteen: Settled Scores

Reconciliation with our enemies is but a desire to better our condition,
a weariness of war, the fear of some unlucky accident.
—Francois de La Rochefoucauld, Maxim No. 82

ADRIENNE HAD GOOD reason to condemn Enguerrand Duprey to death. She had heard him implicate himself, repeatedly, with his own lunatic words. He was from the future, he was her unborn grandson—and most compromisingly—he had prophesized the most bizarre and improbable death for her daughter-in-law, who was now dying of the same Lacaillian fever this raving bedlamite had foretold.

She was no believer in curses or Thinwalkers, and neither did her practical mind waste much time pondering how this particular maniac had managed to infect her beloved Sophie.

She only knew that this man calling himself Enguerrand, an obviously criminally deranged crackpot in the employ of the one of the many and creative enemies of the Dupreys, was a walking, talking weapon who had been wound up and sent into their family so as to cause confusion and heartache.

He had accomplished his backstabbing task, as Sophie, the dearest thing in her life was now lingering at death's door with her unborn son's life in the gravest peril as well. As for the Duprey's enemies, they had failed miserably. They had sown no confusion; she signed her faux grandson's death warrant with more surety than anything she'd ever green-lighted. She gave not the slightest credence to her own son's eyewitness account of Enguerrand having been swept away and beyond her reach or anyone else's.

Louis Duprey, however, who had looked deeply into the eyes of Enguerrand seconds before he disappeared, who had heard his last words, was on the other hand just as certain of the opposite. He couldn't erase the sight of the man who called himself his son being yanked out of existence before his eyes— nor did he wish to. Instead, he swore he'd get to the very bottom of this whether he'd have to move heaven and Earth or both.

It turned out to be much easier than that; as simple as knocking at the air lock of *Ultramariner*, left orbiting Arcadia above. Now that his core protocol was deemed at an end, the only entity on board, the ship's amanuensis, an Otto-matic, had no interest in scuttling the vessel and was calmly and patiently waiting for his next legal instructions.

They came.

"What do you know about the former captain of this ship?" Louis Duprey inquired.

Otto, of course, knew quite a bit, and before he finished divulging every incredible fact, the boarding party of Arcadian free-rangers was dumbstruck amid a silence rivaling the ethereal hush that pervades the epicenter of the Corona Borealis void.

Only Louis Duprey could finally find his voice.

"So you are the only person, creature, article, thing, individual—biological or mechanical—left in existence in a copy-cosmos from twenty-five years in the future?"

Otto was pleased to hear Louis put the matter so succinctly.

"Indeed, Mr. Duprey, the distinction is quite noteworthy. I've been calculating the probability that such a peculiar and singular description should have come my way. The results should interest you."

The results didn't interest Louis Duprey.

No one present realized it, but everything changed from that instant—everything. It was the incipient moment of a great watershed for the human race, one that would hold back furious oceans that otherwise threatened to overwhelm mankind.

Every free-ranger on board *Ultramariner* that day had his or her blood chilled to a temperature that made liquid hydrogen seem positively balmy. The true significance of every slogan, campaign, plebiscite, insurrection, victory, defeat, every life and death struggle formerly deemed more important than the very gravity holding the Milky Way together was instantaneously seen for what it was: trivial.

It was trifling enough to be swept into the same cauldron of less than nothing on the other side of the pulsar portal—into a realm that now didn't even exist. Humanity was fortunate that one such as Enguerrand Duprey had held the tiller during the cosmic storm that had just broken and even more providential that his father took the helm now.

Louis Duprey grabbed it with both hands.

"Your son, Mr. Duprey, I don't mind telling you," Otto confessed, "was quite a remarkable man. Very unlike many humans with whom I've served."

Louis nodded sadly in agreement, and then forced himself to ask. "What was that thing?"

This was a topic that piqued Otto's imagination to no end.

"What your son called the Karnifex? I must tell you that I've come to the most astonishing conjecture as to its identity."

The machine paused.

"I feel foolish saying this, but considering that all the potential answers are scientifically impossible, the best speculation is a terribly unscientific one."

"What was that thing that took my son?"

"An angel, Mr. Duprey?" Otto said straight out. "What humans have called angels since time immemorial."

Otto shrugged his shoulders and tilted his head.

"What else to call what *Homo sapiens* has purported to have witnessed for thousands of years? Aren't they divine messengers, utterly omnipotent, unimpeded by time or space, residing nowhere and everywhere, impossible to elude, upon one in a nanosecond and gone the next? My best answer is that your son was taken by an angel."

Louis Duprey at first said nothing but the look on his face spoke clearly enough. Of course, there could be nothing to add to that except to ask if Otto were serious.

"I interacted with it, Mr. Duprey," Otto now had more of a look of surety on his face. "There's no wrestling with those things, no matter what Earth's sacred texts say."

Louis asked the only question he could. "Taken...where?"

Otto gave him the only answer he could. "Home, Mr. Duprey. It would have taken him home."

Otto left a few terribly silent moments for the astounding supposition to sink in before perking right up again.

"He'll be born in a few days though. Let me be the first to congratulate you!" Just as quickly though, the happy smile on the mechanical's face was replaced with a somber look. "And, allow me to express my condolences for the impending death of your wife. I am so sorry for your future loss."

No amanuensis was supposed to talk like this. Louis wasn't sure if not just his son had been disassembled and put back together, but this Otto-matic as well who had taken the same surreal ride.

"Do you suppose," Louis was dazed to hear himself inquiring of a construct of circuitry to elucidate things for him, "do you think they'll be the same...person?"

Even Otto was set back by the question.

"You mean your newborn son and Enguerrand Duprey?" He gave an animated shake of his mechanical head. "Oh, no. I think not. There can only have been one Enguerrand Duprey. He was only put in this world to do something, he was chosen, and once he accomplished it, he didn't belong and had to go away."

"But why him," Louis asked, "why was he chosen?"

"Oh, Monsieur Duprey, if we have no access whatever to the mindset of a Choser, there's little hope of fathoming how those who are selected come to be so, *n'est-ce pas?*" He repeated his earlier comment on the topic. "Your son was a quite remarkable man." Noting the effect on Louis, Otto graciously added a qualifier. "But, I'm certain your son will be a fine man too, monsieur. Again, my congratulations."

Otto thought for a moment and gave a last piece of upbeat speculation.

"It will all be just like it never happened now, couldn't that be the case?"

It wasn't though.

No one in that party of free-rangers listening to Otto was changed quite like Louis Duprey. It was he who had watched his son evaporate before his eyes, ignored his cry for help only seconds before, heard his last words asking absolution for his faithlessness, calling out to his father with his last breath.

Louis was a changed man from that moment forward, determined to atone for his deafness, forcing a calling onto himself that would reverberate throughout Creation and the Free Range.

Louis Duprey soon buried his wife, spent hours gazing into the green, green eyes of his new-born son just to imprint onto his soul the sort of assurance he required, and then leaped into the fray with even more single-minded determination than his dead son had.

Otto-matic was the only receptacle for the co-ordinates of the pulsar portal, and now Louis Duprey possessed that immensely important information.

He assembled the greatest minds in the Free Range and put this remnant of the super-advanced ghost-race that created it under a microscope of ferociously intense scientific examination.

After only the first year, mankind's knowledge—and the free-rangers' technological acumen—was leap-frogged a century into the future. But Louis Duprey did something astounding with that advantage, something that required the unstoppable force of his personality to accomplish against the collective angry cries of every other free-ranger alive: he shared it.

Instead of attempting to conquer or annihilate the enemies of the free-rangers, he approached Creation with the gift of real knowledge and offered for the first time something that both sides finally were ready to consider accepting with grudging sighs of relief: compromise.

"The charity and goodwill of every faith in existence demands it," he told all the flabbergasted recalcitrants around him. "We will never convince them of their humanity unless we demonstrate ours."

This wasn't easy.

His first problem was a woman as headstrong as any who ever lived. Adrienne was as addicted to power as any Byzantine empress, dowager queen mother, or Ottoman valdide. Enguerrand's own mother, Adrienne, would never, could never agree to anything less than total war, complete victory or "death before inoculation." Louis saw to it that she would spend the rest of her life under a very pleasant but permanent house arrest, ending her days like so many jilted ex-sovereigns—fuming, plotting, complaining and cajoling but to no end.

Then there was the other great mind who had no part in even laying eyes on the pulsar portal, much less investigating it.

Louis didn't hold Nils Rimbaut culpable for scuttling an entire cosmos that lost its claim to being, yet still he was cashiered immediately from his positions and placed under the greatest surveillance of any human alive.

Rimbaut couldn't pick up a screwdriver or gaze through a microscope for the rest of his life without a committee of spies knowing about it and discussing its significance. To have taken his life, Louis believed, would have been a crime.

And, he already was imperiling his soul by the transgression he was indeed determined to commit, one last piece of personal business, an affair of honor.

Louis Duprey spent many periods and hundreds of thousands of credits biding his time and setting his trap. When sufficient bodyguards and paramours had either been removed or corrupted, Louis Duprey himself paid Brabec Van Maanen Alexis, Alpha C-15307 a visit. Brabec was enjoying a massage in one of the five-star hotels on the pleasure planet of Beta Hydranis-5.

"I want you to know that this is for what you did to my son, Enguerrand Duprey."

A bewildered Brabec protested.

"Enguerrand Duprey? I don't know any Enguerrand Duprey."

Of course, Louis was aware of that and gave a last helpful explanation.

"You brutalized him—and his wife and daughter. You attempted to murder my son, my daughter-in-law and my grandchild…twenty-five years from now."

Brabec's mouth hung open, his eyes wide.

"Strangle you with Orion's Belt. What *is* this?

"Retribution," Louis answered, the last word Brabec Van Maanen Alexis, Alpha C-15307 ever heard.

Those were the only scores Louis saw settled.

As for the rest, he spent every breath, brought his word, his power, his credits, every reward, threat and inducement under his control toward an impossible mission to end the greatest feud of them all—the one that had smoldered for centuries between Creation and the Free Range.

At a hundred conferences held to come to terms with just what the "compromise" and "peace" he championed should mean, whenever the self-deluded, pontificating rabble-rousers screamed for all or nothing, Monsieur Louis Duprey, Grand Marshall now, speaking for Arcadia and all Vela Eridani, and in effect for all free-rangers everywhere, son of Adrienne, re-discoverer of the portal, had an apt rejoinder to chill the marrow.

"If it's all or nothing one seeks, it can easily be found. We have a poignant reminder of what it looks like and where it is. It's on the other side of the pulsar portal for anyone who would like to get a closer look at it."

He was his mother, and it turned out, then some. His star streaked across the skies from Alpha Centauri to bands of outlanders so far out in the Big Black that they lacked place-names.

The marshal used the pulsar portal as his cudgel. It languished in space, broken, now only half of what it was, with one anchor in something and the other in nothing, a horrific memento of how close all of humanity—all of existence—had come to the end. Louis used it to sound a heart-stopping "beware!" to mankind. Everyone listened intently now, perhaps for the very first time in all of history.

The naysayers who declared Louis Duprey a dilettante, false prophet, a fool on an impossible errand, wound up on the wrong side of the swiftest reversal of public opinion since the Canum Venaticorum Bubble burst, sending over a hundred million investors into bankruptcy.

All of a sudden, with the urgency of a chain reaction once critical mass has been reached, a powerful set of allies saw The Event, as it was called, for what it was and rose up, virtually as one, and not only joined Louis Duprey, but placed themselves in his vanguard.

That Louis' son had single-handedly forced the arrow of time one way and not the other seemed the clearest portent from Heaven itself. Every fair-minded person with the slightest decency became deeply ashamed of the rancor that had bedeviled dozens of star systems for far too long.

However, it had come to pass, the zeitgeist just changed. These were humans, after all, their spirits moved them in the end—more than reason, platitudes, inducements, or anything else—and nudged the worldline itself.

For those who believed that something came out of the void to snatch away Enguerrand Duprey after having done its bidding there was the simplest choice to make, and for those doubted, the terror of being wrong caused them to acquiesce as well.

One last hard look at the Home Sector did wonders for Louis' cause too. Most averted their eyes from the ghastly ennui that infected this small part of the cosmos.

Louis Duprey dug his strong hands into the collars of every regular working man and woman, each head of average households, the man and woman walking the streets of Chi Orionis A9 or Kappa Ceti 3—and yanked their attention to the most hideous sight of their darkest nightmares.

"Is this what you will leave as your legacy? Is this the place to which you will consign your progeny?

It was not.

Everyone walked away a little disappointed and humbled after all was said and done—that usually being a sign for the better. The inertia for peace was too strong, crushing the appeal of the hive-mind or boundless freedom. The Wars ended, just like that, and not with a bang but with a whimper.

There would be no Generation Eleven of nanites—or twelve, or thirteen. The human race came together and paused, and decided there had to be a middle ground and that it would be found.

Both sides gave much, and gained much as well.

For the free-rangers, they were obliged to muzzle the Luddites among them. There were many excellent reasons to host certain nanites, the kind that bestowed unparalleled benefits in health, safety, education, efficiency, convenience. And there were just as many grounds to ban other nanites that snooped into the realm of emotion, sexuality, morality, privacy and one's very thoughts. The former were to be embraced—by everyone; the latter to be prohibited—everywhere.

A long, thorough, carefully thought-out and adjudicated, painfully specific list of what was allowed and what was proscribed was hammered out, signed and delivered, and put into effect in every star system in which a footprint of a human could be found.

Blessed peace descended upon the inhabited spiral arm of the Milky Way, and lasted.

Enguerrand Duprey had feverishly wondered if an angry universe had struck out at its previous offspring, the pulsar portal builders. He wondered if the same cosmos were warning the current race of children now set to range into vast sections of the Milky Way that such an august entry could not be allowed as a virus-like form of swarm-life.

If cosmic repugnance were real, it might be seen on the wrong side of the portal in a universe consigned to the trash heap of failed existence, complete with a vacuum wrung dry of its last erg of energy. Tantrums let loose by infinite and eternal constructs would be boundlessly risky, perilous enough to unleash the partings of seas, the raining down of fire and brimstone on degenerate cities—or even the erasure of entire universes.

Louis Duprey didn't wonder; he knew.

But mankind had only tread to the edge and then wisely retreated. Now a great peace and happiness descended upon the entirety of humanity's vast abode, a delight born of liberty, choice, autonomy, privacy—moderated by the most responsible concessions.

That well-being was now as real and pervasive as it had ever been. Perhaps this itineration of super-advanced life in the cosmos would achieve its final nirvana without partaking of the forbidden fruit and ending their tenure evicted from paradise.

Enguerrand Duprey grew up a far different boy in a much-changed world. No ferocious battles raged as he learned his first words of French and New English, no populations disappeared from existence in flashes from the storied planets he'd only just come to know from his studies.

He wasn't raised to meet every challenge with Spartan courage, to stand his ground and defend it to the death. No one whispered constantly in his ear to either come back victoriously bearing his shield or being borne upon it.

This Enguerrand would not kill his first man at the age of fifteen and go on to slaughter a hundred more. The human race simply vaulted right past that chapter in history which now was destined never to be written at all.

Some things, however, never change—not in the here and now, the then and there, or anywhere else.

When he was ten years old his father caught him doing something of which he strongly disapproved. It didn't matter to him that so many other boys used slingshots to pursue sludgeskimmers. It wasn't that Louis was unaware of how much fun Arcadian boys got out of targeting sludgeskimmers, but that these bizarre creatures—half insect, half bird, part firefly, mostly alien hummingbird, actually exploding like fireworks in the oxygen-rich air much of the time if they were hit properly—were sentient creatures.

"But, they're just sludgeskimmers, Father!" Enguerrand protested.

Louis had remembered almost to the word the lecture he was told ten years prior he'd be giving at this moment.

"All sins, every piece of ugliness that ever existed or ever would, all the dark, evil, debilitating defeats and failures of mankind, in every age, all stemmed from the same primal, spiteful poison: unreasoned violence. This was not only the great offense to righteousness, but brute force hid the true shortcomings of laziness and stagnation, since it was easier for the dull and sluggish to steal what they thought they required than to create it. Envy, theft, murder and finally warfare and annihilation—these and other weaknesses, vices, and crimes were nothing but the exposed gangrene of violence, let loose on the body of humankind."

After all these years Louis remembered his dead son's words in the Cave, delivered to be heard by none other, protected by a tensilated Jansen cage, almost to the letter.

"Violence and death should hold no terror for the man I'll see you become. That man should fight to the death when it is required but no son of mine will ever treat the killing of any creature as sport."

Louis paused to let the words sink in.

"Do you understand, Enguerrand?"

Ten-year old Enguerrand had his head bowed, pouting, but shaking his head in the affirmative.

But, Louis knew he didn't. The father knew, of course, that the son was fibbing.

"Isn't there something you wish to confess to me now, Enguerrand?"

The boy raised his head, meeting his father's soul-piercing gaze, one formed in another reality and waiting a decade for this very moment. Enguerrand looked up, bit his lip, and came clean.

"I have another slingshot, Father," he admitted.

"Is it your favorite, hidden away in the fort in which you and your companions play? That one?"

Enguerrand was less shocked by Louis' prescience than by the sight of seeing his immovable, impermeable, titanium-hard father trying mightily to restrain tears.

"You must be faithful to your word, Enguerrand, you're Quebecois. Always remember that."

But just as tears streamed unaccountably from the prior version of Enguerrand Duprey that Louis had known, the twenty-five year old young man—having arrived from the mists of the future desperate for his assistance, now that curse of the son was visited on the father.

There were many moments too poignant for human endurance that wrung salty proof from Louis' eyes that he wasn't fashioned from titanium at all, but instead from very vulnerable flesh and blood. Every night the vision of the entity that was still his son, the one he had failed in the end, this was the apparition that Louis saw when he closed his eyes.

"It's hard not to like you some," he recalled telling his son.

He also remembered only too well Enguerrand pressing the father's hand to his heart, repeating all the love, respect, devotion and loyalty this version of his son had displayed. The beaten, scarred, war-weary, wounded version of his son, when needing him the most, he'd turned away. This awful spiritual burden Louis Duprey carried alone for the rest of his life.

It would have killed any less of a man.

Chapter Nineteen: Gaia

However men pride themselves on their great accomplishments, such acts are often not the result of design, but of pure chance.
—Francois de La Rochefoucauld, Maxim No. 57

MANY VISITORS ARRIVED on Earth to celebrate the New Year in 10,000 AD, many more than the usual billion or so sightseers in the average year.

The guests far outnumbered the full-time residents of Earth.

"The last time there was this few people on Earth might have been in the year 10,000 as well—only that it was 10,000 BC."

His quip wrung smiles and chuckles from the tourists.

The Pre-Ancient era was a crowd-pleaser for all the tourists, starting around twenty thousand years ago at a site they'd be visiting called Gobekli Tepe in a region of Old Earth named Turkey.

But nothing took the breath away like the blood-curdling walk-throughs of historic Terra in its most disgraceful period, as the fetid, stinking, wretched trash-heap of a squalid planet, as

Earth was approaching the Third Millennium AD. A small piece of the sluice was kept as a relic, a physical reminder for visitors.

People in every era have always loved horror stories, and this one was the mother of them all.

It shocked the children and not a few adults as well. All were awe-struck and asked their parents in hushed tones, "Did people really live like that? Is this really true?"

They did, the lecturers were constrained to admit, and it was true. What they couldn't fully explain were other queries.

"But how could such a thing have happened? It must have taken so much time to turn Earth into an open sewer populated by dead-eyed hordes crowded together like bacteria in a petri dish. Didn't the people see that as it was happening and do something about it?"

The docents tried to give sensible answers—using the analogy of frogs slowly being boiled who fail to perceive the water temperature slowly rising until too late. Sometimes those answers worked, but most of the time visitors simply scratched their heads—and shielded their eyes. The guides also wished to move on, much more disposed to draw their charges' attention to the great miracle that had brought Mother Earth back from the brink.

Of all the monumental feats achieved by the race of man, now wielding the power to turn stars on and off, there was little to rival their most enduring and prideful mega-project. This breed of demigods, in the end after many prodigal millennia, had the pure decency to remember their mother.

When they took their first tentative and furtive steps away from Earth, they had been as weak and vulnerable as newborn kittens; they returned as the greatest single force in existence within the vastness of the entire Milky Way.

They laid eyes on their ancient cradle and cried torrents of bitter tears. A terrible shame fell upon the titans, for even though Earth could not speak, the results of their ancestral misdeeds were on display. The most beautiful jewel in the exquisite crown of creation had been allowed to be defiled, ravaged, violated. Their own mother planet had been abused more brazenly than the worst doled by the most black-hearted taskmasters of the deepest, darkest molyserilium mines.

"By the opening of the tenth millennium, the Terra Project began to gain billions of adherents all across the galaxy." The docent elucidated a human saga like none other. "The Project was initiated at one of the most extreme nadirs in Earth's intensely erratic population swings—taking advantage of what the Alshanian Pox had already accomplished, turning the planet into a vast graveyard. The reformers swept in at this moment of opportunity, resettled the remaining population, and began to put the planet right. This was done surprisingly quickly. By the end of a century the planet was all but unrecognizable."

That was the official and sanitized version of the greatest event ever to take place on Earth. The docents left out the details and gave the broad strokes. The lecturers weren't there to harp on whatever controversies and missteps connected with the retransformation of Earth. They were adept at avoiding those patches of weeds, stressing how gentle, righteous, and humane the Project was while still being effective as well.

Of course, it wasn't quite as simple and straightforward as that—remaking planets hardly ever is. But humanity, even now having evolved into a super-race, still clung with stubbornness to some of its ancient ways. Propaganda, as old as civilization itself, had yet to be left at the wayside. When it came to forgiving and erring, they were still something less than divine.

When Earth's long-estranged relatives returned from the edge of the stars, they'd been changed by the journey, but not so much as they had altered the galaxy. In their footprints were left soul, life, order, bounty, commerce, science, art, love, security and—peace.

Earth, on the other hand, had been abandoned long ago to

take a different path.

Both sides of the family met again after so many millennia to put their collective inheritance in order. The invincible titans who tamed the cosmos had come home after all this time and decreed that their ancestral birthplace was to be completely remade now. Doing what needed to be done came easily to them after so much practice clearing asteroid belts, deflecting comets and moving planets out of the way of their designs.

Mankind's age-old fear of aliens someday arriving and repossessing their planet actually came true. The only twist was the one no one saw coming. The aliens were—themselves.

Their cousins' relentless focus accomplished it, leaving an epic tale without parallel in their wake.

The real work began with a bustling tempo that took aback even the very workers engaged. Colossal swaths of the globe were ripped up, knocked down, smashed to bits and plowed under. Much of the entire planet's infrastructure was pulled from the ground, pounded, shredded, dissolved and vaporized to the point where it was determined that nature would soon be able to take over and quickly finish the chore with ease.

It was one of the greatest demolition job ever attempted and accomplished. Before long, the jungles, forests, and open prairies were made the most unlikely recrudescence. Earth's antediluvian beauty was restored to her.

"Naturally, the sacred monuments of the human race were rescued, cleansed, brought back from the brink," the docent was quick to add. "You'll be seeing all of them shortly." She gave the abbreviated list. "The Great Pyramid, Machu Picchu, Angkor Wat, the Acropolis, the Great Wall, Stonehenge and many more."

After such a Herculean task was completed, the final phase started with undertakings at least as daunting.

"The oceans were filtered, cleansed and brought back to life. The atmosphere was reconstituted with the optimum proportion of gases in just the right percentages, made to reflect what Earth's skies must have tasted like close to the very birth of our species at around 330,000 BC. And the millions of pieces of flotsam and jetsam orbiting just above those skies in the Trash Zone—all this refuse was either vaporized or blasted out of its trajectories and sent into the Sun."

The tourists murmured their approval.

"Thankfully, some prudent people in the distant past had the foresight to catalogue the DNA of all the countless species of plants and animals that had then gone on to utter extinction. This heroic piece of stewardship was the saving grace for all the flora and fauna that grow and roam on New Terra at present."

The sightseers burst into spontaneous applause.

"They gave New Terra back to the millions of species from whom it had been stolen," the young, fresh-faced docent explained, smiling broadly as she narrated the spectacular, sublimely uplifting part of the epic tale.

She had good reason to be so upbeat. It was an almost impossibly implausible dream to be a docent on Earth. She most certainly was the daughter of someone very, very important. She would never forget her time as a full-fledged legal resident of New Terra; it was an honor allowed to but one in a billion.

"It's said that they knew their labors were close to complete when one of the chief architects flying over a place once known as the Yangtze River Basin remarked to his fellow engineers," she paused for the gravity of her next sentence to be marked well. "This must be what the place looked like at the end of the sixth day, I think we can take the next day off."

Of course, that was just one of many apocryphal stories and quips having sprung from the greatest accomplishment in the history of the species of mankind—the restoration of Earth. No one knew if it was true or not, but it was so ingrained in the consciousnesses of trillions that the words had to be pronounced, especially here and now.

"I can assure you, all the stories you've heard about lions, giraffes, elephants, whales, rhinoceroses, sequoia, and all the rest—you'll be thrilled to know they're perfectly accurate, all completely true to the letter."

This almost never failed to produce the desired effect.

"I want to see a cheetah!" one of the excited youngsters called out.

"And so you shall, young man," she responded cheerily. "So you shall."

An elderly man raised his hand.

"Yes," she pointed at him. "You have a question, sir?"

He returned her smile.

"I'm here from Vela Eridani and want to ask you something about some very antique history that comes from my star system."

She gave him the best look of feigned interest she could manage; this was part of her job.

"About the original impetus for the Terra Project, in Vela Eridani there are chronicles that go back to The Wars indicating that free-rangers in our system had been pointing to the Home Sector and screaming for something to be done as early as the beginning of the fourth millennium."

This kind of question made her wish the boy would call out for the cheetah again. She turned to the lead docent, making ready to offload the subject to him.

"What an excellent question," she pretended.

She had heard many hundreds of crackpot ideas and conspiracy theories dealing with Old Earth. It was to be expected in her line of work, what with Terra being the oldest settled planet in the entirety of space, the place where everything started. It was no surprise that thousands—perhaps millions—of bizarre half-truths bounced out from this wellspring of history, science, philosophy and everything else only to spend thousands of years mutating and transmogrifying into anything that could be imagined.

Only yesterday she had leaned on the much more seasoned lead docent to settle yet another little-known controversy. A very adamant tourist from Lambda Serptentis D-4 wanted to know whether the tour would be taking in the "Roswell" site in Mexico, and what had happened to the extraterrestrial artifacts that she had been told were at hand.

The lead docent was superbly informed about many astoundingly arcane pieces of Old Earth lore, sufficient to correct her and set straight that the place to which she referred was in a locale then known as *New* Mexico, not Mexico. He'd heard about this one before and every other just like it.

"No, unfortunately, we won't be taking in Roswell," he said gregariously, "but we will be visiting Mount Rushmore. It's not far from Roswell's former coordinates."

He dismissed the artifacts, certain that he wouldn't be able to convince her of anything no matter what he said.

The young guide was out of her league when it came to this sort of mumbo jumbo and always backed away.

"All the way back to The Wars and…free riders? Is that what you called them?" She pretended to give over her rapt attention. "I'm curious myself." She handed off to the lead docent. "What about that?"

Her superior hadn't the faintest idea what had or hadn't happened over seven thousand years ago and dozens of light years away from his highly-prized quarters overlooking Petra in an arid desert once known as Jordan. Nonetheless, he had an excellent stock answer. He'd have responded the same if the questioner had hailed from the swamplands of Horologia or anywhere else.

"You bring up a very interesting question. You're right too. People in systems across the Spiral Arm played indispensable roles in the Terra Project. Vela Eridani, one of the oldest and most important systems, did more than its fair share.

Again, welcome to New Terra."

Blessed rescue came in the form of the ten year old.

"When are we going to see cheetahs?" he called out again.

Everyone laughed and the docents used the levity to their advantage.

"Well, alright then, let's move on, shall we?"

The lead docent had given short shrift. That Earth now was a pristine museum rather than a reeking cesspool was a legacy of the free-rangers, and they owed a debt to many who came before them.

Over many millennia, there were few philosophers, priests, dreamers and believers who hadn't pondered humanity's role in the universe, why we were here at all, and what the meaning of our existence was. Earth alone had given birth to the only sentient creatures who could pose those questions, even though they had never been truly answered.

They wondered ceaselessly about creation since they'd exited from Neolithic caves, asking numberless questions for untold ages.

Receiving no answers, they struck out into the vast, dead, silent void, converting it into an abode for life, love, and wonder. Stately Earth had indeed produced a quasi-divine brood of incomparable children whose destiny was to leave a verdant, green vivacity in their footsteps across the bleak chaos of the galaxy.

They transformed the Milky Way into the awe-inspiring image of their glorious mother Earth and only internecine conflict, fratricidal violence and war could stop them now.

There *were* true perils in the infinite universe—against which humanity must forever remain united, strong, supremely armed and invincible.

But they were now more than a race of beings; they were a stupendously powerful force of nature and well on their way to becoming even something greater.

And God looked over everything that He had made, and behold, it was good.
—Genesis 1:31

The End